PENGUIN BOOKS
OUR STORY ENDS HERE

Sara Naveed is the author of *Undying Affinity*. Being a writer has always been her dream. Having written in many fiction forums, Sara's interest grew and her writing skills improved. She currently resides with her family in Lahore.

You can follow Sara on Twitter (@SaraNaveed), like her on Facebook (www.facebook.com/saranaveedwriter), visit her official website at www.sara-naveed.com or her blog, www.saranaveedwriter.blogspot.com.

Our Story Ends Here

SARA NAVEED

PENGUIN BOOKS

PENGUIN BOOKS

USA | Canada | UK | Ireland | Australia
New Zealand | India | South Africa | China

Penguin Books is part of the Penguin Random House group of companies
whose addresses can be found at global.penguinrandomhouse.com

Published by Penguin Random House India Pvt. Ltd
7th Floor, Infinity Tower C, DLF Cyber City,
Gurgaon 122 002, Haryana, India

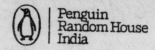

Penguin
Random House
India

First published in Penguin Books by Penguin Random House India 2017

Copyright © Sara Naveed 2017

10 9 8 7 6 5 4 3 2 1

ISBN 9780143428176

Typeset in Sabon by Manipal Digital Systems, Manipal
Printed at Thomson Press India Ltd, New Delhi

www.penguin.co.in

My family, my friends, my loved ones and my readers.
To all those who believe in love.

Prologue

Do you know what it feels like to live without a heart, a soul and *her*? It's affliction. Deep affliction. I've been feeling this way for so many years that it doesn't feel unusual any more. I think it has become a permanent part of my life now. But for the faintest moment, I'd like to experience what life would have been if I had been with her. Not a day, not even a single moment goes by when I don't think about her. Those hazel brown eyes, pink cheeks, loose curls framing her face . . .

I suddenly came out of my reverie as a motorbike zoomed past me, blowing a puff of smoke on my face. I slowly slid the sunglasses over my eyes and observed the usual rush at the local bazaar. Sweat trickled down my forehead as I walked past a couple of shops. It was warm, and I suddenly realized that wearing a brown, leather jacket on a sunny day was not really a great idea.

I made sure nothing looked out of place. I looked around one more time and then finally went and sat inside a roadside eatery. A young boy, aged between fourteen and fifteen years, sat next to me. He was busy playing a game on a brand-new cell phone. Suddenly it rang out loud, compelling me to look at him.

'Yeah, what is it now? I have already told you that I
will be home in an hour. Stop calling me every minute!' the
young boy yelled at the caller.

I looked at him incuriously.

He paused, listened to what the caller was saying and
then spoke again.

'I took permission from Abba and Amma. Now stop
calling me again and again. Bye.' He cut the call and gasped
for breath, looking in my direction as I was seated next to him.

'Getting calls from home?' I asked nonchalantly.

'Yes, bhai,' the boy said. 'It sucks. I mean, it's really not
easy being a teenager, you know.'

I smirked, looking away.

'First, my parents were reluctant to buy me a phone
and when they finally did, the calls just don't stop,' he
complained.

'Maybe because they care for you, considering the
incidents we hear of—bomb blasts and accidents,' I
shrugged.

'Ah. That. I get your point. They're my family after all.
They will be scared and worried. But I never get scared.'

'Really?' I raised my brows in amazement. 'Does death
never scare you?'

'Not at all. I'm not scared of death,' the boy shrugged.
'I've been brought up tough. I know how to fight my fears.'

'That's impressive, brother. How do you do that?' I
asked, fishing out my cell phone from the pocket of my
leather jacket.

'My sister, you know, she once told me this cool trick.
It really helps in dealing with your fears.'

'And what's that?' I scrolled through a couple of
messages on my phone as I listened to his story.

'Whenever you feel scared, just close your eyes, take a
long, deep breath, hold yourself together and pray to god.

The fear will subside slowly,' the boy said, demonstrating each step with gestures.

Before I could absorb his words, a blinking message on my cell phone diverted my attention.

'Hey, I gotta go now. It was nice talking to you, brother. I think you should leave for home now. This place seems a bit crowded. Doesn't look very safe,' I said, pursing my lips together.

'Why not? What's wrong here?' he asked, shrugging his shoulders.

'Just leave. Do as I say,' I said, getting up from the chair and walking away from the crowded area. As soon as I reached the other end of the bazaar, I dialled a number.

'Haider, listen to me. I don't think this seems like a safe move. We need to plan this somewhere else,' I said, concern filling my eyes.

'What the hell are you talking about, Sarmad? We have already set the entire plan in motion. The bomb has been planted,' Haider said.

'What the heck are you saying?' I said, trying to keep my voice as steady as I could.

'Sorry, Sarmad, but this is what we were asked to do. Just move away from that area as soon as you can. The bomb will blow up any time now,' he told me and then ended the call.

I stood there motionless; the phone still glued to my ear. But my mind was somewhere else. I closed my eyes to remember what he had said.

'Whenever you feel scared, just close your eyes, take a long, deep breath, hold yourself together and pray to god. The fear will subside slowly . . .'

It suddenly dawned on me that I recognized that advice. I remembered that trick. It was mine. I owned it. That boy knew the trick. *She* must have told him . . .

I opened my eyes and turned around, frantically searching for the boy. To my relief, he was still sitting in the same spot, his eyes glued to his phone. I let out a sigh of relief and ran towards him.

'Hey!' I called out. I was only a few inches away from him now. Before I could see the reaction on his face, there was a huge explosion, throwing me to the ground. The entire area was covered in thick, grey smoke. I choked as I looked around with my blurred vision. I tried to look at the spot where he was but couldn't find anything. The metal pieces of his phone were on the ground along with a black, tattered leather wallet. I reached out with my wounded arm and got hold of the wallet. I slowly opened it and found a black and white photograph inside. She beamed at me—innocent and beautiful. Her laughter rang loud in my ears. I tried to smile back at her but soon lost consciousness. Within a few seconds, I lost track of everything. I lost the young boy. And with him, I lost the only possible hope of getting her back.

Mehar

'Swat, a river valley and an administrative district in the Khyber Pakhtunkhwa province of Pakistan, is almost 685 kilometres from Lahore.'

'Queen Elizabeth II, during her visit to the Yusafzai State of Swat, called it the "Switzerland of the east".'

These results popped up on Wikipedia and other websites when I typed the name of the beautiful tourist destination on Google. I had been fascinated with that place since childhood. I had always shared a strong bond with it. Whenever I heard its name, I felt that strong association. However, I failed to understand or remember the reason behind that unusual feeling.

I immediately closed the browser window and looked around. It was the end of the winter season; flowers had already started blooming all across the front yard of our institute. I sat cross-legged with my friends, Laraib and Asma, on the moist grass of Kinnaird College and pretended to study for our finals We were studying less and babbling more.

'What are you checking so keenly on Facebook?' Laraib asked Asma. For a minute I thought she was asking me.

'Have you checked iTravel Pakistan's page on Facebook? They arrange sightseeing trips to the northern areas of Pakistan,' Asma informed.

'Really? That's amazing!' Laraib exclaimed.

'One of our seniors told me that the members of this group are genuine, extremely reliable and arrange successful trips. I was thinking of going on a trip with them after our final examinations. What say?' Asma asked us.

I shut my book and looked at her. Their conversation had piqued my interest.

'Sounds exciting! Where are they going next?' Laraib asked, getting excited.

'They are going to Kalam, Swat and Malam Jabba next week! It's going to be a ten-day tour!' Asma announced as she read from her laptop screen.

'Wow! I really want to visit Swat Valley. Let's make a plan!' Laraib said, getting excited.

Flabbergasted by her words, I instantly looked down at the book lying on my lap. Was this a coincidence?

'I've been there a number of times in my childhood,' I interjected, looking at Asma. 'Times were different then. Don't you think going there will be a bit dicey now, considering how it's under the influence of terrorism?' I questioned.

'Of course not. I've heard the government and the army have worked on improving the tourism sector of Khyber Pakhtunkhwa. Otherwise, the travel agencies wouldn't arrange trips to these areas,' Laraib said.

I nodded thoughtfully.

'Will you get permission, Asma?' Laraib asked.

'I think so. My parents have never objected to going out for school or college trips.'

'That's great,' Laraib smiled. 'What about you, Mehar?'

'Uh . . . I think it's going to be a problem for me, guys. I haven't been there without my family. I don't think they would want me to go all by myself.'

'But you can talk to them about it, right?' Asma asked.

'Yeah, I will try,' I nodded.

My father, retired general Haissam, had an authoritarian personality, but he was generous and kind towards his family. He loved my mother and had devoted everything to his family. Though he was a retired army officer, he had managed his household well. We were in a good position financially. We were two sisters and one brother. My father had become more protective towards us after the demise of my younger brother, Omar.

I waited at the college gate for my chauffeur, whom Abba sent every day to pick me up. Though I had learnt how to drive, I never practised. The sight of my friends and other girls driving all by themselves made me jealous at times.

I lived in a farmhouse on Raiwind Road, far away from the hustle and bustle of the main city. As the car pulled into the driveway, I got out and looked at our lush, green and manicured garden. Amma was fond of gardening, and she loved to decorate our garden with different plants. However, since my brother's death, she had lost interest in looking after them. It was mostly done by the gardener now.

Inside, I found my mother in the prayer room. I walked up to her and sat silently across her. I observed the wrinkles on her forehead and the dark circles that were forming under her eyes. Since Amma had fair skin, the dark circles were more prominent. She did not look after herself at all. This bothered me as I wanted her to look as beautiful as ever.

'You are home?' Amma asked as she sensed my presence in the room.

'Yes,' I whispered.

She mumbled a prayer and blew on my face.

'Amma, why do you always do this?' I asked, narrowing my brows and folding the prayer mat.

'To keep you safe from *buri nazar*,' she replied.

'Amma, there is no negative energy surrounding me. I'm safe as long as god is with me.'

'That is not a justified reply. Why don't you pray five times a day?' she asked.

'I will make it a routine very soon, Amma. Only a semester is left now. Then I will be free.'

'These are all your lame excuses.' She rolled her eyes.

'No, I'm serious,' I grumbled.

Out of habit, after returning from college, I usually met her and then Abba. He was reading a book in the library.

'There you are!' He took off his spectacles and reached for my hand.

'Salaam, Abba *jaan*!' I sat on the floor beside his rocking chair.

'*Walaikum asalaam*, did *miyan* come to pick you up on time?'

'Yes,' I said.

'That's good,' he replied with a smile.

'Have you had supper?'

'Yes, your mother just gave me a cup of tea. Go and have something to eat.'

'Sure.'

'When are your exams beginning?' he asked.

'From tomorrow.'

'Good luck with them and make me proud.' He smiled.

'Inshallah.' I gave him a weak smile again and then walked out of the library.

I wanted to talk to him about so many things but refrained from uttering anything because I did not want to spoil his good mood. Abba's anger was as unpredictable as his mood.

Sarmad

Who said life in Kabul is unproblematic when you are a part of a fundamentalist political movement? Certainly it was not easy for a person like me who wanted to live in a free world; a place that was free from all evils and political propaganda. At twenty-four, I thought I had seen most of the world. However, it wasn't true. I had only seen the tribal areas of Afghanistan and some parts of North Pakistan such as Muzaffarabad, Naran, Kaghan, Swat and Hunza Valley.

Sitting in a cart among my tribesmen, I squinted at the sun that glistered on my face. As the cart progressed on a muddy path in Kabul, I thought deeply about my true identity. I was not mortified at being an important part of an extremist group; people who were commonly termed as terrorists. I knew I had an uncertain life that could end any moment, yet I was ready to embrace death.

This was the kind of life that I had chosen for myself; this was my destiny.

Kabul was the largest city as well as the capital of Afghanistan. I resided in an old house with the other tribesmen and their wives who were also a part of the extremist group.

Hakem Ullah, commonly known as Mullah, the leader of our group, ran a house of eleven members who were fully trained in spreading violence across the country.

I was a part of Mullah's clan, and he was the person who had taken care of my necessities since I was a child. He hadn't married and didn't have a family of his own. Instead, he had adopted ten children at a very young age.

Nafisa, twenty-one, was one of them. She secretly fancied me. I knew this and so did everyone else. However, I paid no heed to her feelings. I had always been like that. Not paying much attention to women. Not that I had any sexual disorder.

Despite having beautiful Afghani looks, she had failed to make a long-lasting impression on me.

On the other hand, Haider, Karim and Ramez were extremely close to me. Though I did not have any family members except Khan Baba, my only blood relative, I had found brothers in these three. All of us lived like a family; a family tortured by our past and grievances.

After observing drone attacks all over North Waziristan and some parts of Afghanistan and the consistent war since 2001, Mullah had ordered the insurgents to team up and move to Lahore. One of the US officials, James Henry, had planned a visit to Lahore to meet the prime minister. According to the grapevine, he was one of the people involved in taking an immediate decision to not end the war in Afghanistan. Mullah loathed this person and could never forgive him. He formed a group that included me, Haider, Karim and Ramez to assassinate him. Karim and Ramez were going to take the route to Peshawar via Jalalabad, whereas Haider and I decided to reach Quetta directly from Kabul.

We had packed our weapons in a way that no one could find them even if they searched our bags. We were well trained to do that.

Everyone at home had always admired my beard as it really suited me. Unfortunately, the young men had to adopt a clean-shaven look as we did not want people to become suspicious.

We had to leave early the next morning. Nafisa cooked shorwa for us, and everyone sat on the floor cross-legged and ate it with nan—unleavened, flat bread. However, I was not present at the dinner table that night. I was inside the room, listening to their conversation.

'Where is Sarmad?' Mullah asked.

'He's getting ready for tomorrow,' Karim replied, taking a bite out of the nan.

'I hope you are aware that this mission could possibly be your last,' Mullah continued.

'Yes, we know that,' Haider said.

'I might not see your faces again,' Mullah's voice trailed off.

I knew Nafisa must have cringed at the thought of losing me. But this was not under her control or mine. This was how our lives were meant to be; to die in the name of god.

'Do not forget who we are and why we are doing this,' Mullah resumed, his voice crisp and clear. 'We are born jihadis, and we will fight for our rights. We will not let our women and children die because of the inhumane drone attacks. Just focus on your mission, *bachchas*. Kill that bloody James Henry.'

'What if we fail in our mission, Mullah?' Ramez asked.

'Then sacrifice your lives before someone else kills you,' Mullah replied with dignity.

'I'll go and look for Sarmad,' Nafisa said hesitantly.

I stood bare-chested in front of the mirror in the lavatory that was used by everyone in the house and observed my face warily. I took a bar of soap in my hands, dipped it in a mug full of water till it lathered. I applied the lather all across my hairy chest and then shaved it smoothly with a sterile blade. On hearing Nafisa's footsteps, I looked outside the lavatory door. She was holding a cup of *kahwa* in her hands.

'Ready to leave?' she asked, leaning against the door.

'Yes, almost,' I replied nonchalantly and then poured the shaving cream on to my hand.

'I'm about to die,' she sighed.

'Why?' I furrowed my brows together.

'I'm going to see you clean-shaven after a long time. You look so bloody handsome like that. Mashallah.' Her eyes sparkled impishly.

Without replying, I just smirked and applied the cream all over my beard. She observed how the six-pack of my clean-shaven abdomen hardened as I swiftly shaved my beard.

'Slow down or you'll get hurt,' she whispered as she stepped closer.

'I'm fine,' I said as I splashed water over my face.

'Mashallah,' she said breathlessly.

'You praise me for nothing.' I walked away, tucking my kurta under my arm.

'And you never praise me,' she said dejectedly.

As I wiped my face with a small cloth and wore the kurta, Nafisa held my arm.

I turned to look at her guardedly.

'Now that you're going away, will you miss me?' she asked.

'I'll miss the entire clan.'

'Will you miss *me*?'

'I have a lot of packing to do.' I pushed her arm away and started putting my clothes in a sack.

'Okay,' she paused and then spoke again, 'This might be our last meeting.'

'Indeed.'

'Can I touch you one last time?'

I stared at her with a blank expression on my face. She had started it again.

'We might not get this chance again,' she said as she crept closer and wrapped her arms around my neck.

'Don't do this,' I warned her as I closed my eyes for a brief second.

'I want to put my soul right into you before this life ends,' she said, running her fingers through my tousled hair.

I wanted to jerk her away but her hold was stronger than I had expected. She held me tightly, digging her fingers into my back. She traced a pattern on my skin with her finger and then touched my lips. I stood like a statue and did not respond. I was not aroused by her affectionate touch. She brought my face closer to hers and then planted a soft kiss on my lips. I shoved her away this time and resumed packing. I don't know why but she could never arouse me.

'Such an ungrateful monster you are!' she scowled at me.

I did not say anything.

Without feeling disappointed by my demeanour, she candidly put her arm around my neck. 'So, you're going to Lahore. A big modern city, right?' she asked.

'I guess so.' I ignored her.

'You'll be meeting new people there. I've heard Lahori girls are very pretty and up-to-date.'

'Who told you that?' I asked her.

'Someone was mentioning it the other day.'

'I don't believe it. It doesn't even matter.'
A small smile flickered on her face.
'What if you fall in love with a Lahori girl?'
I smiled crookedly, and she knew that the smile was not from my heart.
'What happened?' she asked.
'Extremists are not born to love.'

Mehar

I ate dinner with my parents in the dining room. There was utter silence in the room except for the rattling sound of forks and spoons against the china plates. I could not muster up the courage to talk to my parents and seek their permission to go to Swat Valley as I knew they would refuse. Abba would never let me go alone on a trip with my friends. I ignored the thoughts and focused on dinner. I finished my food quickly and went to my room.

I lay the bed and switched off the lamp on the side table. In complete darkness, I felt relieved and found inner strength. What if I left my presumptions and spoke to Amma and Abba? What if they agreed? But when should I talk to them? Will they allow me to go for a tour with my friends? I was sure Asma and Laraib's parents were non-conservative and would let their daughters go on a ten-day tour but what about mine? Would they agree?

I knew my parents would not let me take the risk. They had lost their only son and now they wouldn't want to lose a daughter too. My mind suddenly took me to the day when we heard the news of Omar's death.

I remember it as a beautiful morning. Fall had already set in and there was a nip in the air. Omar was an O-level student. At fifteen, he had started looking like a young man. His moustache had started to appear and his voice had deepened, which indicated that he was no longer a child. Omar's school friends had urged him to go to the Old Food Street to take part in a kite festival and later devour the famous golgappas from the local cart shops. At first, Omar had refused because our parents usually did not allow him to go to places that were far away from home. Consider it his misfortune, but that day when Omar asked for Abba and Amma's permission, they readily agreed without creating a scene. This surprised him the most. However, I did not want my little brother to go out to such a crowded place.

'I promise we'll fly kites on our terrace today.' I smiled with gleaming eyes as I tried to persuade him.

'You always lie to me,' he said. He tied his shoelaces and then rose from the bed.

'I'm not lying this time!' I raised my arms in surrender. 'I promise.'

Omar heaved a sigh.

'Let me go this time, and I promise I'll fly kites with you tomorrow,' he said in a pleading tone. 'Okay?'

I was helpless and I knew I could not stop him from anything.

After a few hours of his departure, there was news all over TV channels about the blast. I remember clearly how Amma had fainted after hearing the earth-shattering news. I had clutched the arms of my elder sister, Sidra, as I was terror-struck. We were not able to contact Omar as we could not connect to his cell phone. Abba had received the news from a few reliable sources. It was a heart-ripping moment for our entire family. Amma did not regain consciousness, and remained in hospital for a couple of weeks. However, Abba acted a bit differently—he became mute. He stopped talking to people around him and preferred to remain in complete solitude. After about six months, Amma considered a marriage proposal for Sidra that had come from Dubai. Both Abba and Amma discussed it and finally agreed to go ahead with it. After meeting Sidra's in-laws-to-be, the marriage preparations began. It was a low-key affair, and only close relatives were invited. After the nikah, Sidra flew to Dubai with her husband. She requested me to take care of our parents in her absence. I would do anything for my sister and vice versa. Sidra was my lifesaver.

I took out my cell phone and typed a text message to Sidra. I knew my sister would give honest advice and would help me in any situation.

After a few minutes, my cell phone vibrated. I knew Sidra would call me as soon as she read the message.

'Hey,' I greeted her in a shaky voice.

'Mehar, my baby, how are you? Are you okay?' Sidra asked from the other end of the line.

'I'm fine, Sidra, don't worry,' I assured. 'I wanted to tell you something.'

'Wait. Wait. Wait. Does this have anything to do with a guy? Did a marriage proposal come up?'

'No way!' I snapped. 'How could you even think that this was about a guy?'

'Well, it just came to my mind. You are young enough to fall in love with someone.'

Fall in love with someone. I don't think I will ever be able to do that.

'I don't really think about all that, okay? Anyway, I don't want to talk about boys. I wanted to talk to you about something else.'

I told her about the upcoming Swat trip and solicited her honest advice. Surprisingly, Sidra did not find the trip unusual at all, and she wanted me to go out with my friends and enjoy my life as much as possible. She promised to talk to Amma and Abba and seek their permission!

Sarmad

The next morning, I woke up from a nightmare. I could not recall the intricate details of the dream but only remembered that someone was trying to push me into a deep, black hole. I rose from the mat and rolled it into a bundle. With the noise in the room, Haider woke up, rubbing his eyes.

'When are we leaving?' Haider whispered.

'In two hours. Get up and pack your things,' I replied, heading out of the room.

It wasn't a room actually. In fact, it was more like a wooden cabin that was lit with lanterns and a few light bulbs. One by one, the boys surrendered their sleep and prepared their minds for the upcoming mission.

I could not recognize myself in the mirror without my beard. I gargled quickly, splashed my face twice with icy cold water and then took a quick bath. Nafisa and the other women were busy preparing breakfast for us. We finished our breakfast and then bowed our heads to seek blessings from Mullah.

'May god protect your kind souls, and may you all succeed in your mission,' Mullah called out a prayer for everyone.

'What if we get caught?' Ramez's question startled everyone in the cabin, especially Mullah.

'How reckless of you to ask this!' Mullah yelled at him.

At Mullah's uproar, Ramez started shivering. I stood by his side and placed an arm over his shoulder.

'I think you were a bad choice for this mission!' Mullah continued to shout.

'Calm down, Mullah sahib,' I interposed. 'Ramez is new. I will explain everything to him on the way to the bus station.'

'You better!' Mullah retorted.

I bent my head and whispered in Ramez's ear.

'Never utter such words in front of Mullah as you know how he reacts. I will tell you why we won't get caught.'

'Okay,' Ramez answered in a low, frantic voice.

'Let's move now,' I ordered and then walked out of the room.

As soon as I exited the door, Nafisa ran after me and clutched my arm tightly.

'How could you go without bidding me goodbye?' she asked, gasping for breath.

I lowered my head and remained silent.

'I'm going to miss you, Sarmad!' she said in a heartbreaking voice. 'Because I love . . .'

'Nafisa . . . these words mean nothing to me! Why don't you get that?' I cut her off and freed my arm from her tight grip.

Nafisa stared at me in bewilderment, making me feel more pathetic.

'Look . . .' I fought for the right words to express myself. 'I respect you as a person. I respect your feelings for me but we both are aware of the fact that none of these things matter to us.'

Nafisa tried to hold back the tears that had formed in her eyes.

'We do not lead normal lives,' I said.

'But we are humans, and we have every right to love. You cannot stop me from loving you.'

'*Khuda hafiz*,' I said, changing the subject entirely.

'I'll pray for your safe return.'

I nodded, and just then Karim, Haider and Ramez headed out of the house. As we marched away, I could feel Nafisa's gaze on me.

We reached the bus station in Kabul. Karim fetched two bus tickets for Jalalabad and two for Quetta. After wishing them luck, I boarded the bus along with Haider. There was fear in Ramez's eyes that disturbed me greatly.

Mehar

After my exam, I joined Asma and Laraib in the cafeteria lounge. They had ordered samosas for themselves.

'Thank god, this is our last semester and tomorrow is the final exam. Otherwise, I would have been dead by now,' Asma said.

I picked a samosa, dipped it into chutney and munched it slowly.

'To hell with the exams, yaar, what about the Swat trip?' Laraib looked at Asma's face and then at mine.

I shrugged nonchalantly.

'I talked to my parents last night and they gave me permission,' Asma replied casually.

'Wow. That's so exciting! My parents have agreed as well!' Laraib announced animatedly.

I let out a low sigh, my shoulders sinking at once.

'What about you, Mehar?' Laraib probed as she tried to gauge my reaction.

'I haven't talked to them yet.'

'What? Why? Are you crazy?' Laraib started bombarding me with questions.

I blinked my eyes in confusion.

'Mehar, you should have asked them by now!' Asma added.

'I know, guys.' Irritated, I spat out the piece of samosa in my mouth. 'Can't you just let me eat peacefully first?'

'Okay, okay,' Laraib held her breath. 'Take your time.'

I first looked at their faces and then gathered my wits to speak.

'See . . . it's quite possible that I might not get permission to go to Swat with you. Considering what happened to my brother in the past, my parents won't allow it.'

Laraib shook her head sadly.

'But I promise that I will talk to them once. I will.'

'Sure?' Asma asked.

'Yes.' I smiled as they continued to blabber about our last exam.

Sarmad

I waited for Haider at the local bus station of Kabul while he had gone to use the public lavatory. The bus to Quetta was about to leave in fifteen minutes. Not wanting to get late, I took out my cell phone and called him.

'I'm coming. Wait up,' he said.

I slid the cell phone back into my pocket and stood cross-armed, leaning on one of the pillars of the bus station. I had been trying to get Ramez's petrified look out of my head but it still lingered. Right then, my cell phone rang.

'*Asalaam u alaikum*,' I answered in a heavy voice.

'Walaikum asalaam. We have completed half the journey,' Karim spoke diligently from the other end of the line. 'We will reach Jalalabad in an hour.'

'Be safe . . . and look after Ramez. He's a kid,' I said.

'He's fine. Don't worry. Stay in touch,' Karim said.

'Khuda hafiz.' I ended the call.

Mehar

I was sure my parents would turn down the trip plan. I considered my friends fortunate as their parents had given them permission to explore an exotic place all by themselves.

When I returned home, I found Amma in the prayer room. Without disturbing her, I tiptoed to my bedroom. I took off my lime-green chiffon dupatta and headed towards the bathroom before praying:

'O Allah, please let me go on the trip with my friends. Let my parents agree. Please.'

Suddenly, I heard a screeching sound in the driveway. I slid the curtains to find Abba getting out of the car.

'I must talk to him today.'

Sarmad

The bus made its way through the epitome of beauty, the capital of Balochistan province, Quetta. The city stood tall and proud like its mountains. Only when you looked closely, the open wounds showed up. The looming presence of terrorism kept people alert and scared all the time. As the bus halted, half-awake, half-asleep, I tried to open my eyes. Through the window, I could see an enormous crowd gathered at the Quetta bus terminal. People were talking endlessly, mostly in Pashto. As I looked to my right, I found Haider getting up from his seat.

'Let's go, brother. We have to find a place to hide,' Haider said in a low voice, to which I nodded affirmatively.

With heavy bags slung across our shrunken shoulders, we managed to hail an autorickshaw. We were not unfamiliar with the routes of the city, so it was not difficult to find a local hotel. We decided to stay at Green Resort for a week as we needed time to devise our dangerous mission. We had selected this one on purpose as it had fewer security checks. Only then could we move to Lahore and execute the plan. After keeping the bags on the floor, I sat on the edge of the bed and looked at it for a minute. We were not used to sleeping on foam-filled mattresses and beds. I grasped the pillow, tucked it under my arm and placed it on the carpet. A fine, white sheet of cloth was enough to cover my body while sleeping.

'Do you want something to eat?' Haider asked as he removed his shoes.

'No, I'm fine. Nuts that we had on the way were enough to satisfy my appetite,' I answered, resting my head on the pillow.

'Are you sure?'

'Yes,' I whispered and soon drifted off to a deep sleep.

I didn't know how much time had passed when I opened my eyes. All I could see was darkness. Haider had switched off the lamps and had made sure that there was no light in the room. I pulled the white sheet off my torso and sat up. I checked my cell phone that was lying on the floor just a few inches away. There were no updates from Ramez and Karim. I got up from the carpet and walked towards the window that was slightly ajar. I slid the curtain aside to get a view of the picturesque town outside. The night was dark, hollow and silent. Despite the frightful environment and underneath the cloud of terror, the city still breathed. It lived life to the fullest. I took a long, deep breath and shut the window because there was no place for beauty in my life. I felt lonely in every city, every country and every place.

Mehar

I could neither sleep nor study. I flipped through my textbook but my mind was somewhere else. Probably the upcoming trip and the excitement attached to it. I wanted to discuss the topic with my parents. I shut my textbook and threw it aside on the bed. I made up my mind. I would talk to them early in the morning at the breakfast table. I switched off the bedside lamp and went to sleep.

I woke up to the sound of sweeping. My maid, Nasreen, was busy cleaning my room. I lazily rubbed my eyes and got up. The lukewarm water felt smooth on my dry skin as I stood under the shower. I let out a deep sigh.

I have to grow up and fight for what I want. I cannot stay mute and let the world throw decisions at me. I am old enough to take my own decisions.

A sudden knock on the door startled me and brought me back to reality.

'Who's there?' I asked, unfazed.

'Bibi, it's me, Nasreen.'

'*Haan*, what is it?' I asked, annoyed now.

'I have to clean the bathroom.'

'Can't you see I am inside right now?'

'Yes, but *bade* sahib is calling you downstairs.'

Now this shocked me. Abba wanted to see me.

'Oh,' I gulped. 'I'll be out in a minute.'

Thankfully, an ironed, red and green salwar kameez was kept in the cupboard. I dressed myself in no time. Without drying my hair, I ran downstairs.

Sarmad

I was used to eating nans and shorwa for breakfast, thanks to Nafisa. Now, there was halwa-puri kept in front of me. Haider had brought it from one of the street shops. As I ate it, I suddenly realized how much I missed nan and shorwa and Nafisa. Yes. At last I had remembered her. I wondered what she might be doing right now. I wanted to call her, talk to her, but I refrained from making any contact with the people back home.

'Is it good?' Haider asked, taking a spoonful of the halwa. I did not want to respond.

'What happened, haan? Missing Nafisa's breakfast?'

Now Haider was crossing his limits and getting on my nerves.

I pushed aside the plate and said, 'What is your problem, Haider? Why can't you mind your own fucking business?'

'Relax, brother. I was just teasing you.'

'No, we don't have a relationship where we can tease each other. Do you understand?' I pointed a finger at him.

'All right.' Haider raised his arms. 'Relax.'

I took a deep breath and calmed myself down.

'I just thought maybe . . . you're in love with Naf . . .'

'No! We're aliens to that emotion. You should know that very well.' I raised a brow at him.

Haider nodded approvingly.

'Anyhow, have you called Ramez and Karim? Where are they?'

'Yes, I talked to Karim in the morning. They've reached Peshawar.'

'Hmm. It is time to work out our plan then,' I whispered.

Mehar

I entered the dining room where Amma and Abba were eating quietly. I held my breath and prayed to god, asking him to turn the matter in my favour.

'Come, *beta*. Why are you standing there?' Abba asked.

I nodded and smiled as I sat opposite him.

'When are your exams getting over?' he asked.

'Today is my last exam,' I said, tossing an omelette on my plate. Amma kept an eye on me.

'Great. Start packing your bags then. We're going to Islamabad for a week,' he announced.

I started trembling, and could feel my cheeks flushing.

'Uh. Isn't it all of a sudden? When are we leaving?' I asked, trying not to choke.

'Tomorrow morning,' he replied.

Am I left with an option now? No! If Abba has decided something, then it has to be done. I have no right to object to his decisions.

'Are you happy with this news?' Amma asked, breaking my reverie.

'Amma, if you're happy, then I'm happy,' I tried to smile but failed. I was 100 per cent sure that my disappointment was obvious.

'No, beta. This is certainly not about our happiness but yours. We've planned this trip for you. Your Khadijah Phupho and her kids, especially Hamza, are eager to see you. We'll only go if you want to.'

This is it. This is the best time to talk about what you want, Mehar. This is the best chance you will ever get. Just say it!

'Abba . . . if it is about my happiness, then . . . I am ready to go,' I said. I couldn't hurt my parents.

'Are you sure?' Abba asked.

'Yes,' I replied firmly.

'I guess we should start packing then,' Amma said.

I sat there, dazed and confused. I had the chance to speak up, tell them what I wanted. I had the opportunity to talk to them about the upcoming trip, but I had chosen to remain quiet. Why? For this question, I had no answer. I could not see my parents getting hurt on my account.

Later that night, I messaged Sidra on WhatsApp.

She wanted to know if I had talked to Amma and Abba about the Swat trip. I told her the truth.

She instantly called after reading my messages.

'Why didn't you ask them?' she asked in an agitated voice. I knew she was quite upset with me.

'I couldn't . . . I couldn't ruin their plan,' I said. 'They seemed so excited after a long time. How could I dampen their enthusiasm, Sidra?'

'But what about you? You were longing for this trip, weren't you?'

'Yes, I wanted to go, but nothing is more important than our parents' happiness. Right?'

'Yeah,' Sidra sighed. 'Right.'

'I am going to sleep now. I have not even finished packing.'

'Okay. Have a nice time with Phupho's family.'

'Yeah, right,' I sighed.

'Especially Hamza,' she giggled.

'Oh god.' I rolled my eyes. Sidra always teased me about Hamza. 'I sure will,' I said with a smile.

As I was about to flip my pillow, my glance darted to the doorway. I was stunned to find Abba standing there.

'Abba?' I shivered.

'Why couldn't you ask for the permission straight away?' he asked with a heavy voice. Behind him, Amma's frail shadow lurked.

'Abba . . . I . . . I just couldn't. I didn't want to hurt you,' I managed to say, looking down.

'I would have given you permission if you would have asked for it, *meri* jaan.' Abba walked towards me and then gently placed his hand on my shivering shoulder.

It took me a minute to absorb this.

'This is your life after all. You're allowed to enjoy it as much as you want,' he said.

'But Abba . . . I thought you would never want me to visit Swat Valley and other nearby areas alone . . .'

'Why not? There's no danger. We have army checkpoints throughout the region. You'll be safe. Don't be scared. You're a general's daughter after all. A brave daughter!' Abba hugged me.

I smiled and then looked down, tears forming in my eyes. I had never thought he would allow me to go so easily.

'But you have to promise us one thing, Mehar,' Amma said, stepping into the room.

I looked at her inquisitively.

'As soon as you return from the trip, we'll get you engaged to your Phupho's elder son, Hamza.'

And there came another major shock. Despite knowing that my cousin had been fond of me since childhood, I couldn't digest the news.

'Hamza likes you and is keen on getting married to you,' Amma declared.

'And we have approved his proposal. I hope we have done the right thing,' Abba concluded.

My eyes became watery the next instant. It was not that I didn't want to get married to my cousin. I liked Hamza. In fact, he was the most respectable and decent fellow in my entire cousin clan. I just didn't want to get married so soon.

'That's why we wanted to take you to Phupho's house so you could meet Hamza, and we could proceed with the engagement ceremony. However, this event can be postponed. We shall await your return from the trip and then continue the *rasam*,' Abba said with delight.

'Are you happy with our decision?' Amma asked.

'Yes, Amma,' I said with a heavy heart. 'I have no qualms about this proposal. I'll do as you say.'

'Mashallah. Great news! I'll go and deliver it to Khadijah right now!' Abba said cheerfully and left the room.

Amma glanced back at me.

'When does your group leave?' she asked.

'Tomorrow morning, 5 a.m.,' I said.

'Is the group reliable?'

'Yes, Amma. Totally,' I assured her.

'*Acha* . . . Let me help you pack then. I don't want you to forget warm clothes and other important items.' As Amma continued to speak, I fell into my own dark world.

Sarmad

I woke up to the sound of horns from across the street. I sat up and rubbed my weary eyes. I realized it was already 4.30 a.m., and going back to sleep seemed like a useless idea.

Setting the bag on the table, I took out the maps where we'd drawn the entire plan.

'You're up quite early,' Haider said as he came and stood beside me.

'We still need to locate some checkpoints. We won't understand their placement unless we visit these areas.' I drew a line over a few checkpoints in order to explain.

'Shall we leave then?' Haider asked.

'The sooner the better.'

Mehar

Abba had already called Phupho to give her the happy news. Phupho, Hamza and other family members were pleased with the final decision. They always wanted me to be a part of their family and now their wish was coming true.

I packed my bags absently. On one hand, I was going to live my life but on the other my independence was going to come to an end. I was distressed but couldn't discuss it with anyone. Amma had told Sidra about Hamza's proposal over the phone the same night. Even she was happy after hearing the news. In fact, she also revealed that she had known this was about to happen. I felt a little agitated as she had never mentioned this to me. Everyone seemed happy except me. I couldn't understand why I wasn't. He fancied me. But, what did I really know about him? Except for his decency and well-mannered behaviour for which he was quite famous in our family.

In the car my mind drifted towards what my parents had told me last night. What would have happened if I had rejected Hamza? How would have Abba reacted? What would have Amma thought? What would have Phupho said to Abba?

'How long is your trip?' Abba asked me, disrupting my thoughts.

'It's a ten-day trip, Abba,' I answered.

'Hmm. Quite long. Take care of yourself. Make sure you stay with your group and seniors.'

'I will.'

'I'll miss you, meri jaan,' Amma said, kissing my forehead.

'I'll be back soon,' I reassured and then hugged them one by one.

'Take care of yourself. May Allah be your *nigehbaan*.' Abba hugged me.

'Khuda hafiz, Abba. Khuda hafiz, Amma,' I said as I stepped down from the car and walked towards the bus.

Sarmad

Without thinking of what the future held for me, I took the journey from Quetta to Mingora, the main town in Swat Valley. That's where all the group members had decided to meet before going to Lahore.

Haider got two bus tickets along with plates of paratha anda.

'What's this for?' I asked dejectedly.

'Breakfast. Aren't you ever hungry?' Haider asked, surprised.

'You're always hungry,' I said sarcastically and then took one paratha roll from him.

The bus jolted into motion. It was going to be a tiring journey.

Mehar

'What? Eight hours?' Asma choked.

'Yeah. That's what our senior says. It'll take us at least eight hours to reach Swat Valley,' Laraib declared.

We were seated at the back of the bus.

'Quite a long journey, huh?' Asma nudged me, as I was completely lost in my own thoughts.

'What's wrong with you, Mehar? Aren't you excited about this trip?' Asma asked worriedly.

'Of course, I am,' I said half-heartedly.

'You seem lost. Why are you so quiet?' Laraib inquired.

'Guys . . .' I struggled for the words. 'I'm getting married to Hamza, Phupho's eldest son.'

'What? Really?' Asma gasped.

I nodded in affirmation.

'But isn't this supposed to be great news? After all you've always spoken so well about your cousin,' Laraib said.

'It's not about Hamza. It's not him. It's . . . me. I guess I don't want to get married so soon,' I said with a glum expression on my face.

'Don't be stupid, Mehar. Consider yourself lucky. Hamza seems like a decent fellow. I'm sure he will keep you happy,' Laraib squeezed my hand.

I nodded and then looked outside the window. I observed the sky as it gradually turned purple. With every passing minute, I felt my heart sink.

'Acha, show us his latest photo!' Asma nudged me again.

'I don't have it,' I declared.

'Check his Facebook or Instagram, *na*,' Laraib said.

'I haven't added him on Facebook yet,' I replied.

'WhatsApp display picture maybe?' Asma asked.

'Yeah, wait.' I opened my WhatsApp and scrolled down my contact list to look for Hamza. To my surprise, I had never had a single conversation with him. I opened his profile and came across his current display picture.

'Here it is. You can see him.' I flashed the mobile screen in their direction.

In the next couple of minutes, they were drooling over his goddam looks.

Sarmad

Half of the journey was over. I rested my head against the window pane. Though my eyes were closed, I could hear everything around. I could hear the chatter in the bus, I could hear the buzz of the passing bus and could also hear Haider breathing right beside me. A loud thud made me open my eyes. All the passengers gasped in horror. After scrutinizing the situation, we figured out that the bus driver had missed a speed breaker on the road.

'Stupid driver. He scared the hell out of me,' Haider hissed.

'He's human after all. He can make a mistake,' I said as I gazed out of the window.

'We'll be stopping at Saidu Sharif for half an hour. You all will have time to get something to eat,' the bus conductor announced.

Mehar

One of the trip coordinators asked the driver to stop the bus at the Saidu Sharif bus stand. We were informed that after the stopover we'd go straight to a hotel in Kalam—a heavenly tourist spot and sub-valley of Swat. Near the bus stand, there was a shop selling cold drinks and other snacks. One by one, the girls stepped out of the bus and headed towards the shop to get some refreshments. I moved away from the crowd and walked towards the toilets. There was an obnoxious stench. I suddenly felt sick as my stomach somersaulted with disgust. I immediately came out, and gulped some fresh air.

'Hurry up, Mehar. We're about to leave,' Asma called from a distance.

'I'm coming,' I replied.

Some of the students boarded the bus while some continued standing around the shop, having chai and parathas. Asma and Laraib ordered some for themselves, but I refused to eat.

'Aren't you hungry?' Asma asked, sipping tea from her cup.

'No. I don't feel like eating anything,' I replied, glumly.

'Listen, Mehar, if you're going to behave like this for the rest of our trip, then I'm afraid none of us will have fun. C'mon, cheer up. It's not like you're getting married tomorrow,' Laraib exclaimed.

I looked at my hands.

'Laraib is right. Cheer up, Mehar. This is our one and only chance to be ourselves. We don't know what the future holds for us,' Asma continued.

'I'm fine, guys. Really.' I tried to smile.

As I looked away, I saw another bus that had just arrived. The passengers getting down from the bus looked more like Pathans with their fair complexion and blonde hair. Suddenly, my gaze stopped on a man with peculiar eyes. He also looked like one of the Pathans—fair, dark brown, ruffled hair with brown, brooding eyes. I observed him till he reached the corner shop. For some reason, he looked familiar. His face looked tired, as if he'd been on a long journey. My heartbeat came to a sudden halt when I realized he'd noticed that I was staring at him.

I shifted my gaze and dropped my hair over my shoulders to cover my flushed face.

'Let's take some pictures. C'mon,' Asma declared.

Sarmad

I have lived in this world for twenty-four years. In this time, I have been to various places and conducted countless dangerous missions. During my journeys, I have met different kinds of people. But no face had caught my attention the way this girl's did. I had never felt attracted to any woman in my life before. Her aura was bewitching. There were old memories attached to her presence. It felt as if I had some strong connection with her. A lost bond. With twinkling eyes, an innocent face and pink lips, she looked at me with curiosity. When I caught her staring, she immediately lowered her gaze and brought her slack curls to cover her face, making it difficult for me to judge her reaction.

'Let's get some chai and get back to the bus. We have our luggage on board. I don't want people to get suspicious. Be quick,' Haider ordered in a whisper, breaking my reverie.

For a while, I had forgotten the world around me. My true identity. How could I forget myself and stare at a girl like that? I felt embarrassed and hated myself for doing that.

Mehar

I found his personality peculiar; something weird but indescribable. Whatever it was, I chose to ignore him. I stood near the cliff, taking in the breathtaking view of the beautiful, gigantic mountains and tranquil lakes. Behind me, Asma and Laraib were busy taking selfies on each other's phones.

To my surprise, the same man stood a few feet away from me. His presence unnerved me; I felt intimidated by him. His crisp, white kurta and the brown chaddar wrapped around his neck gave him a complete northern look. Despite being uncomfortable in his presence, I wanted to initiate a conversation with him and inquire whether he was also en route to see the beautiful Swat Valley. I struggled to find the right words to say to him.

I checked the time on my cell phone but its battery had died out.

'Damn,' I hissed. 'Need to charge my phone.' I turned to see if he had heard me but he seemed oblivious to my presence. He hadn't moved an inch. It seemed as if he wasn't even breathing.

'Umm . . . seems like my phone's battery has died. Could you please tell me the time?' I asked him.

He looked at me in confusion. He couldn't believe I was talking to him. He glanced at me and then turned to face the other side. I felt greatly insulted. This person had clearly ignored me. I looked down at my hands. I didn't want to look like an idiot so I tried once again.

'I asked you something. I hope you're not deaf,' I said.

But there was no response from his side. His cold response made me angry. I wanted to bash him for his rude demeanour.

'You're really weird. I just asked for the time because my phone is not working. You're acting as if I asked you to kill someone!' I said in a frustrated tone.

'What's your problem? Can't you see I'm not interested in talking to you?' he spoke at last, his voice all husky and dry. His blazing eyes scared me for a moment.

'What's my problem? What's your problem? Can't you talk politely with strangers? Is this what your parents have taught you?'

All of a sudden the anger disappeared from his eyes. His broad shoulde shrunk and wrinkles formed around his eyes, making him look older. He turned his face and looked the other way. There was silence. I felt dejected once again and decided not to bother him. I turned to walk away but his voice made me stop.

'It's 2.30 p.m.,' he whispered.

'What?' I looked at him with surprise.

'The time. It's 2.30 p.m.,' he repeated.

This made me smile for no reason.

'Thank you. Are you also on a trip to the Swat Valley?' I asked, taking advantage of his not-so-sulky mood.

He nodded and then looked away.

'Me too,' I added.

He glanced at me sideways and then nodded.

I heaved a long sigh and then looked at the beautiful landscape.

'I love adventures. I love travelling. That's why I am here!' I told him.

I could feel his eyes lingering on me.

'I think you should be there . . . with your other friends. Why are you standing here alone?' he asked in a brisk voice.

I didn't know what to tell him. Why was he suddenly interested in knowing me?

'I want to be here at this moment. It is making me happy,' I answered.

He nodded and then looked to the other side.

'And you?' I asked.

'Huh?'

'What about you? Why are you standing here all by yourself?'

'I'm . . . accustomed to being alone. There are times when alone is the best place to be. I enjoy my own company.'

'Oh,' I muttered. His answer had confused me.

One of the buses was ready to depart. Perhaps his. Without saying another word or looking at me, he strode towards the bus.

'Being alone is not better than being with someone who completes you. Wish you a safe journey. Take care,' I said.

He stopped for a second to hear what I had said but didn't turn to look at me. Without saying another word, I went to join my friends.

Sarmad

I had to walk away from her. What other option did I really have? Her words had made me uncomfortable.

Despite my determination, I glanced back over my shoulder. Her friends were busy taking pictures, but she looked at them silently.

I sat in the bus quietly as Haider took a bite from the sandwich. The driver of the other bus also requested the passengers to get on board as it was ready to leave. We were only a few minutes away from Mingora. The bus in which the girl sat with her friends overtook ours. I tried to catch a glimpse of her but failed.

Mehar

Despite plugging in my headphones and listening to loud music, I couldn't get his picture out of my mind. It made me frustrated. I was aware of the fact that he was travelling in the bus right behind mine. If only I could see him again . . .

What if he's also heading to Kalam like me? Will I get to see more of him?

I poked my head out of the window and turned to look at the bus behind ours. Unfortunately, I could only see the front of the bus.

The bumpy ride started making me queasy. I got up from my seat and walked down the aisle to stand near the bus door that was partly open. I breathed deeply, relishing the cool air that hit my face. But, life is really unpredictable. You never know what a moment holds for you unless you experience it.

Right then, one of the front tyres of our bus burst; it spun across the road, making the passengers scream in horror. I was thrown out of the door and on to the rough road. Next thing I knew I was falling off the cliff.

In a blink, everything turned upside down.

Sarmad

The sudden accident of the bus ahead caused havoc in our bus. The driver immediately stopped the vehicle and stepped down to see what had happened.

Haider and I picked up our bags and got down from the bus to see the damage. Few other passengers from our bus also followed.

The other bus had turned turtle.

Some of the passengers had managed to escape from the vehicle. A few others were trying to get out. I heard one of them calling for an ambulance. So far, there were no serious casualties. I didn't try to go inside the wrecked bus to look for her as I knew she had fallen out. I had seen her tumbling towards the cliff.

I ran towards the edge of the cliff but couldn't find her anywhere.

Where did she go? Is she . . . even alive? Oh god . . . No . . . I have to look for her. I need to find her. I can't let her die so easily . . . I can't.

Within a few minutes, ambulances arrived. Their blaring horns could be heard in the distance.

Stretcher-bearers from a nearby hospital laid a few injured passengers on stretchers and moved them to the ambulance.

Confused, I scanned the cliff. My eyes settled on a red piece of cloth which I assumed belonged to the same girl. Without thinking of the consequences, I stepped down and pushed myself lower. Haider warned me, even screamed at me, but I ignored him.

Mehar

Far away from the chaos, I lay on the ground, unconscious. I tried to open my eyes but it seemed difficult. My entire body ached. I moaned lightly in my unconscious state.

When I opened my eyes slowly, I could only see unfamiliar surroundings. Everything around was fuzzy. Suddenly, an arm, stretched out in my direction, tried to get hold of me. I wanted to respond but couldn't as there was no strength left inside my frail, injured body. In that moment, I experienced a sense of déjà vu.

Sarmad

I didn't know why I was helping her. I didn't understand why I had even come after her. I had not planned to rescue her. I did not belong to her. Did I? I had just followed my instincts. I knew I had to. I knew Haider would be pissed off as I'd left without informing him. I had left my mission to save this girl; a girl who didn't even know me properly. She lay breathless on the ground. I took her hand in mine and checked her pulse. To my relief, she was alive. I swiftly wrapped her arm around my neck and grabbed her from the waist. Carrying her in my arms, I carefully walked along the rough path to reach the place of the accident. Since the ambulances were already present at the site, I knew she would get medical attention on time. As I trudged along the road in search of the main road, my shoulders started hurting. I had also carried my bag, which to my surprise seemed heavy now. Beads of sweat trickled down my face. I felt out of breath. I stopped for a while, took deep breaths and then looked around. The girl still lay limp in my arms, unconscious.

Even after looking in all directions, I couldn't see signs of the main road anywhere. Perhaps, I had taken a wrong turn that had led me towards another road.

After walking for almost fifteen minutes, I spotted an old, wrecked jeep. I carefully laid her on the side of the road and made an attempt to stop the approaching jeep. Thankfully, the jeep stopped midway. A middle-aged man, who was seated on the driver's seat, popped his face out of the window. A woman sat next to him, her face clouded with concern.

'Salaam, bhai. Is there a problem?' he asked, lowering his shades.

'Uh . . . yes. I . . . uh . . . our bus met with an accident on the Saidu Road and she tumbled off the cliff . . .' I said as I frantically pointed at her unconscious body.

'Aziz! See that poor girl lying on the road! *Ya* Allah *khair*! What happened to her?' the woman asked, getting out of the car. The man, probably her husband, also followed her.

The two of them circled her. The woman got down on her knees to check her pulse.

'She's . . . fine . . . she's alive. I got her here,' I told them, my voice faltering.

'Aziz, please get the water bottle from the jeep. We must give her some water to drink.'

Aziz did what the woman told him to do.

'What happened to her, bhai sahib? Is she your wife?' she asked, looking at me.

'Uh . . .' I didn't know what to say. Clearly, I couldn't blurt out something that would make them suspicious.

'Yes . . . she's . . . my wife,' I nodded.

Aziz brought the bottle from the jeep and quickly handed it to his wife.

'Honeymoon?' she asked as she opened the bottle.

'Yes, right,' I nodded my head.

She held the water bottle to her lips. However, the girl did not take in much.

'She needs proper medical attention,' Aziz told me.

I looked at him, dazed.

'Bhai sahib, I can feel her pulse drop. Listen . . . we have a family doctor who is staying at our house in Mingora. Our house is only a few miles away. If you agree, we can take you with us. Once her condition stabilizes, you both can leave,' the woman suggested.

Damn, no. That didn't sound like a good plan. I couldn't stay anywhere. I had to get back to my mission. I had to call Haider and tell him where I was. I had to move on.

'House? Oh, no, no. I don't think that's required. I don't want to trouble you. You can just drop us to a nearby hospital,' I said.

'There's no trouble, bhai sahib. It's completely all right. This way you don't even have to bear any hospital charges. My mother-in-law, Bari Aapa, will be pleased to welcome you at our place. Please come with us,' the woman said.

Suppressing my dilemma, I let out a deep sigh and then walked away a few steps to think over the possibilities. Just then my cell phone rang in my pocket. It was a private number.

'Hello?'

'Sarmad!'

'Mullah sahib!' I exclaimed in surprise.

'*Shuker* Alhamdulillah, you're safe, my boy!'

'Why, what happened?' I furrowed my brows in confusion.

'Don't you know? The army has started a new search operation in the major northern areas of Pakistan. They're looking for militants everywhere and shooting them on the spot. Haider is missing. We can't locate his number. I believe he's . . .' Mullah stopped speaking.

I felt a deep pain in my chest. My entire body trembled with shock.

'Just be careful, son: Hide somewhere safe. Make sure the army doesn't reach you. You need to be careful as this operation might take some days. I will call you again once the situation is clear. You can then resume your mission and go to Lahore.'

'But I was heading towards Mingora because that's where we had to meet . . .'

'No. You can't meet the others at this point. Just hide somewhere for a couple of days and wait for my call.'

'Ji, Mullah sahib. As you say . . .'

'Allah hafiz.' Mullah ended the call.

A spasm of shock went through my body. I didn't want to believe that Haider was taken because he was at the accident scene. What if someone had caught him right there? I instantly made up my mind and glanced back at the girl, who was still lying unconscious on the road. Aziz and his wife were looking at me expectantly, waiting for my final decision. I knew where I had to go as I was left with no other option. I had to take that decision.

For a moment, I felt aimless. I didn't know what on earth I was doing here. I shouldn't have been here. I had saved her because she was in trouble, I kept reminding myself. But how many people had I really saved before? None! Why her then? Why had I put myself in great danger because of her?

Mehar

Day 1

I don't know how long I'd been unconscious for. It seemed like a lifetime. It felt like I had been thrown into darkness forever. I had been on the way to Swat Valley with my friends when the bus tumbled off the road and I fell out of it. I don't know what happened after that. When I slowly opened my eyes, I tried to take in the surroundings. My mind tried to process the information around me. I was lying on a neatly made bed in a clean, spacious room. The walls were covered with light beige paint, with lilac-coloured curtains hanging over large windows. I could hazily see a balcony through those windows. As I looked around the room, three unfamiliar faces, all women, gawked at me with expressions of concern. Who were these women? How did I end up here? Where was the rest of my group? Where were Asma and Laraib? Were they fine? I started fidgeting, trying to get rid of the bandages but a young woman, probably around my age, stopped me.

'What are you doing?' the young woman asked, getting hold of me.

'Who are you? Let me go!' I protested weakly.

'You can't leave, beta. Not until your condition is stable,' an elderly woman, standing beside the young woman, told me.

Feeling helpless, I stopped fidgeting and took a deep breath. These women did not look dangerous. They seemed polite. Knowing this was not the way I was going to get my answers, I tried to calm down.

'I had an accident. How did I end up here?.Who brought me here? And where are my friends?' I tried to sit up on the bed, tensed.

'Your husband brought you here,' the young woman said as she helped me sit up.

'What?' I choked with shock. 'Husband?'

'Yes, he did. He's standing outside. I must say he's really worried about you, beta,' the elderly woman said.

My head exploded with this revelation. Who was this person? Why had he saved my life? And more importantly, why had he claimed to be my 'husband'?

Sarmad

Day 1

I had done my job. I had saved her life, though I had had to lie to this family. A few minutes ago, their family doctor had visited her and assured me that she was all right. There were no internal injuries—just a few bruises here and there. I could hear her voice from the bedroom. She was alive, breathing again. It was pointless to sit outside the room now. Aziz and his younger brother, Faisal, were also seated beside me. I closed my fist tightly, heaved a long sigh, and thought about my next plan of action.

Bari Aapa, Aziz's mother, came out of the room, looking for me. Aziz's wife and another young woman also followed her.

'Beta, your wife wants to see you,' Bari Aapa told me.
I hiccupped at her words.

These women must have told her. She knew about my lie. How was I going to face her now? I had made up a story without even asking her. But what other option did I have? It was obvious for them to consider us a couple. I wanted her to understand this.

'And, don't worry. She's completely fine now,' she said, patting my back.

I half-heartedly smiled at her and went into the room, closing the door behind me.

Mehar

Looking at my injuries, I realized that I wasn't badly hurt. There were a few scratches and bruises on my legs and arms. Other than that, I felt completely fine. But where were my friends? Were they safe? What if they had informed Amma and Abba about the accident? I didn't want to tell them as they would get unnecessarily worried. I looked around to find my luggage but couldn't find it. My handbag and cell phone were also missing. How would I get in touch with my friends now?

My head still whirled with confusion. Who was this person who had saved my life and then claimed to be my husband in front of these people? Where was he?

Just then, a man in an off-white kurta, with a shawl wrapped around his shoulders, walked into the room. I held my breath for a moment, trying to place the familiar attire and that face.

Wasn't he the same person I had met at the bus stop?
I gasped, the hair on my neck and arms standing.
When did he become my husband?
'Uh . . . hi.' He looked at me, embarrassed.
'Who are you? Why did you bring me here?' I asked him, my head exploding with questions.

'You fell off the cliff. I saved you,' he said in a low voice, without blinking.

'What?' I was shocked at his casual demeanour.

'Yes. I met this family on the way to the spot of the accident. You were unconscious. They insisted on taking you to their house instead of the hospital. So yeah, that's how I got you here,' he said, looking away. He couldn't even meet my eyes.

'But why? You shouldn't have listened to them. You should've taken me where my group and friends were!' As I tried to get up from the bed, a severe spasm of pain hit my left leg.

'Ow! Oh no . . .' I cried. Instantly, he was by my side.

'Are you okay?' he asked, his brows furrowed.

I shot him a furious look.

'No! I'm not okay,' I lashed out at him, ignoring the pain. 'I don't even know you or these people. What am I even doing here? I don't get it . . . I just need to go back. I need to talk to my parents. I need to go to where my friends are.'

'Fine, fi_____. I will get you back there. All right?' He ___ed to calm me down.

'You better!' I brushed away the strands of hair that had fallen over my forehead and then looked away. He contemplated something for a few minutes and then turned away. I attacked him once again.

'And how dare you call yourself my husband?' I fumed.

He turned to look at me again, this time with a calm expression on his face.

I was expecting him to be furious, to throw a fit. To my surprise, he remained calm and eerily quiet.

Sarmad

Despite her accusations, I did not even cringe. I found it hard to rebuke those beautiful, caramel brown eyes. I knew I couldn't be angry with her. I knew it, but didn't have an explanation for it. Before I could say something in my defence, someone knocked on the door and then stepped inside.

'May I come in?' It was Aziz's wife.

'Sure, please,' I whispered.

The girl, whom I had saved, shot me a bewildered look.

'Hope I am not disturbing you,' she said, warily. A boy of around five or six years stood right behind her. Probably her son.

'Not at all,' I reassured, half-smiling at the boy.

'How are you feeling now?' Aziz's wife asked her. 'I think you should rest.'

'I am fine, much better. Thanks,' she told her, biting her lip.

'By the way, I'm Rukhsana, Aziz's wife.' She passed her a warm smile as she introduced herself.

'I am so sorry that you two had to go through such a misfortune. You even lost your luggage.'

Both of us shared a quick, bemused glance.

'But I must say, your wife is indeed lucky, ji. She has such a caring husband like you.'

I looked down, not wanting to see the girl's reaction.

'I have brought some clothes for you to pass the night.' Rukhsana said, glancing at the stack of clothes in her hands.

'Oh . . . no . . . we are fine. I mean . . . we could have managed something ourselves . . .' I broke in. The girl shot me a furious look, and I instantly understood what she wanted me to do.

'In fact . . .' I said, looking at the girl. 'We should leave now. You've already done a lot for us. We can't thank you enough . . .'

'That's not a problem, ji. We felt it was our duty to help you. Don't worry about going back. You can comfortably stay here for the night and then leave tomorrow. It's completely dark outside, and it's getting cold. Therefore, I'd suggest you stay over. Rest is up to you.' She smiled once again and kept the stack of clothes near the bed. The little boy tugged at her dupatta and hid his face.

'And I've also arranged dinner for you. One of the servants will bring the food to your room. Actually, we have a wedding in our family that is keeping us busy.'

I tried to smile at her.

'Acha, I'll take your leave now. Let's go to sleep, Jamil. You have school tomorrow . . .' She stepped out along with the boy and closed the door behind her.

I ran my fingers through my hair, heaving a sigh of relief.

'Why didn't you tell her that you aren't my husband?' The girl started accusing me again.

'What?' I asked, shocked.

'You could have easily told her the truth and we could have left right away. Now I am stuck here with you throughout the night!' She sat down on the bed, cradling her head between her hands.

'Listen . . . even I don't want to stay here with you. I had no intention of spending the night with you in this bloody room.' I shot back at her. I had to. She had got me fired up.

She looked at me, her expression softening. The fear in her beautiful eyes bothered me.

'I can't stay here even for a microsecond. I need to get out of here as soon as possible because I also have some bloody work to attend to.'

She looked down, not meeting my eyes.

'Instead of being thankful for what I did for you, you've been accusing me constantly. Don't make me regret saving you because I never regret my decisions!'

A look of remorse spread across her face.

'What else could I have said to the family who brought us here? They wouldn't have believed me if I had told them we aren't married. I did what seemed reasonable and justifiable at the time of saving you. You have no reason to accuse me like that. If you can't pretend for a night or can't handle the situation, then just walk away.'

I could see the guilt washing over her face. I soaked up her flawless beauty as I continued to stare at her. The innocence in those brown eyes; the fragility of her dainty hands; the nervousness evident in her body language. Now she made me regret my words. Her forlorn expression made me feel guilty.

'Let's just spend the night somehow. I'll take you back to your friends tomorrow morning,' I told her.

She looked up at me, tears glistening in her eyes.

Those sad eyes broke me from inside.

Without looking back at her again, I grabbed my bag from the floor and walked towards the balcony.

Mehar

I rushed into the bathroom and locked the door from inside. Tears rolled down my cheeks. I quickly turned on the water tap and cried my heart out. I didn't want him to hear my wails. I splashed water on my face to calm myself down. Without turning off the tap, I sank down on the floor and cried more.

Why was I stuck here? I had to get back as soon as possible. I hope my friends are safe . . .

I shouldn't have shouted at that guy. He was the one who saved my life after all. He was the one who brought me here. Had he not helped me, I would not be breathing at the moment. I shouldn't have blamed him. He did what he felt was right. Perhaps I would have done the same if I had been in his place. I must apologize to him. I must . . .

Sarmad

She probably thinks I'm some evil guy trying to take advantage of her. But she's right in a way. I'm a monster who is not capable of doing any good for anyone. I brought her here for my own personal motives. I had to take shelter in this house in order to hide from the army. I couldn't stay outside and get caught. I have to stay here till the situation clears.

But how would that be possible? She wants to return to her friends and family. I have to make her stay for a few days. How will I do it? How will I stop her from leaving?

It was 2.30 a.m. Outside, rain tapped against the roof. It had started with a few drops but later turned into a heavy downpour. The cold wind battered the balcony window, sending chills down my entire body. I walked back into the room and saw her sitting on the carpeted floor, her head resting on her knees and arms wrapped around her legs. The sound of thunder filled the room; the lightning from the dark clouds lit up the sky for a second before vanishing.

She hadn't eaten the food Rukhsana had sent to our room. I ate it silently, without offering her anything. We hadn't spoken since our last squabble.

After finishing dinner, I walked into the washroom to clean up. Later, I took a blanket and pillows and set them on the couch. All through, I observed her from the corner of my eye. Without saying another word, I lay on the couch and covered myself, head-to-toe, with the blanket.

Mehar

After calming myself down and mustering some courage, I changed my worn-out clothes and wore what Rukhsana had brought for me. How kind and humble she was. In fact, the entire family. I tiptoed from the washroom and sat down on the carpeted floor. He ignored me. He ate his dinner silently and then went to sleep. How could he sleep after ruining my mood? How ill-mannered and discourteous he was!

I couldn't fall asleep with him in the same room. Despite feeling terrified by his presence, I couldn't help but appreciate the fact that he had left the bed for me and was sleeping on the couch. I looked at him to make sure he was asleep and then sighed. I decided to call Amma and Abba the next morning and inform them about my condition. I also had to check on my friends.

Sarmad

Day 2

I woke up around 5 a.m. Removing the blanket from my face, I turned my head to check on her. To my surprise, she'd fallen asleep on the floor. I got up from the couch and walked towards where she lay. I stared at her for a long time. A few strands of hair had fallen over her face, making her look even more beautiful. Every single feature of her face took my breath away. I surely hadn't seen a more beautiful living creature than her. I stared at her face for a few more minutes.

How could someone be rude to her when she deserved all the good things in the world? She didn't deserve wrath but something else . . . but I was not capable of giving her that. All I could do was be nice to her and apologize for my rudeness.

Mehar

Day 2

A sudden knock on the door woke me up. My eyes first scanned the entire room to look for him but he was nowhere to be seen.

Where was he? Had he left me alone here? Had he walked away?

My heart pounded loudly in my chest as I walked towards the door. Right then, I heard the sound of the shower in the bathroom and felt relieved; he was having a bath. However, the knocking on the door persisted until I unlocked it and peered outside.

'Good morning, how are you feeling today?' a young girl, probably a few years younger than me, asked. She had a tray of breakfast in her hands.

'Hi . . .' I tucked my hair behind my ears. 'I'm feeling better now. Thank you for the help.'

'I'm Sufi, by the way! I'm the one who's getting married.' She rolled her eyes dramatically.

'Oh. Congratulations, Sufi. I'm Mehar.' I smiled at her, slightly taken aback. She looked too young to get married.

'Nice to meet you, Mehar! I have brought breakfast for you. Actually, Bari Aapa sent this for you.' She giggled.

'It wasn't required at all, Sufi . . . I . . .' I was amazed by her bubbly personality.

'Should I keep it on the table?' She ignored my comment.

I nodded and moved aside, allowing her to step into the room. She set the tray on the table and looked at me.

'Do you want to have a look around the house? It's being decorated at the moment. Come with me. I'll take you through the wedding festivities.' She took me by my arm and, despite my reluctance, led me downstairs.

The entire staircase, along with different areas of the mansion, had been decorated with beautiful flowers and fairy lights. I couldn't stop admiring the beauty of the place. It seemed like heaven. Girls, sitting cross-legged in the living room, were busy applying henna on each other's hands. Some of them grooved to wedding songs. while others played the *dholki*. Trays full of flowers and mehndi were kept in the centre.

'Everything is so beautiful . . .' I said dreamily.

'Mehar, why don't you stay with us till the wedding?' Sufi asked, turning towards me.

Her question startled me.

'Stay?' I looked back at her, perplexed.

'Yes! I don't have too many friends here. I would be really happy if you attended my wedding. Please stay, na! It will be so much fun!' she insisted.

'Good morning, young lady, how are you feeling now?' an elderly woman—perhaps Bari Aapa—asked as she appeared out of the blue.

'Very well, thank you so much. You've all done a lot for me,' I replied, smiling.

'You should thank your husband, not us. He was the one who brought you here.'

The word 'husband' sent thousands of chills down my spine. I looked down, feeling slightly embarrassed.

'Where is he?' Bari Aapa asked.

'Uh. He is taking a shower upstairs,' I said, tucking strands of hair behind my ears.

'Bari Aapa, please ask Mehar to stay with us till the wedding. Please request her, na!' Sufi started insisting again.

'*Arey* haan, this seems like a brilliant idea! Beta, why don't you stay with us till the wedding? We would love to have a young couple like you. It will be a wonderful way for you to spend your honeymoon as well. Trust me, I would be delighted if you stayed.'

'No, I think we're fine, Bari Aapa,' he interrupted. 'We have other business to attend to.'

He had come out of nowhere; seeing him made my heart skip a beat. With washed hair, glowing skin and neat clothes, he looked different. The fresh, white kurta and crisp salwar looked heavenly on him. For a second, I couldn't take my eyes off him. Was he really the same person? He narrowed his eyes at me to understand my reaction. Embarrassed, I looked away.

'But beta . . . this wedding will be a lot of fun. I'm sure this would be the best wedding you have ever attended! It will be very different from those Lahori weddings of yours,' she chuckled.

'I don't think that's possible, Bari Aapa . . . We have to get back today,' he said, trying to gauge my reaction.

I could see that Bari Aapa and Sufi were disappointed with his reply.

'But . . . it's just a matter of a few days . . .' Sufi whined.

'I wish we could stay till the wedding but we have to go back. Our parents will be waiting for us,' he said as he looked at me.

I did not want this to happen. I wanted to stay here. I wanted to witness a wedding in Swat. Since I was already here, I wanted to experience something new; something that would remind me of the good old days. But the current situation seemed to be taking away this golden opportunity from me. I could not let this opportunity slip away. I instantly thought of a plan and then replied.

'I think . . .' I looked at his face and then continued. 'We will be staying here till the wedding.' I nodded at Bari Aapa and Sufi.

He shot me a surprised look.

'Really?' Sufi exclaimed.

'Yes, really,' I said, darting a serious look at him. He stared back at me with anxious eyes.

'Amazing news! It's decided then. You two are staying here till the wedding. I'll inform the others as well. I need you two to get ready as all of us are going down to the Swat River. We'll have breakfast near the banks of the river.' Bari Aapa patted both of us and then walked away.

'Yay! I'm so happy!' Sufi took me in her arms. 'I'll ask Rukhsana Chachi to arrange more clothes for you.'

As I hugged her back, I saw a surge of resentment in his eyes. He stomped off to our room.

Meanwhile, I asked Sufi if I could use their telephone. I had to check on Asma and Laraib. When I called on one of their numbers, Asma quickly picked up the phone.

'Asma! How are you and Laraib?' I asked, not even waiting for her to speak first.

'Mehar! Oh god! You're fine! Thank god. Where are you? We tried your number so many times but it was switched off.'

'I'm totally fine, Asma. Don't worry. Are you two all right? And where are you now?'

'We're fine. We came back to Lahore today morning.'

'What happened after the accident?' I asked her, getting curious.

'We were rushed to the nearby hospital where we were treated. Thankfully, everything was fine. We spent one more day with the rest of the group in Swat and then came back today. What about you? Where are you?'

'I was also rushed to the hospital and luckily got rescued by my relatives here. I'm staying with them now,' I lied to her. If I told her the truth, I knew the story would somehow reach my parents which I didn't want. I didn't want them to know what had happened.

'Oh, that's great.'

'Just take care of yourself, Asma. I'll get back to you when I return to Lahore.'

'Sure, buddy. Take care.'

After talking to Asma, I called up my parents and talked to Amma. I told her that I was fine and would come back after a few days. I felt bad for lying to her though. I realized what a terrible liar I had become in the last few days.

Sarmad

I did not understand why she said yes to Bari Aapa. *Was she a fool?* Last night she was dying to go back to her friends and today she suddenly changed her mind. She'd just come out of a huge problem and now wanted to plunge into another.

'Why did you say yes to Bari Aapa when you knew we were not going to stay here till the wedding? Why? Are you out of your mind?' I asked her when she got back to 'our' room.

'I said yes because I wanted to . . .' she said in a low voice, closing the door behind her.

'What? God!' I anxiously ran my fingers through my hair. 'You wanted to go back! What made you change your mind all of a sudden? May I know, please?'

'I don't know myself . . .' she said, hazily. 'I just didn't want to turn down that offer. It . . . it kind of excited me.'

'What? Excited you?'

She nodded.

'What about me? What made you think I would want to stay here with you till the wedding?' I crossed my arms across my chest as I questioned her.

'You can . . . just leave if you want to,' she shrugged.

'What?' I frowned.

She stood motionless, her face clouded. Clearly, she was running out of answers.

'And what about your friends? Your family?' I continued probing her.

'I've already spoken to them. My friends are safe.'

'I've also informed my parents. I can stay here till the wedding.'

I did not want to push her further because whatever she had decided was ultimately in my favour. I could easily stay here and work on my mission without getting caught. Having her by my side as my fake wife was an added bonus, as Bari Aapa's family would not suspect me.

'All right . . .' I nodded, looking at her. 'If that's what you've decided.'

She nodded in return and walked away.

I hurried towards the balcony and fished out my phone from my pocket. There were no missed calls or unread messages from any of my group members or Mullah sahib. I got worried. I dialled Haider's number to check on him. After a few rings, and to my surprise, he picked up my call.

'Haider! Where are you?' I asked, without waiting for him to say anything.

'Sarmad . . . where did you vanish all of a sudden?' he whispered. 'I'm hiding somewhere in Batkhela. What about you? Where are you?'

'Thank god you're fine . . . I'm sorry I had to leave unannounced. I am badly stuck in Mingora but I'm safe. Don't worry about me,' I told him, heaving a sigh of relief. I kept my voice low because I knew she was in the room.

'We need to hide and stay safe for a few days until the search operation stops,' he said.

'Yes, I know . . .' I whispered, turning back to see what she was up to. She was busy pulling out clothes from a suitcase.

'Just be safe, my brother. *Rab rakha*.'

'Rab rakha,' I whispered, taking in a deep breath.

Mehar

Later that day, Rukhsana sent a suitcase to our room that contained enough clothes for the two of us. I rummaged through the suitcase till a multi-coloured piece of cloth grabbed my attention. I took out the cloth that turned out to be a pheran, a knee-length gown worn by Pashtun women. The gown had embroidery on the front panel and on the edges. I loved it and decided to wear it. I'd seen pictures of Pashtun girls dressed in pherans but had never thought I'd wear one myself.

I wanted to stay for a while in Swat so that I could reminisce about the past. This seemed like the last golden chance to live my life freely and to the fullest. My parents were already getting me married to my cousin. I would never get the chance to live on my own terms. This seemed like my last trip on my own, and I wanted to make it memorable. It didn't matter if it only involved witnessing a wedding in Swat.

After a few minutes, he came back to the room. I'd seen him talking to someone on the phone, but I didn't ask anything. Why would I?

'Everyone must be waiting for us downstairs. Maybe you should get ready,' he said, not looking away.

He held my eyes for a long time as he waited for my reply. His stare unnerved me.

I hastily nodded my head, without looking him in the eye, and rushed to the washroom.

Sarmad

As she came out of the washroom, dressed in a Pashtun dress, my heart fluttered. I wasn't sure if I'd seen such beauty before. She looked beautiful, simply beautiful. She looked ethereal in the multi-coloured pheran. I observed her from head to toe but when I realized that my stare was making her uneasy, I blinked my eyes and then turned my head to the other side. She dried her hair and combed it neatly. Even without any make-up, she looked beautiful.

Within a few minutes, she was ready to go. Without saying a word to me, she just signalled that she was ready to leave. I followed her outside the room and then joined the rest of the family members. Jeeps stood in the driveway to take us to the river. Since everyone had to be accommodated, we sat close together. I knew the proximity between us made her uneasy, but I was helpless. As soon as her fresh scent hit my nostrils, I felt mesmerized. She let out a silent gasp when my shoulder touched hers. We shared a quick nervous glance, and I tried my best to create space between us. Deep down I knew what I'd done to her last night was not right. I felt apologetic and hated this feeling.

Mehar

Bari Aapa's mansion was beautiful in every way. The outside pavement was decorated with expensive flowers. I couldn't believe I was about to experience a wedding in Swat. This could be a once in a lifetime experience for me. However, *he* made me nervous. I did not want to sit in the same jeep as him.

What else could I do? What other choice did I have?

Since I was pretending to be his wife, I had to sit next to him. Every time his shoulder brushed against mine, I winced. Across me, Rukhsana sat with her five-year-old son, Jamil. Aziz, her husband, was behind the wheel. Jamil constantly shot nervous glances at me and then him. For him, we were new people. When I smiled at him, he hid his face in his mother's lap.

'I think he's just scared.' Rukhsana smiled at her son's gesture.

'Yeah, that's what I thought too,' I mumbled, smiling.

He pretended to remain oblivious to the entire conversation, but still looked at us through the corner of his eye.

'You don't have to be scared of me,' I continued, trying to gain Jamil's attention. 'I'm your friend.'

Jamil looked at me groggily while sitting comfortably on his mother's lap.

'Will you be my friend?' I asked him in a sweet tone.

Jamil seemed confused; he looked up at his mother to get her confirmation. She gestured him to go ahead. And then again he glanced at me.

'Please? I'll be your true friend. I'll also give you chocolates,' I told him.

'Really?' Jamil spoke at last.

'Yes,' I nodded animatedly.

'Then we're friends!' Jamil said, getting out of his mother's hold and sitting next to me.

I shook hands with Jamil, and he started talking to me. I could see that *he* was not interested in our conversation, so I chose to ignore him. The cool gust of wind on my face made me feel alive and happy. The beautiful sight of the gigantic mountains, roaring rivers and fascinating waterfalls brought a smile to my face. I seemed lost in its endless magnificence. Between admiring the beautiful place around me and chit-chatting with Jamil, I didn't notice that we had arrived at the river. A jolt of excitement fired through me.

Sarmad

All of them got down from the jeep one by one. Aziz helped his wife, Rukhsana, and then he took his son in his arms. I stepped down after them and adjusted my clothes. Along with everyone, I started walking towards the valley but something stopped me. I couldn't feel her behind me. I turned around to see what had happened. To my surprise, she was still in the jeep, waiting for someone to help her get down. I huffed and shook my head as I walked towards the jeep. She looked uncomfortable. Perhaps she was scared of heights. Without looking at her, I held out my hand so she could hold it and step down easily.

'No . . . I'm fine, thanks,' she muttered. 'I don't need your help.'

'Don't overreact and just hold my hand,' I said, getting irritated at her childish behaviour.

She shot me a nervous glance.

'Step down!' I told her. This time it sounded more like an order.

She quickly agreed, held my hand nervously and then stepped down, but she suddenly tripped—her arms tightly wrapped around my shoulders and neck. This little accident brought colour to her already pink cheeks. She flushed and felt embarrassed. I could see mortification on her face. I could smell her fragrance and hear the loud thudding of her heartbeat. For an instant, our eyes locked. She quickly shoved me away. We were too embarrassed to say anything. Bari Aapa called out to us. She immediately rushed towards her, leaving me alone to deal with the embarrassment. I can't describe how I felt at that moment. She had touched me unwillingly, but still she had touched me. I could still feel her cool breath on my face and smell her fragrance on my collar. She was driving me crazy. I tried to ignore this fact but failed.

Mehar

I felt a jolt of embarrassment. All my excitement vanished. I couldn't believe that I had just been so close to him. I had touched his body against my will. I had never felt this way before. I had never come so close to a stranger. I stood beside Bari Aapa, feeling embarrassed. Within a few seconds, he also joined me. For obvious reasons, I loathed his presence and wanted to run away from him. I wished I could go back to Lahore. I regretted staying with the family till the wedding. Coming to Swat was my own plan. But now, just because of him, I felt like reversing my decision. The family members busied themselves in taking pictures of the beautiful landscape. The women, including Rukhsana, laid down a mat on the lush green grass and opened their food baskets. I also helped them out to distract myself. The gushing river surrounded us. Gradually, the breeze turned chilly, and the sunlight shone on the valley like a million little glittering specks. Across the banks of the river, children played and women worked in fields. The perfectly aligned wooden houses looked straight out of picture postcards. I could feel the serenity of the place and felt completely separated from the rest of the world. Deep down, it gave me unadulterated happiness coupled with peace. Ignoring his presence for a while, I tried to feel happy. I tried to enjoy my freedom. Being here reminded me of my childhood—those carefree days. This also triggered a memory which I'd put at the back of my mind. I tried to remember it but failed.

Soon, I indulged in the delicious desi breakfast that the women had laid out—hot tea served with baqerkhani, omelettes, parathas and samosas. As I took a samosa along with a cup of tea, my eyes landed on him. Everybody was busy eating except him. He stood near the river bank, lost in his own thoughts. Beside him Jamil sat on one of the rocks, busy playing with sheets of paper. I wanted to sit next to them. I arranged a breakfast plate for him and excused myself from the rest of the family members. As I walked towards them, I could hear the gushing blue waters of the river flowing on one side and the waterfall on the other.

Sarmad

I felt an excruciating craving for a cigarette but unfortunately couldn't find one. My thoughts still revolved around my other companions. I waited for Mullah's second call every passing second. In an attempt to distract myself, I turned my attention towards Jamil, who was sitting next to me. Blank paper sheets were scattered all around him as he tried to make something out of them.

'What are you trying to make?' I asked, bending down to sit next to the kid.

'I'm trying to make a bird but it seems difficult,' Jamil mumbled, making a glum face.

'Where did you learn it from?' I asked, curiosity rising in my tone.

'My teacher taught me in school. I think I have forgotten it. My bad,' Jamil made a face again, crumpled the paper in his hand and threw it away.

'Don't give up so easily. Wait a second. Let's give it another try.' I took a fresh piece of paper from his notebook. Just then, she walked up to us and stood there, witnessing the scene. From the corner of my eye, I could see the amazement on their faces. Slowly and with ease, I successfully made an origami paper crane.

'Wow. This is unbelievable!' Jamil clapped his hands in excitement.

A smile flashed across my face after seeing him happy. She also smiled.

'Will it fly?' Jamil asked me innocently.

'Do you want it to fly?' I asked, cocking my eye.

Jamil nodded.

'Let's do it then.' I took the bird from Jamil's hands and then threw it across the river. As it flew, Jamil clapped more enthusiastically.

'Look, look, Amma. There goes my bird!' Jamil called out to his mother, Rukhsana.

The entire family left their breakfast and looked at the flying origami. All of them felt extremely delighted for the child. A small smile played on my lips but in the next moment I hated myself for even showing the trick as I knew she had been staring at me the whole time.

Mehar

Seeing his behaviour towards Jamil made me happy. But what caught my attention was the origami crane. It reminded me of something from my own childhood.

The night had turned chillier. With a cup of green tea in my hands, I stood under the starry night in my room's balcony. We'd returned from the river right before dusk.

I had almost forgotten to call my parents that day. I didn't have a mobile phone as I had lost mine during the bus accident. Thinking of my parents brought tears in my eyes. I sniffed and tried to control my tears but they came rolling down. I didn't realize when he came in and stood beside me. We glanced at each other briefly before I averted my watery eyes. I knew he'd seen the tears.

'I really miss my parents,' I said, killing the silence between us.

He didn't turn to look at me.

'This is the first time I've been away from them for so long . . .' I whispered.

'You shouldn't have come then, knowing it would be difficult for you to live without your family,' he retorted.

Wiping my tears, I shot him a contemptuous look.

'I wonder how your parents let you come on this trip,' he said. 'Girls of your age shouldn't be allowed to step out of their homes.'

'You should be ashamed of your thoughts,' I said, facing him now. 'Do you really want women to stay confined within the boundaries of their houses? I don't understand why men are so against women's freedom. Men should support them in every possible way. This is the reason why women have not prospered in our country. It is because of men like you that there is no equality!'

He shot me a fuming look but I ignored it. This time, I was not scared of anything.

'My father is a man of principles. He never wanted me to come on this trip but he did it anyway because he wanted to see me happy,' I said. 'Despite being in the army and having rigid principles, he never imposed anything on his wife, son or daughters. He let us live a liberal life.'

There was a certain discomfort on his face when I told him about my father. I could clearly see it.

'Army? Is your father an army officer?' he asked, out of curiosity, and then looked away.

'Was. He has retired now.'

'What's his name?'

'Retired general Haissam Uddin.'

Sarmad

I winced on hearing her father's name.

'What happened, do you know him? I'm sure you must have heard about him,' she said in an affirmative tone.

'I guess I have,' I mumbled, my jaw muscles tightening. We remained silent for a while.

'I really. don't have anything against independent women . . . it's just that I wasn't brought up in a household where women were given the right to live according to their own will.'

'Where have you lived all your life?' she asked, her voice getting intense.

I did not want to reveal so much information about myself. Though I felt safe telling her everything, I wasn't allowed to break the rules. Therefore, I stayed silent. My silence answered her question.

'It's okay if you don't want to share anything with me. But I don't know why I don't feel awkward sharing everything with you,' she said, looking into my eyes.

There was genuineness in her eyes; I could feel it at that moment. I no longer felt any animosity towards her.

'I don't know anything about you except that you're from Lahore,' I said, changing the subject.

'Oh yes.' She smiled, happiness glimmering in her eyes. 'I'm from Lahore. I've lived there all my life. I study journalism at Kinnaird College. Have you heard of KC?'

'No.' I slowly shook my head.

'Oh okay,' she muttered. 'Seems like you're not familiar with Lahore.'

I did not say anything in return and did not even shake my head.

Silence prevailed once again as we looked straight ahead.

'I was thinking about something,' she murmured.

I cocked my head to look at her.

'Since we're staying here till the wedding and pretending to be a happily married couple, why don't we behave like normal people? We don't necessarily have to be mean towards each other. I mean . . . we can be friends as well.'

Her words rocked me from inside. I couldn't believe what she'd just blurted.

'I know you might find it odd but what's wrong in it? If we behave nicely towards each other, nobody would ever find out the truth. What do you say?' she asked, facing me.

Her question had startled me. She was right. I had to survive for a couple of days and take shelter in that house. And for that I had to be on good terms with her. She noticed that I was lost in thoughts.

'What are you thinking?' she asked.

'Maybe you're right . . .' I said, coming back to reality. 'We shouldn't be mean towards each other.'

She smiled in return.

'I'm sorry . . .' I whispered.

'For?' she asked.

'For being rude to you the other night,' I confessed.

'I think I should apologize too. I also overreacted.' She bit her lip.

I stared at her for a long time.

'Thank you . . .' she said.

'For?'

'Saving me and then bringing me here.' She smiled.

As a response, I nodded my head lightly and then looked straight.

'It's so weird that we've been together for so long and still haven't asked each other's names,' she said, chuckling.

I looked at her once again. This was the first time I'd seen her laughing. God, she was so beautiful.

'I'm Mehar. Mehar Haissam Uddin. And you?'

'I'm . . . Sarmad,' I said.

She smiled after hearing my name; I don't know why though.

'Nice to meet you, Sarmad,' she said as she held out her hand.

I stared at her hand for a long time before shaking it. I noticed the silver bangles on her wrist. They clinked together when she brought her hand forward. The clinking sound amused me. Her hand felt soft and warm against my rough skin.

What was happening to me?

'Can I ask for something?' she asked, to which I nodded.

Anything, my heart said.

'May I borrow your cell phone for a moment? I need to call my mother.'

'No. Sorry, I can't,' I replied curtly, cutting her in between.

There was a look of shock on her face.

'But why? I won't talk for long!' She frowned.

'I'm sorry but i can't.' I raised my hands in defence and then remained mute.

She took a deep breath and then nodded, staring down at the floor. I walked away.

Mehar

< *> >

I couldn't understand why he didn't give me his phone. All I had asked for was one call. His demeanour seemed strange. Nevertheless, I didn't overthink and went to bed. For some unknown reason, I felt more at ease after I got a bit familiar with Sarmad. *Sarmad*—a name that had become a part of my life. I felt strange for not asking his name earlier. I watched him as he made his bed on the sofa and went to sleep. Somehow, I no longer felt scared in his presence; I felt comfortable. He was my saviour after all. He couldn't be dangerous. With these happy thoughts, I dozed off too.

Sarmad

I couldn't sleep that night. I kept changing sides on the couch. The thought of getting friendly with Mehar disturbed me. I wasn't here to make friends. I was on a mission which was still incomplete. I fished out my cell phone and switched it on. There were no new messages or calls from our leader.

Right then I remembered that Mehar had asked for my phone earlier. I couldn't give it to her. I just couldn't. It wasn't a normal phone but a secret device. I could never let her know about my operation. I turned my head to see her sleeping peacefully. I thought of her beautiful, shy smile. I couldn't take that clinking sound of her silver bangles out of my head; her silver nose ring still sparkled in my eyes. I remembered her neatly manicured nails and the warmth of her hands. When I thought of her long, smooth and delicate curls falling over her shoulders, my heart fluttered. The way she stared at me made my stomach knot into a tight ball. I didn't like the effect she was having on me. An unknown apprehension hit me.

Mehar

Day 3

It was raining when I woke up; the raindrops tapped softly on the window pane and the roof. The fire, which had spread warmth before, now lay silent. I felt cold now. I immediately covered myself in the warm duvet while listening to the rain tapping against the window panes. The wall clock showed it was only 7 a.m.

The sound of the door opening distracted me. Sarmad, wearing a towel around his waist, slowly tiptoed out of the washroom. I gasped and then closed my eyes because the sight of him half-naked was obscene. My heartbeat quickened and my stomach turned a somersault. I couldn't take it. However, some part of me craved to see more. I slowly opened my eyes, making sure he didn't know that I was prying on him. Wrapped in a fresh, white towel, he looked undeniably hot; he looked like a Greek god in that towel. Drops of water glistened on his messed-up hair. My heart raced as I observed his well-built and toned body. He stood in front of the mirror, running his fingers through his wet hair. His muscular chest seemed smooth and unscathed. I suddenly shut my eyes as he dropped the towel on the floor. My heart fluttered with nervousness. The sight was enough to set my pulse racing.

How could he stand naked when he knew I was in the same room? Gross . . .

As I opened my eyes, he caught me staring at him. Horror was writ on his face. Our eyes met for a brief moment. Suddenly, there was no shame left. No embarrassment felt. I didn't close my eyes and neither did he pick up the towel from the floor. Our eyes were locked. I suddenly dropped my gaze and closed my eyes. With images of his naked body in my mind, I tried to sleep again.

I didn't know for how long I slept. I woke up groggy and miserable; my hair fuzzy. I tried to loosen my knotted hair but failed. I needed a shower. I threw the quilt off my body and put my warm feet on the cold floor. It was then that a shiny, silver box placed on the side table caught my attention. I wondered whom it belonged to. I scanned the entire room to look for Sarmad but he was nowhere in sight. Out of curiosity, I opened the box. On seeing what was inside, I covered my mouth with my hand and gasped. A brand new cell phone lay inside. A shy smile played on my lips; it was a nice surprise. Setting the phone aside, I got up from the bed to look for him. As soon as I reached for the door knob, the door suddenly creaked open and he stood right in front of me.

My heart almost skipped a beat.

'Hi . . .' I said, breathless.

'Hi,' he whispered, confused at my reaction.

'I wanted to . . . I wanted to thank you for the . . . phone,' I smiled.

'That's okay. I figured you needed one,' he said, his tone flat.

'Thanks, Sarmad,' I said, not looking into his eyes.

'You're welcome.'

I stepped aside so he could come in. As he walked by, I looked at him and then smiled to myself.

Sarmad

Day 3

She surprised me with something new every time. I was still feeling ashamed about the little incident. I didn't really have the nerve to look her in the eye. She had seen me naked, I wondered how embarrassing it would have been for her. Setting aside my thoughts, I summoned enough courage and walked towards our room. That day I saw the hidden coyness in her eyes when she opened the door for me.

I had no choice but to get her the phone. Had I not bought the phone, she would have asked for mine again. I didn't want that to happen. Therefore, I had walked to the main bazaar of Mingora early in the morning while she was sleeping. I watched her as she dialled a number on her phone and slowly tiptoed to the balcony.

Mehar

I talked to Amma and told her about my tour. I made up a long story, but also felt bad for lying to her. I couldn't do anything else. I promised to return soon. After talking to her, I felt relieved and pleased. Everything seemed fine. I was happy my parents weren't as worried as I'd thought them to be. I walked back to the room and found him sitting on the sofa. He was busy writing some notes. I watched him from a distance, trying to gauge his mood. I wondered what he did for a living. When he sensed my gaze on him, he turned to look at me. As soon as our eyes met, I lowered my head. I could feel my cheeks burning. There was a look of surprise on his face when he found me standing there. Without uttering a single word, he raised his eyebrows, his eyes asking, 'What happened?'

'Thank you,' I mouthed.

He shook his head slowly and then resumed his work. I could see a slight smile playing on his lips.

Sarmad

Day 4

Getting up in the same room as her had become a routine. I waited till she got ready, making sure the washroom was free, and she waited till I finished getting dressed. We walked downstairs, trying to be amiable towards each other. I could feel that it wasn't difficult for her to pretend but it was for me. I was living a life I wasn't accustomed to.

We had to join the family at the breakfast table. She chose to sit next to me. Dressed in a maroon salwar kameez, with her hair tied up in a loose bun, she looked simple yet beautiful. Everything was so natural about her. I managed to catch sight of her from the corner of my eye. However, she remained oblivious to me. The breakfast table was full with various dishes—parathas, omelettes, sheer khorma, cereal, lassi, milkshakes, green tea and normal tea. A few moments later, a girl in her teens joined us.

'Two days from now we'll be having the mehndi ceremony at our place. I want all the arrangements to be done. Right, Aziz?' Bari Aapa said.

'Yes, Amma jaan. Don't worry,' Aziz confirmed.

The family dispersed after the meal. Some of the young girls, including the bride, Sufi, took Mehar along with them to a common room. I wandered in the living room in search of something to do. I stepped out and entered the lounge to see the arrangements for the upcoming event. The weather had turned cold in the last few days. Just then, I saw Aziz and his friends trying to hang lights on the poles. I walked up to them and offered help.

'Would you like some assistance?' I asked.

'Sure, why not brother,' Aziz said. 'We might need a little help from you.'

I nodded.

'Faisal,' Aziz said to his cousin brother. 'You can ask Sarmad to put those light bulbs on that pole.'

'Sure, bhai jaan. Sarmad bhai, please come with me,' Faisal said.

I followed Faisal.

'Faisal . . . what is a mehndi ceremony?' I asked, confused.

Faisal smiled.

'Sarmad bhai, didn't you have one during your wedding?' he asked, a smile forming on his lips.

I shook my head.

'Well, this ceremony takes place before the main wedding. It's all about rejoicing and dancing. The groom's family will also be invited.'

'Oh okay.' I tried to take in the idea but soon dismissed it. I wasn't here to get involved in such stuff but was forced to.

Soon I got busy hanging light bulbs around the poles. While doing so, my eyes caught Mehar's. Standing on the balcony with the other girls, her eyes were on me. I realized that she had been staring at me the whole time. I got off the stool, landed softly on the ground and placed the light bulbs on the floor, my eyes still on her. My heart skipped a beat as she passed me a smile; I looked away. I didn't know how to react in such a situation. I didn't want to appear friendly and give her the wrong impression. But I was helpless.

Mehar

Day 4

I don't know why he shies away from me all the time. Whenever I try to be nice to him, he never acknowledges it. Why does he run away from me? Am I that bad?

'Mehar . . . Mehar!'

I turned around to see who was calling me.

'We're waiting for you. Come here,' Sufi called.

'Coming!' I said as I glanced at Sarmad for the last time; he was still busy finishing his tasks.

'Do you have anything to wear for the mehndi ceremony?' Sufi asked.

'Uh . . . no . . . actually we came in a rush . . .'

'That's all right. I'll give you some clothes. Consider them yours,' Sufi smiled as she handed me a packet.

'But . . .' I protested.

'Hush! I just hope you like them. I'm sure you will look beautiful in this dress!'

I felt helpless but couldn't decline her offer. I smiled instead.

'And don't worry about your husband. My brothers will look after him,' Sufi giggled along with the other girls in the room.

'Mashallah, your husband is so handsome, Mehar Aapi!' one of the girls gushed.

'Oh, um . . . thank you,' I didn't know what else to say.

I had no idea that girls here were secretly swooning over him.

'You're really lucky!' the other one said.

I acknowledged each and every comment and blushed.

Sarmad

I was on my way to the Mingora bazaar with Aziz and Faisal to get a few things when Aziz asked, 'So, Sarmad sahib, how did you meet her?'

His question startled me as I didn't know what to answer. I did not want him to become suspicious.

'What happened, Sarmad bhai?' Faisal asked, nudging me. 'Are you feeling shy to share your love story with us?'

I looked at him and then looked ahead, my mind racing with innumerable thoughts.

'Seems like Sarmad is lost somewhere,' Aziz giggled.

'Tell us na, Sarmad bhai? How did you meet her? When did your love story start?' Faisal continued to probe me.

'The relationship I share with her . . . is something that cannot be defined,' I whispered, finally mustering up the courage to speak. The words just spilled out of my mouth. 'My heart's string is attached to hers. Words can't describe the feelings I have for her . . . it's complicated,' I half-laughed, mostly at myself.

I have a love-pain relationship with her. Love that caused more pain and pain that changed me.

Aziz nodded as he listened to what I was saying.

'That's quite deep, bhai. What you feel for her seems quite surreal,' he said.

I looked at him and then smiled.

Yes. Deep and surreal.

Mehar

I spent the entire afternoon with the girls in Sufi's room. They gossiped and discussed random stories about love, relationships and marriage. I wondered how young girls like them knew so much about love. Later in the evening, all of them went out to finish their chores except for Sufi and me. Both of us lay on the bed, still chatting.

'Mehar . . . should I be scared?' Sufi whispered.

'Scared of what?' I asked.

'Of marriage . . . '

I sat up straight, crossed my legs and faced her.

'You're getting married to your cousin. You shouldn't be scared at all. He seems like a fine gentleman.'

'I know but I still feel a bit strange. I'd never thought I'd get married to my cousin. All of my life I've considered him as my own brother. It was really difficult to change my perspective.'

For a moment, everything went blank in front of my eyes. I thought about what Sufi had just said. She was going through the same dilemma I had faced a few days ago when my family had decided to get me married to my cousin, Hamza. All my life, I had considered him as my brother, but all of a sudden our relationship changed forever.

'Mehar . . . where are you lost? What happened?' Sufi probed, bringing me back to reality

'Uh, nothing.' I turned back to her, smiling. 'Don't be scared. Everything will be fine. Whatever your parents have decided for you will be the best,' I assured.

'Is Sarmad bhai your cousin too?' Sufi inquired, moving closer to me.

'Uh . . . no . . .' I mumbled, dazed by her question.

Within a minute I had to shift my thoughts from Hamza to Sarmad. There was a huge difference between the two. One was soft-spoken, calm and composed and the other was rough, wild and infuriating.

'Then how did you both get married? Was it a love marriage?' she asked me.

I turned a little so I could look away. My head was full of questions. But I stopped on two words—love and Sarmad. I leaned my head on the backboard of the bed and thought hard.

'I don't know what love is . . . I really don't know . . . but all I know is . . . he saved me, gave me a new life, a new meaning. If he wasn't there, I wouldn't have been here talking to you. I wouldn't have been living in this world. I wouldn' have been breathing. All I know is that I owe him. I owe him a lot. I don't know how I'm going to repay him for everything he has done for me so far . . .' my voice trailed off.

'That is love, Mehar. That is love!' Sufi exclaimed in a low whisper.

I looked at her with shock writ on my face. Sufi had read my mind and she knew that it only revolved around Sarmad. I was amazed. How effortlessly had she told me what I felt for him. How had she listened to my heart when I had refused to listen to it all this time? I felt embarrassed.

It was 9 p.m. but Sarmad had still not returned. I kept looking at the clock and waiting for him. A few blank papers

were scattered on the bed beside me. I had been trying to
make an origami bird out of them but had failed. I wish I
could make one just like him.

After some time, he opened the door slowly and tiptoed
in, not wanting to disturb me.

'You're back . . .' I said, catching my breath.

'Yes, did I disturb you?'

'I am getting accustomed to your footsteps . . .'

He remained silent.

'Have you had dinner?' I asked, changing the topic.

'Yes, I had it with Aziz, Faisal and the others.'

'Oh okay,' I muttered under my breath.

I felt hugely disappointed because we had been eating
all our meals together since we arrived here.

'What about you?' he asked.

I did not expect him to ask me, and so this question
really took me by surprise.

'No, I haven't yet . . .'

'Why not?' He narrowed his brows.

*Because I've been eating all my meals with you, and it
felt wrong to eat without you! Don't you get it?* I thought
loudly in my head.

'I'm not hungry,' I lied.

'Okay.' He sighed and then walked into the washroom,
leaving me disappointed yet again.

Sarmad

She can't even lie properly. When the truth is transparent in her eyes, why does she have to lie? She is growing dependent on me, and I can't take it. She won't even eat without me now. Damn. I fucking hate this!

I hit my fist hard on the washroom wall.

I quickly took a shower and got dressed. When I came out, I found her asleep on the bed. She lay without a quilt on her body. As I was about to unfold the quilt placed near her feet, I saw a pile of papers placed on the bedside table. I picked them up and realized what she had been up to. She had been trying to make origami cranes. A wry smile spread across my lips as I placed the papers back on the side table and unfolded the quilt. She smiled in her sleep when I spread the quilt across her body. I loved her smile. Just when I was about to move away, she held my hand and stopped me.

I looked at her face in astonishment. Her grasp was firm.

'Thank you . . . for everything,' she mumbled, smiling. Her eyes were closed.

I briefly nodded at her as I tried to free myself from her hold. She remained reluctant and did not let go of my hand.

I narrowed my brows in confusion as I tried once again to free my hand. She looked at me, an angelic smile spread across her lips. She seemed half conscious.

'Never let me go . . . ever,' she whispered.

I winced, aghast at her confession.

I jerked her hand away and took a few steps back, my eyes still on her. She briefly smiled at me once again and then dozed off.

She is definitely asleep, I thought, looking at my hand that was in hers just a minute ago.

Mehar

Day 5

Once again my eyes opened in the middle of the night. I couldn't tell the exact time but I was sure it was around dawn. As I tilted my head to the other side, I was shocked to find Sarmad on the prayer mat offering his *fajr* prayer. I couldn't blink my eyes even for a second as I didn't want to miss any move. Before me, a beautiful man was sincerely praying to god. His eyes were closed, his lips moved slightly and his hands were raised as he finished his *dua'a*. I couldn't take my eyes off him. Seeing him in this position gave immense relief to my eyes. As he finished his prayer, he wiped his hands across his face and then slowly opened his eyes. I smiled at him as he turned to look at me.

'You're . . . up,' he whispered, his eyes wary.

I nodded.

'Come. Offer your prayer then.' He got up from the floor, folding his prayer mat.

I couldn't find any reason to turn down his order. I quickly agreed and walked into the washroom to perform my ablutions. As I splashed warm water on my face, the sweet memory of our recent interaction flashed across my mind.

Though I was asleep, I clearly remembered holding his hand. I smiled at my own naivety. At that point, I really did not care what he thought of me. I just concentrated on the feeling that I had experienced when I had held his hand in mine. After completing my ablutions, I walked out of the washroom. To my surprise, I found Sarmad standing near the balcony, my cell phone jammed against his ear. It seemed as if he was talking to someone. As soon as he saw me, his expression immediately changed.

'I'll speak to you later, Khan Baba,' he whispered, ending the call.

I could not decipher the name he'd said as I was too dazed to notice anything.

'Uh . . .' He stepped towards me nervously. 'My call package expired, so I had to use your phone. Sorry,' he muttered, putting down the phone on the side table.

'Never mind.' I smiled at him and then laid out the prayer mat to offer namaz.

Sarmad

Day 5

There was just a day left for the mehndi ceremony. I knew I had to help the family out with the wedding arrangements. Before Mehar woke up, I tiptoed downstairs to get some breakfast for her. I knew she hadn't eaten last night and felt guilty as I thought I was the reason behind her starvation. I requested Rukhsana to set a plate for Mehar. I took the plate to the room. With one arm tucked under the pillow and the other stretched out, she was snoring peacefully. I smiled as I placed the breakfast tray on the table and then walked to sit beside her on the bed. For a few minutes, I kept looking at her face and couldn't help but admire her natural beauty.

What are you doing to me, Mehar? Don't do this to me again . . . You've given me what I was always looking for . . .

A wisp of hazelnut hair hung over her forehead, and she brushed it back in her sleep. I realized how much it disturbed her. Just when I was about to brush that strand away from her face with my fingers, she opened her eyes. My hand froze mid-air. She gasped after seeing me and immediately sat up on the bed. I knew my presence affected her. I instantly got up, feeling ashamed.

'I brought breakfast for you. Thought you might be hungry,' I said, looking away.

She tucked her hair behind her ear as she tried to look in my eyes.

'I know you haven't eaten anything since last night.' I looked back into her eyes. 'Please don't do this again.'

She looked at me in amazement.

'There will be times when I will come back late. So you need to eat with the rest of the members. Is that clear?'

She nodded after giving it a thought.

'Good,' I mumbled. 'Your breakfast is on the table. Eat it.' I walked to the washroom.

Mehar

How does he win my heart every time?

I smiled looking at the plate that he had kept on the table. I hurriedly got out of bed and started eating. Perhaps god had sent him because I had done some good deeds in my past life. After breakfast, I opened the cupboard and took out a black-coloured salwar kameez for him. The kurta was plain but the neckline was embroidered. Sufi had given me clothes for Sarmad as well. Moreover, I wanted him to look good since he was pretending to be *my* husband. The thought of it brought a smile to my face.

Dressed in an off-white salwar kameez, he stepped out of the washroom, his hair still dripping wet. I flashed a smile at him and then showed him his new clothes.

'What's this?' he asked, looking at the black salwar kameez.

'Sufi was kind enough to give us these clothes. This one's for you. I don't know if you consider my opinion important, but I want you to wear this tonight,' I said, my heart thumping loudly in my chest.

He looked at me for a long time but I kept my eyes down. Our fingers touched for a brief moment when he took the suit from my hands. That's when I looked into his eyes—the eyes that made me smile.

All the family members were busy with the arrangements. I helped the other women with household chores, while Sarmad was busy helping the men with the decoration. He ran errands for everyone and gladly helped others. I was distracted in his presence; I caught myself staring at him more than once. I wondered why he amazed me so much.

Bari Aapa asked everybody to get dressed before the guests arrived. I waited till Sarmad got ready. I was glad to see that the black salwar kameez fit him perfectly. However, I wished I could fix his unruly hair somehow; it was always messed up. Perhaps that's what made him look exceptional. The moment he stepped downstairs, his eyes met mine. As he took a step towards me, someone grabbed his arm and took him outside for some work. I sighed and felt a bit anxious; I wanted to know why he had walked in my direction. However, pushing my thoughts aside, I headed towards the room to get dressed for the night.

Sarmad

The temperature had started to drop; it was relatively low that evening. I, along with the other men, placed gas heaters in the lounge so that the place remained warm. This way the guests wouldn't shiver and they could enjoy the ceremony with ease. After getting done with the arduous task, my entire body felt tired. It seemed I would collapse any time. Before I could think more about this, I saw Mehar stepping down the stairs along with the other girls. Awestruck by her beauty, I almost tripped but held the staircase railing for support. I can't describe how beautiful she looked that evening. It wasn't because of the clothes she wore—a short, heavily embroidered red kurta, an embellished orange salwar and a netted green dupatta. She was beautiful the way she was. Her hair was tied in a French plait that ended up in a fancy *paranda*. She caught my gaze and smiled warmly but I didn't smile back. I immediately shifted my gaze and looked in the opposite direction, making her believe that I wasn't taken in by her at all. She frowned in disappointment, furrows wrinkling her brow. I wished I could tell her how beautiful she looked at that moment.

Slowly the hall started filling up with guests. Bari Aapa and the rest of the family members greeted the groom's family with warmth and affection. I was also one of them. I had to put on a fake smile and greet the guests. I caught Mehar staring at me; in fact she was laughing at me. She'd seen how I was pretending to smile. I felt a bit embarrassed and tried to ignore her.

All the girls gathered at the centre of the lounge and sat cross-legged on the carpeted floor. An elderly woman sat in the middle with a dholki on her lap. As the girls started singing wedding songs, the elderly woman tapped the dholki, filling the air with music.

I stood far away with the other men, near the light pole, taking in the breathtaking scene. This was the first time I was attending a wedding. Everything was new for me. I had never seen a proper family gathering or a religious festivity, let alone a wedding. Everything about the ceremony, each and every ritual, left me speechless. I watched as the girls stopped singing and slowly took positions on the dance floor. They tied their shimmery dupattas around their waists and swirled to Bollywood numbers.

The music set the tone for the evening, breathing energy into everyone's body and urging them to dance. Mehar was slowly getting into the mood of the moment. She stood along with the other girls and imitated their dance steps. I observed her as she danced. I noticed the dangling silver anklet on her foot that sparkled in my eyes. I could not look away even for a second as she looked ethereal from where I stood. Slowly the lights turned dim, disrupting my view. The music turned louder and more people came up on the dance floor. It became difficult for me to locate Mehar among the others. As the drumbeats became louder, I finally caught her view. As I took a few steps towards her, I noticed that she was losing her balance and was about to fall. Fortunately, I reached on time and broke her fall. Both of us fell on the floor, and Mehar howled in pain. The tears in her eyes and the pain that shot across her face made me wince.

Mehar

My loud wail made the DJ stop the music, and within no time everybody gathered around me. I cried in pain as Sarmad tried to calm me down. I shuddered as he wrapped his arm around my shoulder. We shot a glance at each other. My eyes were filled with pain and his with deep concern. Though he had tried his best to save me, I had sprained my ankle. Bari Aapa came rushing when she heard about the accident.

'What happened to her?' Bari Aapa asked, sitting beside me and stroking my leg.

'She fell while dancing, Amma,' Rukhsana informed.

'Oh god . . . you should have been careful, beta. You just recovered from the accident,' Bari Aapa said.

'I know . . . I'm sorry . . .' I muttered in pain.

'Sarmad beta, please take her to the room immediately and make her lie down. I will send a home-made ointment. It will give her immediate relief,' Bari Aapa told him, to which he vaguely nodded.

He looked frantically across the room and then his gaze stopped at Sufi.

'Sufi, can you please help Mehar get back to the room?' he asked her.

Without a question, Sufi agreed and helped me to my feet.

Bari Aapa's brows creased in confusion.

'Wait! Why Sufi? You are her man, Sarmad. You are supposed to take your wife to the room,' Bari Aapa interjected.

A look of shock shot across his face. He nervously looked at me but I averted my eyes.

'But Bari Aapa . . . how can I . . . ?' he asked nervously, his lips quivering.

'Arey, what's wrong in it? She's your wife. Just hold her in your arms and take her to the room. Hurry up before her sprained ankle hurts her even more. C'mon.'

He once again looked at me to get my approval. I couldn't say anything and looked at him with pleading eyes. My heartbeat quickened when Bari Aapa asked him to carry me in his arms.

Without wasting another second and making others suspicious, he softly grabbed my arm, wrapped it around his neck and lifted my body off the floor. Now his strong arms were around me. With his one arm cupped under my thighs and the other folded across my shoulder, he walked towards the room. Every time he took a step, I felt his grip becoming stronger against my body. I felt his warm breath all over my face.

His lips were only a few inches away from mine. Throughout, he didn't look into my eyes and I couldn't look away from his. A sensual heat radiated from his body as he walked. I knew I wouldn't fall as I was safely wrapped in his arms. I held him tight and put my arms around his neck. I grabbed the back collar of his kurta and leaned closer. I could almost hear the throbbing of his heart and the quickening of his breath. The fragrance of his cologne lingered on his collar. It maddened me and made me forget the pain for a while.

On reaching the room, he opened the door slowly and stepped inside. He made me lie on the bed carefully. As he did, a few strands of my loose hair got stuck in the top button of his kurta. When he moved away, I squealed softly.

'Ow . . . !' I squealed in pain, yet again.

'Oh . . . I'm so sorry,' he whispered, trying to open the tangle.

Our faces were close now. We looked at each other for a moment and stayed still. He looked so beautiful in that instant that I felt like grabbing his unruly hair from the back and planting a soft kiss on his lips. Our lips almost touched. I could feel his cool breath on my lips. My lips quivered with the sensual tension, and he saw it.

'Let me get this done, all right?' he whispered, breaking the silence between us.

I slowly nodded, still mesmerized by his good looks.

He tried to untangle my hair from his button but failed. Every time he tried, his eyes locked with mine, distracting him. I tried to help him. Our fingers entwined, eyes locked. However, a sudden knock on the door disrupted our moment of intimacy.

'Shall I come in?' Rukhsana asked, smiling.

She stood near the door with Sufi in tow.

'Yes, please,' Sarmad replied briskly, finally able to untangle my hair from his button.

'Amma has sent this home-made ointment for you, Mehar. You'll feel better once you apply it.' Rukhsana handed the ointment to Sarmad. He took it from her diligently.

'I hope you can apply the balm on her foot now without feeling embarrassed.' Sufi teased him.

I caught the embarrassed look on his face and smiled.

'Yeah . . . I think I can,' he whispered, running a hand through his ruffled hair.

'Great. Mehar, I'll send over a glass of turmeric milk for you. Drink it. You'll feel all right by tomorrow,' Rukhsana said to me.

'Yes, we need to see you super active at the wedding!' Sufi exclaimed joyfully.

'I'll be all right, Sufi. Don't worry,' I replied, still feeling the spasms of pain shooting down my foot.

'Apply the balm quickly, Sarmad.' Rukhsana lightly patted Sarmad's shoulder, and then left the room with Sufi. They closed the door behind them, leaving me with Sarmad yet again.

He stood silently with the ointment in his hands.

'Ow . . .' I cried out in pain, touching my sprained ankle.

'Uh, let me take care of it.'

Sarmad opened the ointment jar and took out a little on his palm. I watched him as he did this swiftly. He sat near the end of the bed and hesitantly picked up my foot and placed it on his lap.

'I think . . . I can do this myself,' I said, my voice breaking.

'You don't have to say this as long as I'm here with you.' He smiled at me.

I closed my eyes, thinking about his words, and winced as he stroked my foot.

He slowly spread the ointment on my sprained ankle and massaged it.

'Does it hurt here?' he asked, looking at me with concern-filled eyes.

'No, a bit up there,' I replied, brows wrinkled.

'Here?'

'Yes . . . I think so.'

'You think so? Not sure?'

'I think I am . . . '

'Right.' He smiled.

A light smile played across his lips. The way he applied the ointment on my ankle was worth noticing. I already started feeling better. The warmth of the ointment relieved the pain and relaxed my muscles. Besides, I could not ignore the exquisite touch of his skin on mine. As he caressed my ankle, I died a little; I didn't want him to stop.

'It's better if you keep it warm for some time,' he said as he tied a bandage around my ankle.

'Where did you get that from?' I asked, coming back from my reverie.

'What?'

'This bandage.'

'Oh, this. It was kept in that drawer near you.' He pointed to the wooden table near my bed.

'Oh . . .'

'It's done. Keep it like this overnight. I'll get that turmeric milk for you.'

He placed the duvet across my body and then shifted to the oth side. I caught his arm, not letting him go. He was caught o ard.

'What happened?' he asked.

'Thank you, Sarmad . . . thank you for everything you've done for me,' I said, my eyes becoming watery.

'There is no need to thank me. I'll do whatever it takes to look after you.'

'But why?' I asked him and then looked down.

'Forget about that. I'll get the milk for you. Be right back,' he said, ignoring my question. He hurriedly left the room, closing the door behind him.

I sighed.

Sarmad

I took a deep breath in as soon as I came out and closed the door behind me. I had felt suffocated in that room. My brain could explode at any moment. I didn't know what I'd done. I had touched her foot, touched her skin. I had touched Mehar without any intention of getting close to her. The more I thought about what had just happened, the more I hated myself. I couldn't stop thinking about her smooth flawless skin. I had revelled in the sensation as I had caressed her foot. The smoothness of her skin had sent currents down my spine. I wanted to get rid of these thoughts but couldn't. I walked down the corridor and made my way to the stairs. I couldn't keep my breathing controlled. I broke into a cold sweat as I entered the kitchen. My sudden entry startled the women.

'Are you okay, Sarmad?' Rukhsana inquired, worried.

'Yes.' I wiped away the beads of sweat that had formed on my forehead. 'I just came to get that turmeric milk.'

'Oh yes. Here it is.' Rukhsana held out the glass for me.

'Thanks.' I took the glass from her. 'I'll make sure she drinks it.'

'She should. It's good for her.'

'Thanks once again.' I exited the kitchen.

Controlling my heightened emotions, I again headed towards our room. I didn't want to get attracted to her. Staying in this house and that too in the same room with her was becoming difficult. Deep down I was aware that I would have to pay a high price for my decision of staying with her.

Still dazed, I stepped into the room and saw her lying on the bed. Though her eyes were closed, her brows were creased, indicating that she was in pain.

'Mehar?' I called out.

My voice woke her up. She quickly adjusted her clothes and sat up.

'I have brought milk for you. Drink it,' I said.

'I'm fine. I don't need it.' She tucked her hair behind her ears.

'It will help in relieving the pain.' I held out the glass for her.

'But . . . '

'Please. Stop behaving like a kid now,' I said, widening my eyes.

'Okay,' she replied sheepishly and took the glass from my hand.

For a moment our hands touched and she froze. Realizing what effect my touch had on her, I quickly withdrew my hand.

'After drinking the milk, I think you should change your clothes. I'll get Sufi to help you change.'

'It's all right. I'm not paralysed. I think I can manage,' she reassured me.

'Let me know if you need anything.'

She nodded, and I walked to the balcony.

The more I go away, the more I am drawn to her. I'm stuck in a dilemma. How do I run away from this situation?

I desperately ran my fingers through my hair and heaved a sigh. All of a sudden, I felt my phone vibrating in my pocket. I took it out and found an unknown number flashing on the screen. I instantly answered.

'Hello?' I said, breathing heavily.

'Be at the Ramkot Fort tomorrow 8 a.m. sharp. Don't be late,' Haider ordered and then ended the call.

Feeling distressed, I looked at my phone. It was finally time to move on with the unfinished business.

Mehar

Day 6

At the sound of the door opening, my eyes flew open.

'Sarmad?' I called, sitting on the bed.

'It's me, Mehar,' Sufi said, walking into the room.

'Oh, it's you. I thought it was Sarmad.' I was clearly disappointed.

'How are you feeling now?' Sufi sat on the edge of the bed.

'Don't worry. I'm already feeling better.' I smiled, my eyes still looking for him. 'Where is Sarmad? I don't think he's in the room.'

'He's not here. He has gone out for some work,' Sufi said.

'Work? How do you know?' I asked.

'He told Faisal bhai before leaving. I guess he had some urgent work and will be back by evening.'

'Oh,' I exclaimed, feeling unhappy.

'Don't worry. He'll come back soon. Why don't you call him?' Sufi continued.

'Uh, yes. I should.' What else could I have told her? I didn't even have his number.

'Then do it. Shall I send your breakfast to the room?'. Sufi asked.

'No. No. Not at all. I will come down in a bit.'

'Perfect. I'll see you then.' Sufi walked out, shutting the door behind her.

Where could have Sarmad possibly gone without informing me?

Sarmad

Day 6

I took a local bus to reach Islamabad, and from there I took another bus to reach the fort. It took me five hours to get to my destination. I had to hire a boat to cross the Mangla Lake. The fort was picturesquely located on the summit of a hill that was surrounded by the lake. A short yet steep climb later I was at the fort. A known figure waited for me at the entrance door.

'I'm glad you have reached on time, Sarmad.' Haider turned to face me.

'Haider!' I exclaimed, embracing him. 'I'm so happy to see you alive. You made it!'

'Yes, brother. I was fortunate that I escaped from the various police checkpoints. And see, I'm here. Standing in front of you,' Haider smirked.

'Mashallah!' I grinned, flashing my teeth.

'Look whom I have brought with me.' Haider pointed at someone standing across the gate.

'Who is it?' I asked curiously.

All of a sudden, Mullah sahib appeared.

'Mullah sahib!' I reached for him as soon as I saw him. Mullah took me in a warm embrace.

'How are you, my bachcha?' Mullah asked.

'I'm fine, Mullah sahib. It's a pleasant surprise to see you here. Mashallah. I feel blessed,' I said.

'You've become so weak, my bachcha! Look at you!' Mullah cupped my face in his hands.

'I'm fine, don't worry.'

'Come, let's go inside and have a chat.' Mullah took me and Haider into a cave built inside the fort.

After a long and strenuous conversation, Mullah rested his back against the wall. Haider filled cups with tea which he'd brought along.

'Where are you staying at the moment?' Mullah inquired.

'I'm staying in Mingora. There's this family—sweet and innocent—that took me to their place and allowed me to stay there for a couple of days. There's also a wedding going on at their house.'

'Is it safe there?' Mullah asked, arching his brow.

'Yes, pretty much. There's also this . . .' Mehar's face flashed in front of my eyes as I thought of her. 'This girl . . . who came on a trip with her friends but on the way met with an accident. I helped her, saved her life. Therefore, I brought her with me to this house.'

'What? Are you insane, Sarmad? How could you allow a girl to stay with you? What if she gets to know of your motive?' Haider interjected.

'She's not a danger to us. I assure you. She doesn't know anything about me or my mission. I've kept her at a distance,' I explained.

Mullah gave me an incensed stare.

'Try and understand, Mullah sahib. I could not stay at their place all alone. This girl and I . . . we are pretending to be husband and wife. Only because of this lie we were allowed to stay there.'

'Where has she come from?' Mullah asked, sipping his tea.

'She is based out of Lahore, comes from an army family. Her father is a retired general.'

I regretted having told them about Mehar.

'And still you believe this girl is not a threat to us?' Haider asked with a twinge of irritation in his voice.

'What's her father's name?' Mullah asked, cutting in between.

'Uh . . . general . . . I . . . I can't remember the name exactly,' I lied.

'Oh . . . '

'Never mind. He is retired anyway. There's no threat,' I said.

Mullah frowned at me.

'Trust me, Mullah sahib. I am safe,' I told him.

'I trust you, my bachcha . . . but be careful.'

'I will.'

Mehar

The clock struck 9 p.m. but there was still no sign of Sarmad. I wrapped myself in a shawl and waited for him. Even Bari Aapa told me that he would be back soon but it had no effect on me. I kept waiting for him, my eyes fixed on the wall clock.

Why hasn't he come back yet? He's been gone since early morning and still hasn't returned. What if he's gone back to where he came from? What if he never comes back? What if he has left me here all alone?

I shivered at my own thoughts.

I sat still on the bed, tears rolling down my cheeks. I started weeping. I'd never missed him so much till now. It was like a part of me had gone missing. I couldn't understand why he had left me alone. I began to assess the mistakes I had made in the past. Last night, he seemed perfectly fine. There wasn't any tension between us. Then what could have possibly gone wrong?

A noise startled me. It was the sound of someone's footsteps. My senses became alert all at once. Despite knowing the current condition of my sprained ankle, I got off the bed and tried to walk towards the door.

Sarmad opened the door and stood before me. He was astonished to see me standing on my feet. Tears spilled from my eyes and ran down my cheeks.

'Mehar!' He glowered. 'Are you out of your mind? Why are you standing? You know you should rest!' He tried to hold my arm but I was already by his side, tugging at his sleeve.

'Where did you go, Sarmad?' I asked, my voice frantic. 'Did I even cross your mind for a moment before you left me here all alone?'

Sarmad seemed stunned by my reaction.

'Please answer me once! Where did you go? Why did you leave me here alone?' I asked, fresh tears rolling down my cheeks.

'Mehar . . . Mehar . . . calm down. I'm here. I never left you!' He tried to pacify me, slightly caressing my arm.

'But . . . where did you go?' I almost shivered.

'I was . . . out for some work,' he declared.

'I thought you left me,' I said, my body becoming weak all of a sudden.

Sarmad kept me from falling as he held me tightly.

'Why would I leave you here? Are you crazy? Remember what I had said to you? I'd never leave you. Not unless you want me to.'

I looked into his eyes for a long time and considered what he'd just said.

'Really?' I asked, sniffing.

'Yes,' he almost whispered.

I instantly realized what I was doing. I let go of his sleeve and wiped the tears off my cheeks. However, Sarmad still held on to me, as he was scared that I might fall again.

'Are you okay?' he asked, concern dripping from his voice.

'Yes, I'm fine.'

'Good . . . how's your foot now?'

'It's fine. It doesn't hurt any more.'

'Well, that's good news then.'

I nodded, tucking my hair behind my ears. I felt comfortable around him.

'I think everybody is expecting us to join them at the dinner table. Would you like to come with me?'

'Yes. Please give me a minute.'

'Okay . . .' He released his hold and let me go.

I walked unsteadily towards the washroom and heaved a sigh of relief.

Sarmad

Our eyes met as she walked out of the washroom. I excused myself and went in to take a bath. As I walked past her, her fragrance hit my nostrils, driving me crazy. I quickly locked the washroom door and sighed. I stood under the shower for a long time, washing away her memories, her aroma, her voice from my thoughts. I hated how she dominated my thoughts, but at the same time I loved it. Mullah sahib may have considered her a threat but only I knew what she actually meant to me. I wanted to protect her in every way. I knew she was getting attracted to me. Despite trying to ignore her, I'd become fond of her.

I cannot betray her . . . not even if I have to risk my life. I will try my best to keep her away from all kinds of danger.

We joined the family for dinner around 11 p.m. Bari Aapa made sure Mehar rested her foot on a stool. My attention was on her all the time. Amid the routine dances and the ceremonial rituals, both of us kept exchanging glances. Every time she smiled at me, I felt an adrenaline rush, followed by the quickening of my heartbeat. I knew I now had a special place in her heart.

Mehar

Day 7

It was 10 a.m., and I was already up. I took a quick shower and got dressed in a traditional pheran. I accessorized myself with some antique jewellery that Sufi had given me. After getting dressed, I found Sarmad still sleeping on the couch—one arm tucked under the pillow and the other hanging freely on the side. I smiled at his unusual sleeping position but also felt bad for him. His creased brow indicated his discomfort. I sat next to the couch, staring at him for a long time. I couldn't even describe how beautiful he looked while sleeping: messy hair spread over his forehead, long lashes almost touching his pink cheeks, lips slightly parted as peaceful snores escaped through them, and chest slowly rising with every breath he took. I wanted to touch his face and make him think of me in his sleep. But I couldn't. It wasn't the right thing to do. I wasn't allowed to think about him romantically. My family's vows rushed into my mind, making me come out of the reverie.

'Sarmad . . .' I whispered.

He slightly groaned in his sleep on hearing my voice and then rubbed his eyes.

'Sarmad, wake up,' I said, controlling the urge to shake him.

'Hmm?' He slowly opened his eyes. 'What happened?' He straightened his back and sat up on the couch.

'Nothing,' I gulped. 'I . . . uh . . . I wanted to go out.'

'Out? Where?' He ran his fingers through his messy hair.

'Bazaar. I wanted to get something for Sufi as a wedding gift. Will you take me?' I asked, batting my lashes nervously.

'What if I don't go out with you? Would you still go by yourself?' he whispered.

His husky low voice startled me. I looked into his eyes.

'I won't have to go alone because I know you'll come with me,' I answered, this time with a lot of confidence.

'How can you be so sure of that?' He frowned.

'You'll never want me to go alone. I know that.'

He studied my face for a few seconds.

'Fine. I will go with you,' he said.

He seemed to be taken aback by my answer. I smiled at him.

'I'll be waiting for you downstairs then.' I bit my lip and then got up from the floor.

I knew my answer had left an impact on him.

It wasn't long before Sarmad came down and joined me. Dressed in a black and white striped pullover, a brown leather jacket and ripped jeans, he looked extremely handsome.

'How are we going to the bazaar?' he asked casually.

'Uh, I think we'll take the local bus,' I replied.

'Why bus? Why don't you take one of the cars?' Rukhsana interjected, appearing from the kitchen all of a sudden.

'I don't think we need it. We'll be happy to travel by bus. That way we'll get a chance to explore Mingora as well,' I said, looking at Sarmad who seemed annoyed.

'Are you sure?' Rukhsana placed her hand on my shoulder.

I nodded gleefully.

'Come soon, then.' Rukhsana smiled back. 'We don't want you to miss all the fun.'

'Don't worry, Rukhsana Aapi. We'll be back soon,' I said.

Before heading out, I gave a warm smile to Sarmad but he didn't smile back.

I kept contemplating the reason behind his smugness all the way to the bus stop. Finally, I grabbed his arm and stopped midway to confront him.

'What?' he asked.

'Why do you seem annoyed? If you didn't want to come along, you should have just told me.'

'I am not annoyed.'

'Yes, you are. Just . . . just look at your face.' I looked away.

'Well, okay.' He crossed his arms across his chest. 'Why didn't you take their car?' There was a twinge of annoyance in his voice.

'I didn't want to sit in a car. I wanted to walk with you!' I exclaimed.

'Yeah, right. We're on an adventurous trip, isn't it?' He looked away.

'Yes, why can't we? I'd love to explore this city with you!' I told him.

He glared at me for a while, biting his lips.

'I'll be fine if you don't want to come along.' I shrugged, feeling annoyed.

He once again gave me a long thoughtful stare.

'I am serious!' I said.

To my surprise, he held my hand while looking into my eyes and walked ahead.

Sarmad

Day 7

Luckily, we got a bus to the Mingora main bazaar but couldn't get a seat. The bus was full as it was a Saturday. Mehar and I stood in the middle of the aisle. A bearded man, standing right behind Mehar, kept staring at her. I sensed his immoral stare, but controlled my urge to smack his face and take him down. I noticed Mehar was feeling uncomfortable as well. I politely asked her to switch positions with me, to which she obliged. A slight smile played on her lips. The pervert did n't seem very happy about this. He just grunted and looked away.

The bus reached the main bazaar within fifteen minutes. I helped her get down. An electric spark went through my body when she held my hand. Amid the buzz, we walked towards the main market area. She decided to stop at a jewellery shop. She tried on a pair of silver *jhumkas* and admired herself in the mirror. She caught my reflection in the mirror as I came and stood behind her. She quickly took off the earrings.

'Shall we leave?' she asked sheepishly.

'Sure.'

A bright orange-coloured kurta caught Mehar's attention in the next shop. The shopkeeper told her that it would cost around Rs 5000.

'Don't you think it's too much for a single kurta?' Mehar asked the shopkeeper.

'Not at all, *baaji*. We're offering reasonable prices.'

'Oh okay. I wonder how it will look on Sufi,' she said and looked at me.

She waited for my answer but I didn't respond.

'Do you want this kurta, baaji?' the shopkeeper asked.

'No, thanks.' She caressed the kurta with her hand and then sighed.

I observed her as she pressed her lips together and then glumly walked out of the shop. I contemplated the situation for a few minutes before fishing out my wallet. In one instant, I bought the kurta and headed out to join Mehar.

I caught up with her.

'What took you so long?' Mehar asked, surprised.

'I . . . ' I hesitated. 'I stopped to get this.'

Mehar's eyes fell on the shopping bag that I was carrying in my hands.

'What's this?' she asked, taking the bag from me.

'The same kurta you liked at the shop. I, uh . . . too think that it would look great on Sufi. So, yeah. We can gift this to her.' I nodded.

She looked at me with disbelief.

'But Sarmad . . . this is so expensive . . . '

'Don't worry about the cost. I got it, all right? Let's head back home,' I said.

'Are you sure?' she asked.

I nodded in return.

She pressed her lips together and gave me a shy smile.

We headed back to the bus stop. There was a bus only every fifteen minutes, so we had to wait. The warmth of the sun felt good on my skin. Instead of waiting, Mehar crossed the road and ran towards an ancient dargah across the road.

'Mehar! Where are you going?' I called out after her.

But she didn't stop, she kept walking towards the dargah.

Fuming with rage, I followed her.

'Mehar! Are you crazy?'

'Shh. You're not supposed to speak loudly here. It's a religious place. Be quiet,' she whispered.

'What?' I frowned.

'Come, let's go inside.'

'No! I'm not coming inside,' I hissed.

'Why?'

'I don't need to explain that.'

'Fine. I'm going then.'

She stepped inside the shrine. I waited for her outside.

After ten minutes, I started feeling distressed about the entire situation. I felt unsafe in that area. My instincts told me it was risky to stay there any longer. I had to get Mehar out and rush back home. Unwillingly, I took off my shoes and entered the shrine. Inside, I saw many worshippers sitting cross-legged on the floor, completely devoted to their prayers. I caught Mehar sitting in one of the front rows and praying ardently with her eyes closed. She looked serene. I sat down among the worshippers in one of the back rows. I wanted to forget the rest of the world and look at her. I watched her pray, with her eyes closed and hands spread out. I felt a sense of calm right then. She finished her prayer quickly and got up. As soon as she walked past me, her mustard chiffon dupatta flew in the air and caressed my face. Mehar, however, was oblivious to it and walked out of the dargah. I had closed my eyes for a brief second to feel the moment. When

I noticed that she'd left, I instantly got up and rushed outside. 'Mehar...' I called out. I was almost out of breath when I caught up with her.

'Hmm?' She continued to walk, without looking at me.

'What did you ask for?' I asked, out of curiosity.

'My amma once told me that all your wishes come true if you pray at this dargah.'

'Do you believe in all of this?'

'Yes, firmly.'

'Wait.' I stopped midway.

'What happened?' She turned around to look at me.

'I'll be back in a minute.' I rushed inside the shrine, leaving Mehar behind.

I walked past the worshippers and found a place to sit.

I closed my eyes and spread out my hands.

Oh Allah! I know that You are everywhere. Please grant Mehar's wish. Give her whatever she has asked for. That's all I want from You.

Mehar

I wondered why he had rushed back to the dargah. My curiosity rose with every passing minute. Just when I decided to go looking for him, I saw him coming out.

'Why did you go back inside?' I asked.

'Nothing. Let's go back.'

'Wait.' I stopped midway.

He turned to look at me.

'What now?' he asked, shrugging.

'I'm hungry,' I said, a little embarrassed.

He heaved a sigh and then looked away.

We took an autorickshaw to a nearby local restaurant. We had an option to sit indoors but I insisted on sitting outside in the open air. Sarmad followed me gingerly as I sat down at one of the tables. The sky had turned purple, and the air had turned chillier. I wrapped a shawl around my shoulders. Noticing my uneasiness, he instantly took off his leather jacket and put it around me.

'I'm fine, Sarmad. You don't have to do this,' I told him, looking into his eyes as he came closer to put the jacket around me.

'I don't want you to catch a cold,' he whispered, his breath warm against my neck.

'Um, thanks,' I said, pushing back a lock of hair. I don't know why but my heart thudded in my chest.

'No problem,' he beamed as he took his seat.

Somewhere, a radio played an old Hindi song. I thought I remembered it from a movie I'd seen when I was a child. I tried to recall the name of the movie but failed. I closed my eyes and tried hard to remember.

'What happened?' he asked.

'Nothing.' My eyes were still shut. 'Just trying to remember the song playing on the radio.'

He didn't say anything, so I continued to concentrate on the song.

'From which movie was it . . . which movie . . . ?' I mumbled to myself.

'*Lag jaa galey, ke phir yeh haseen raat ho na ho . . .*' He started singing the song.

I opened my eyes and stared at him.

'*Shayad phir iss janam mein mulaqaat ho na ho . . .*' He stopped as he looked at me. 'It's from the Hindi movie *Woh Kaun Thi.*'

I kept staring at him in complete shock.

'Released in 1964, it starred Manoj Kumar and Sadhana Shivdasani in lead roles,' he told me.

'Oh my!' I exclaimed, covering my mouth with my hands. He passed me a casual smile in return and shrugged.

'You have a sharp memory, Sarmad! You remember everything! I didn't know you were fond of Hindi movies. I'm so impressed.' I clapped for him.

He let out a soft chuckle.

'Shall we order the food now?' he asked. 'I thought you were hungry.'

'Sure, sir. Why not.' I gave him a salute which made him laugh again.

I wish I could see him like this more often . . .

We reached home before dusk set in. Everyone at the house was discussing the grand event that was to take place the next day. The big fat Pakistani wedding. I felt excited just thinking about it.

Late that night, I packed Sufi's gift with utmost care. The packet looked beautiful. I couldn't stop looking at it.

'All ready?' Sarmad asked, startling me.

He had gone to take a shower and had just come out of the washroom.

'Yes,' I replied, a bit dazzled by his appearance.

'Good,' he murmured, rubbing his wet hair with a towel.

I smiled at him, shyly.

After getting done with all the work, I offered the night-time prayer. I prayed for the well-being of my family and myself. However, this time I made an exception and also prayed for Sarmad's well-being. It didn't matter that we were strangers to each other, he was important to me now. He'd done so much for me already. I didn't know how to pay him back. With a strong positive feeling, I drifted off to sleep.

I was surprised to find myself surrounded by an exotic bloom. I got up, flowers scattered in my hair, and I found my parents standing in front of me. They were smiling. Surprised, I walked towards them, my hand pressed against my smiling lips. It was hard to believe that they were right in front of me. I held them in a long embrace.

'Come with us,' Abba said.

I instantly agreed. All three of us walked hand in hand. A shadowy figure lurked ahead of us. The man stood with his back to me. I knew who he was. A smile passed across my face when he turned around. Sarmad. He was Sarmad. I knew it the moment I laid my eyes on him. He smiled as he saw me.

'Abba jaan . . . that's Sarmad,' I said, my voice dripping with excitement.

'I know him,' Abba replied.

I was stunned at his reply.

'Go, Mehar. He's waiting for you,' Amma said.

With questioning eyes and a heavy heart, I let go of my parents and walked towards Sarmad. He held out his hand to hold mine. The moment I held his hand, I felt peace like never before. He firmly took my hands in his grip, and we walked down the field. Smiling all the way, we strode along the flowery pathway. Everything seemed fine until we found a trench a few feet away. I let go of his hand and took a few steps ahead to examine it. I shrieked in horror when I found my brother's dead body lying in it.

'Sarmad!' I bellowed.

Within a second, Sarmad came and stood next to me.

'Sarmad . . . Sarmad, that's my brother . . . my brother . . .' I cried, covering my face with my hands.

'I'm sorry, Mehar . . . I'm sorry . . .' Sarmad whispered in response. I looked at him with horror.

I gasped as I woke up from the nightmare. Sweat trickled down my face, wetting my cheeks. I looked around the dark room frantically for Sarmad, but he was nowhere to be seen.

'Sarmad? Sarmad?' I called out, but there was no response.

I got off the bed and ran out barefoot. Beads of perspiration rolled down my face as I ran down the staircase. The lounge was empty and dark, not a single soul was in sight. I reached the main door and was surprised to find it unlocked. My heart thudded in my chest with fear. With shaking fingers, I clasped the door knob and opened it slowly. To my astonishment, I found Sarmad playing with the children in the front lawn. A breath of relief escaped me.

Seeing me sweating badly, a crease of concern appeared on Sarmad's forehead and his smile disappeared.

'What happened? Are you okay?' he asked through his eyes.

'Yes ... I'm fine. Don't worry,' I responded in the same way.

We smiled at each other for a fraction of a second before I turned around to go back to the bedroom.

Sarmad

Day 8

The wedding day was finally here. I sat on the couch, silently drawing out a plan for our delayed mission on a piece of paper, while Mehar got dressed for the ceremony. I had been in touch with Haider and Mullah sahib since our last meeting. Every now and then, I got a new message from them, asking me to keep a low profile as the army was on the lookout for militants in every possible area. If the situation stayed like this, we would never be able to complete our mission. It did worry me. At times I thought I was wasting my time living in Swat. But mostly I felt happy; Mehar's company made me feel content.

Standing in front of a full-length mirror, she adjusted her dupatta; I was awestruck by her beauty. I grabbed a packet from my bag and took out a pair of silver jhumkas from it—these were the same jhumkas she had tried on at the market yesterday.

'Mehar . . .' I whispered, standing behind her.

Her body stiffened when she looked at my reflection in the mirror. I could feel her tremble.

'Yes?' she murmured, looking at me in the mirror.

'I got these for you . . .' I held out the jhumkas.

A flicker of surprise flashed across her face when she saw them.

'I would like you to wear these tonight,' I said.

'Oh! They're beautiful. I'd love to wear them,' she said, smiling.

I smiled back at her.

'You know this is not right. You're spoiling me,' she complained.

'How?' I pulled my brows together and crossed my arms.

'By making my every wish come true.'

'Trust me. This is the least I could do.'

'No, Sarmad.' She turned around to look at me. 'You've no idea how much you've done for me.'

Our glances met. I was sure there was something in those eyes for me. As I tried looking for more answers in those beautiful eyes, a sudden knock on the door distracted us.

'Uh oh. I think we should go downstairs,' Mehar suggested as she smiled and then turned to look in the mirror.

Once again she started adjusting her dupatta. She folded it and put it on her shoulder as I watched her.

'Wait . . .' I reached out for her dupatta, leaving her baffled. 'May I?' I asked, politely.

She nodded as she stared at me. I took her dupatta in my hands and began to unfold it. She watched me with amazement. I spread out the dupatta and put it across her head, covering her hair.

'It looks good here,' I whispered, observing her.

Mehar blushed at her reflection in the mirror.

The wedding started and ended in a blink. Bari Aapa included us in all the main ceremonial rituals and treated us like a significant part of her family. Thankfully, the cold didn't play a spoiler to the ceremony and its rituals. Finally, it was time for Sufi to bid goodbye. Everyone had moist eyes as she left the house. Mehar cried too. She had become quite attached to Sufi within a short span of time. I understood her plight; I knew how it felt to get attached to someone. I wanted to stay away from this pain as much as possible.

Without touching her, I tried to console Mehar. Tears rolled down her cheeks as she looked at me with deep distress on her face. I couldn't even hold her in my arms and console her. I took out a handkerchief from my pocket and offered it to her.

'It's all right. Stop crying. We need to go back to our room,' I told her.

She sniffed and nodded.

I made sure she stopped crying before going to bed. I kept checking on her throughout; I didn't want her to cry in her sleep. The fact that she was also a daughter and would have to leave her family one day had made her unhappy, I thought. She knew she had to face that day in this lifetime. She could easily relate to Sufi's feelings. I returned to the couch with these thoughts clouding my mind.

'Are you still awake?' she asked, surprising me.

'Yes . . .' I whispered. She sniffed once and then silence engulfed the room.

'Can I ask you something?' I asked.

'Hmm?'

'What happened to you last night?'

'When?'

'When you came down . . . you seemed out of breath. Were you scared?'

'No . . . I . . .' she hesitated. 'I had a nightmare. It scared me. When I didn't find you in the room, I got more frightened.'

'And when you found me downstairs . . .'

'I was relieved . . .' she whispered.

'Did you think I'd left you again?'

I could hear her soft chuckle.

'Maybe . . .' she replied.

I smiled at her straightforward reply and then closed my eyes.

'Sarmad?'

'Hmm?'

'How long are we going to be here?' she asked. I had no answer to her question.

'We'll be leaving soon,' I said.

'Okay . . .'

'*Shaba khair* . . .'

'Shaba khair.'

I shut my eyes and dozed off. Within seconds, I drifted off to another world in my sleep. Once again, I had a dreamless night. I was surrounded by profound darkness. The sound of thunderbolt hit my ears, causing me to wake up in fright. I sat up and removed the quilt. My entire face was covered in sweat. I huffed, trying to control my shivering body.

'Sarmad? Are you okay?' I found Mehar sitting beside me. She must have sensed my troubled state of mind.

I nodded as I tightly hugged my knees. The rain continued to fall hard outside.

'Are you scared?' she asked.

I looked at her face and remained silent; I did feel jittery.

'Are you?' she asked me again, her voice almost a whisper.

I slowly nodded my head.

In the next moment, she leaned closer to me and carefully wrapped her arms around my neck. My heart fluttered at her sudden touch. I had no idea what she was about to do. I felt her warm breath on the nape of my neck. She brought her lips closer to my ears and muttered, 'Just close your eyes, take a deep breath, hold yourself together and pray to god. The fear will slowly go away . . .'

She held my hands and brought them together.

I slowly closed my eyes and did what she said.

'Feeling better now?' she asked, our hands still intermingled.

I nodded with my closed eyes. A small smile played across my lips but I did not want her to see it. It was my own private moment.

Mehar

Day 9

I woke up to the booming sound of the television. Rubbing my eyes, I got off the bed to see what was happening. Sarmad stood in front of the TV, his hair dishevelled and a disturbed expression clouding his face. I walked to his side and saw the headlines.

'Unknown militants attack school in Peshawar; children and staff members dead.'

I choked after watching the news. I knelt down on the floor, my body drained of all its energy. I couldn't believe what I had just seen. I felt Sarmad's body stiffen. He took out his phone and headed towards the balcony. I prayed loudly for the children as tears rolled down my cheeks.

Sarmad

Day 9

I dialled Haider's number as soon as I saw the news on TV.

'Hello?' Haider answered in a dry voice.

'Who did it?' I whispered, making sure Mehar didn't hear my voice.

'We don't know. They're not a part of our clan. Even Mullah sahib is disturbed by this news.'

'How could they? I mean, how could they target innocent children?' I asked as I seethed with anger.

'Yes, children are not our target. I wonder who did this,' Haider said.

'Find out who this group is and why they've done it.'

'Whoever they are, our motive is the same.'

'Same motive? What do you mean?'

'They're against the army just like we are.'

'But we're not against innocent children! If they wanted to seek revenge from the army, they could have adopted some other bloody strategy!' I exclaimed, trying to keep my voice as low as possible.

'Perhaps they've done this in the wake of the "Exterminate Terrorism" mission started by the army.'

'There will be tighter security now. We're in danger, and the authorities are on a constant lookout. Just be safe wherever you are. Don't reveal your true identity at any cost!' I ordered.

'Will do. Allah hafiz.'

'Allah hafiz.' I ended the call.

Mehar was still crying when I walked back into the room. Right then, Bari Aapa came in along with Rukhsana and Aziz.

All of them expressed their grief, while I remained lost in my own thoughts. I kept wondering which group could be behind this barbaric act.

There was a day's break between the wedding and the reception, so all the family members stayed inside the house with their eyes glued to the news. Amidst the rising tension in the house, the cook prepared dinner and requested everyone to eat. Totally shaken by the news, Mehar excused herself and went to the room. Bari Aapa asked me to take her dinner, to which I obediently agreed.

When I entered the room, I saw her lying quietly on the bed.

'Why don't you eat something?' I asked, as I closed the door behind me.

'When can we go back?' she asked, sitting on the bed and wiping tears off her cheeks.

'What?' My heart sank after hearing her question.

'I don't think we have any reason to stay here any longer. It was a stupid decision to come here. I shouldn't have done this anyway,' she confessed, looking straight.

There was a blank look on her face.

'What are you saying? Are you okay?' I sat on the bed near her and looked her in the eye.

'Yes . . .' she whispered, tears forming in her eyes. 'I just talked to my mother a few minutes ago. She said that Abba is angry because I haven't returned yet.'

I pressed my lips together and looked down.

'I shouldn't have come here . . . I shouldn't have asked you to stay . . .' she said, wiping her tears once again.

'Look . . . I know you're upset because of what happened in Peshawar today. I know you miss your family at this moment but the people you're living with right now are also your family. They care for you . . .' I tried to explain.

'I know . . . I still want to go back, Sarmad. Please take me home,' she said, fighting back her tears.

'Hey . . . stop crying, all right?'

I didn't know how to calm her down. I wanted to hold her, to touch her, and to take her in my arms.

'I will take you back within two days. Okay?'

She looked into my eyes as fresh tears rolled down her cheeks.

'I will. I promise,' I said, not breaking our gaze.

She sniffed and then nodded.

'Now, eat this.' I put the plate in front of her.

'Thank you . . .' she murmured.

The hot water from the shower helped me wash away the disturbing images and video clips I'd seen on TV earlier that day. I thought about the group behind the cruel attack and Mehar's plea. What if I failed in *my* mission?

Mehar paced inside the room with a mug of tea in her delicate hands. She then went to the balcony and stood staring at the sky. I made a cup of instant coffee for myself and followed her.

She shivered when she felt me near her.

'Are you okay now?' I asked, starting a conversation.

'I don't know . . .' she whispered, looking straight. 'I wonder what made the terrorists attack the school.'

'They're against the army since the "Exterminate Terrorism" operation started,' I stated as I gulped down the coffee.

She shot me a glance.

'What the army did to their families in the past cannot be forgotten easily,' I continued.

'What did the army do to them?' she asked.

'The constant bombings in North Waziristan.'

'Don't forget that the terrorists were the ones to spread terror across the country. What the army did was to eradicate terrorism.'

'No! The army started the violence. Militants didn't want to kill innocent people; they just wanted some of their demands to be met. It was all in the name of jihad.'

'Oh c'mon! I don't believe you're siding with the militants. You saw with your own eyes what they did today. They've shot children! Children! Can't you see? They're so weak that they chose children to fight with!' she exclaimed.

I could see the anger in her eyes.

'And how can you forget 2002 when the army moved to South Waziristan and killed several innocent families for no fucking reason?' I asked, anguish reflecting in my eyes.

'No, Sarmad! That's totally wrong. My father was in the army when the Waziristan operation took place in 2002. I remember it very well. He told me how the army conquered that area and succeeded in taking down the militants. They didn't harm the innocent. In fact, two officers and eight soldiers lost their lives in that mission. One of my father's close friends was one of them,' she said.

I became quiet for a moment, tears forming in my eyes.

'The army has always been against terrorism. They can never become a threat to the citizens. How could you even think that? They're the ones protecting us all the time.'

I cast down my eyes.

'I know what the army has done to protect our country. I've seen them fight. I know it very well because my father has worked all his life to protect the people of this country. He neglected his own family for the sake of his country. He lost his own son in a terrorist attack. I know what it takes to lose a member of your family . . . It's not easy living with that pain.'

'You lost . . . your brother in a terrorist attack?' I asked.

'Yes,' she winced.

'When did your brother die . . . ? I mean which terrorist attack exactly?' I asked, shuddering with fear.

'Omar died in a suicide bombing at Lahore Bazaar in 2013,' she said slowly.

I looked down, avoiding her eyes.

'We all loved him so much. He knew that being the only son and that too the youngest. I wish he was with us today. Abba has not been the same without him. He misses him every moment of his life,' she said with tears in her eyes.

I stood motionless.

'Uh, excuse me . . .' She walked back into the room or probably into the washroom to cry her heart out.

I rushed inside and opened the bag I'd brought along. After rummaging through, a black leather wallet caught my attention. I had kept this wallet with me for a long time now. With shaky fingers and teary eyes, I opened it. A black and white group photo of three fell out. A teenaged boy with two beautiful girls beamed at me. Mehar was one of the two girls. It was a photograph of Mehar with her two siblings—Omar and her elder sister. I sank on the couch, closing the wallet. I was there—my group was responsible for that attack. I shut my eyes as tears rolled down my face.

Mehar

Day 10

It was 11 a.m. when I woke up from a dreamless sleep. When I got up, my eyes drifted towards Sarmad who was still asleep. I wondered why he had not woken up yet. Ignoring the thought, I went to take a hot shower and got dressed. I wanted to wake him up but resisted. He seemed to be in deep sleep. Perhaps, he was dreaming about something. Without disturbing him, I quietly walked out of the room. On my way down, I bumped into Rukhsana's son, Jamil.

'Hey . . . where are you headed?' I dropped to my knees to talk to him.

'I'm going to meet Sarmad bhai,' he replied in his adorable voice.

'But he's sleeping.'

'No worries. I will wake him up.'

'But why do you want to see him?'

'My cousins and I are playing a game and want Sarmad bhai to join.'

'Oh, that's sweet. You can go inside the room and wake him up,' I said with a smile.

'Do you think he will be angry if I wake him up?' he asked innocently.

'No, he won't be. Go now!' I patted him on his cheek.

'Thanks.' He quickly gave a slight peck on my cheek and ran away.

I shook my head and smiled as I climbed down the stairs.

I found Bari Aapa sitting with the other women in the garden; I decided to join them.

'Good morning, Bari Aapa,' I greeted her and the other women.

'Good morning, *mere bachchey*. Come, have breakfast with us,' Bari Aapa said cheerfully.

I took a seat alongside them.

'How are you feeling this morning?' Bari Aapa asked.

'Better . . . but I still haven't forgotten what happened yesterday.' I pursed my lips together.

'The army is trying its best to exterminate that terrorist group. Hopefully this will not be repeated again,' Bari Aapa said.

'Hopefully,' I said.

'Where is Sarmad today? I didn't see him,' Rukhsana asked, looking for him.

'He's still sleeping,' I told her.

'Must be tired . . . I'm really impressed by how efficiently he managed the wedding arrangements. I wonder what Faisal and the others would have done if he wasn't there,' Bari Aapa said.

I smiled on hearing it.

'How is Sufi?' I asked.

'She is fine . . . we'll be meeting her tonight at the reception,' Rukhsana said.

'Great. It's good that I am meeting her today, because we might leave in one or two days . . .' I said.

'Really? You are leaving so soon?' Bari Aapa asked, getting upset.

'Yes, Bari Aapa. We can't stay here any longer. We have to go back to our home. I think we've had enough fun; our honeymoon has lasted more than it should have.' I tried to smile when I said it, even though it was a pure lie.

'I hope you had a good time here with us,' Rukhsana said.

'Yes. I loved being here. Every second of it.' I smiled.

Meanwhile, Jamil and his friends had managed to wake up Sarmad and drag him downstairs. As I took a sip of my tea, I saw Sarmad coming out with the kids. He looked stunning as usual in his loose white T-shirt and faded jeans.

'There he is. He has a long life!' Rukhsana smiled. 'I'll go and get more breakfast for you all.' She walked away, leaving me with Bari Aapa.

I did not break my gaze and kept staring at Sarmad. However, he didn't look back. Bari Aapa caught me staring and smiled. I laughed as I watched Sarmad running along with the other kids in the garden.

'You love him a lot, right?' Bari Aapa asked thoughtfully.

Surprised, I looked at her as blood rushed to my cheeks. I didn't have anything to say; I didn't know what to speak.

'The way your eyes don't leave him even for a second only proves how much you love him . . .' Bari Aapa said.

'I . . . I was just watching them play . . .' I confessed.

'Don't try to hide your love from me. I know what you feel for him. It's real. He is devoted to you too.' Bari Aapa looked at Sarmad.

'How can you say that?' I asked, suddenly interested in knowing Bari Aapa's perspective.

'Just look at the way he's staring at you at this very moment. You will understand what I mean.' She was right.

He was staring right at me, his eyes burning with passion. As soon as we shared a glance, he immediately looked away, pretending to be interested in the game. I couldn't gauge his feelings for me. Even if he felt something for me, he would never say it; I was sure of that.

What if it's only an illusion? What if he doesn't feel anything for me? What if I'm taking it too far? I don't want to be shattered and get hurt if he doesn't reciprocate my feelings. I don't want to live my life pining over unrequited love.

Perhaps Bari Aapa heard my silence.

'You should have faith in god and leave everything to Him. He will show you the right path to love,' Bari Aapa said, smiling.

'But how will I know if it's the love I have been looking for?' I asked.

'He will tell you. Just follow His directions. He will take you to love,' she said.

Bari Aapa's words had a profound meaning. They unravelled the mystery of love.

Lost in her words, I slowly stood up and started walking towards Sarmad. They were playing a game of blind man's buff. It was his turn to wear the blindfold. He held out his hands and tried to catch the other players running around him. I walked slowly on the grass, staring at him dreamily. I didn't realize when I came and stood right next to him. Not missing the chance, Sarmad grabbed my arm and pulled me closer. My face was only inches away from his, our mouths nearly touching, our breaths intertwined. In that one moment, the world stopped around us. Still blindfolded, he wrapped his arms around my waist and beamed at me. With my heart skipping a beat, I removed the blindfold. Our heartbeats grew faster as our glances met. I drew closer to him, pressing my body against his. I watched as he closed his eyes and felt every inch of me. I shut my eyes as I pressed my lips against his.

'Mehar!' Rukhsana brought me back from my reverie.

'Uh, yes?' I asked, stunned and embarrassed at my lustful thoughts.

'I called your name so many times. Where are you lost? Ask Sarmad to stop playing with the kids and have breakfast. We have to get ready for the reception.'

'Oh . . . okay . . .' I muttered, my cheeks red with embarrassment.

Instead of asking Sarmad directly, I told Jamil to convey my message to him and rushed back to the room.

Sarmad

Day 10

I noticed the way Mehar ran up to the room. I hurriedly gulped down my breakfast and rushed to the room. As I climbed the stairs, I received a text message from Haider who wanted updates on our mission. Instead of going to the room, I headed towards the terrace and dialled Haider's phone number.

'Salaam, Sarmad. I have been waiting for your call. What is the General's daughter up to?' Haider asked.

I hated the fact that my team members knew about Mehar. I shouldn't have told them about her.

'Nothing . . . I haven't been able to get much information out of her. I don't think she knows anything. Apparently her father had kept everything hidden from his family,' I said.

'What? That's not good. Mullah sahib is not going to be happy with this news. What do we do now?' Haider asked, sounding disappointed.

'We do nothing and wait for more clues. I will try to get as much information as possible. Just wait for my next call.'

'All right. Keep an eye on this girl. She could be very useful for our mission.'

'Do you have an update on James Henry?' I asked. 'Try to track him as well.'

'Will do. Khuda hafiz.' I ended the call.

Before Mullah sahib or any other team member suspects anything, I have to get Mehar out of this mess and take her back to Lahore. I cannot let her know the truth about me. Never . . . it's not safe for her to stay here. Not any more . . .

Soon the evening set in. Everybody started getting ready for the reception which was to be held at a venue in Mingora, not far away from the house. When I came back to the room, I saw that Mehar had already occupied the washroom. I grabbed my clothes and went to the other room to get ready. When I came out, I found Mehar standing near the door. Dressed in a simple yet elegant ivory-coloured dress, she looked beautiful. I passed her a smile and then signalled her to walk with me. She smiled and obliged.

Mehar

My heart skipped a beat when I saw him dressed in a grey suit. Bari Aapa's words rang through my head as I laid eyes on him. It was hard to believe her words, but at the same time I could not deny my feelings for Sarmad. I could not fight with my heart any more. Whatever I felt for him was real. If there was one person, apart from my family, who could do anything for me or go to any extent just to make me happy, it was him. I knew I had lost myself to him, completely. However, I didn't know what to do with these feelings. Should I tell him about it? How would he react when I did? Did he also have similar feelings for me? What if he rejects me? Oh god . . . I didn't even know where he had come from or what his background was. I did not know where he lived and what he did for a living. I knew nothing about him, and yet I felt something for him. What if I had to live a life without him, a life full of misery? Soon, it would be time for him to leave. How would I stop him? How could I stop him considering there was no relationship between us?

'Mehar . . .' he said, breaking my reverie.

I looked at him in a daze as I stepped off the stairs.

'We need to leave tomorrow morning. We should not delay it any more,' he said in one breath.

On hearing this, disappointment flickered briefly in my eyes. Here I was thinking about my confused feelings, and he was already making plans to leave.

'Tomorrow morning?' I asked, slowing down my pace.

'Yes. I need to go back to where I came from. I'll drop you at Lahore tomorrow evening and then come back the same day.'

I didn't respond.

'I need you to pack your things tonight. All right?'

He got into one of the family cars and told me to join him. But I needed some time to think. I needed to be alone and think about the possibilities. I excused myself by saying I wanted to sit with Rukhsana. Sarmad agreed and told me to be safe.

As the engine started, my heart fell down an abyss of sadness. Suddenly, I hated the idea of being separated from him. I hated the idea of leaving him.

How could I fall for a person I barely knew? How could I think of another man when I was almost engaged to my cousin? I could not disappoint my father. Sometimes, it is better if the secrets of the heart remain unsaid and unheard. It will save you from heartbreak. As I looked outside the car window, a tear rolled down my cheek.

Sarmad

I knew what she was going through at that moment. Her feelings were written all over her face. Clearly, she felt something for me and did not want to leave me. But what about me? She didn't even have the faintest idea what I felt for her. I didn't have an explanation for these feelings. I was not allowed to fall in love. I was not here to get involved in a romantic relationship but to work on my mission. But how could I disregard my feelings for Mehar? I could not see her in pain or see tears in her eyes. I'd do anything to protect her. But the question was, for how long could I do that? Soon, I would have to take her to her house in Lahore and walk out of her life. Everything will be finished. The glorious days of an otherwise dull life will forever come to an end. But that's how it is supposed to be. One thing was clear—I was a monster. I didn't deserve her love. I was not capable of becoming the hero of her life. I was the villain of her story. This was my reality. A reality that would ruin her completely and destroy her life.

The reception was an open-air event, and everything was set under tents. Despite the heaters placed in all the corners, it was uncomfortably cold. Throughout, I had my eyes fixed on Mehar but she didn't look back at me. I wondered if she was ignoring me deliberately. I watched her as she hugged

Sufi, who was dressed as a bride, and spoke to her on the stage. Her face remained solemn the entire time. I could not see her like that. I hated that expression on her face. As the event progressed, some people immersed themselves in long conversations, whereas the others got busy eating. Aziz introduced me to a couple of his friends.

'This is Sarmad. Consider him a part of our family,' Aziz smiled as he introduced me to his friends.

'Nice to meet you, Sarmad,' one of the men sporting a goatee greeted me.

'The pleasure is all mine, sir.' I shook hands with him.

'Your face looks familiar . . . it seems I've seen you somewhere,' the man said.

All my senses became alert, my face reddened, and I became conscious.

'Really? I don't know . . . maybe you're mistaken because we haven't met before,' I replied, looking away.

'No, bhaijaan . . . I am sure we've met before.'

'Maybe. I don't remember,' I replied curtly. 'Excuse me, gentlemen. I will be back in a minute.' I excused myself and walked away.

Even I thought I'd seen that man somewhere. The way he stared at me, it seemed he knew a lot about me. I was worried that he might get suspicious and warn Aziz. Without wasting another day, I had to run away before any of the family members learnt about me.

As the time passed, it got colder. The guests departed one by one. I remained aloof throughout the event. Bari Aapa and the rest of the family members got into their respective cars and drove back to the mansion. This time, Mehar sat next to me. She squirmed every time my body brushed against hers. Noting her uneasiness, I shifted a little to create some space between us. We reached home sooner than I had expected. Sitting next to Mehar in complete silence seemed like a lifetime even though our journey lasted only a few minutes.

As soon as the driver killed the engine, she ran out, without looking at me.

Stunned, I drew a deep breath and got out of the car to follow her. Right then, Aziz grabbed my arm.

'Yes, Aziz bhai?' My face turned red as I faced him.

'I heard you're leaving tomorrow. Is that true?' Aziz asked me.

I studied his face before answering his question. There weren't any traces of suspicion on it.

'Yes,' I whispered.

'Okay. Let me know when you will be leaving. I will arrange a car for you.'

'No . . . we won't be needing a car. We will catch a bus in the morning.'

'Are you sure?' He put a hand on my shoulder, a sign of brotherly affection.

'Yes, Aziz bhai. We will be fine,' I reassured him, trying to end the conversation as soon as possible.

'Okay, as you say.' Aziz forced a smile.

'Thanks. Goodnight.' I quickly went inside.

The room was dark when I stepped in. There was no sign of Mehar.

'Mehar?' I called out, shutting the door behind me.

Right then, a figure appeared from the balcony. It was her—dressed in the same ivory-coloured outfit. If she hadn't changed her clothes, what could she possibly have been doing all this while? She remained quiet despite me asking her.

'Mehar . . . are you okay?' I asked, taking a step towards her.

'Yes . . . I was trying to look for things to pack but I just realized that I don't have anything. Nothing belongs to me,' she said slowly.

I half smiled at her response.

'There must be something that actually belongs to you. You might want to take something back with you,' I said.

'Nothing belongs to me but memories . . .' Tears welled up in her eyes as she spoke.

Without saying anything further, she rushed to the washroom and locked it from inside. I closed my fists tightly and grimaced.

I quickly changed my clothes. I picked up a notepad and started sketching—I wanted to capture her beauty on paper. I was not an expert artist but sometimes drew for my own satisfaction. I sat cross-legged on the couch and closed my eyes. As soon as I had her face in my mind, I started sketching.

Mehar

In the washroom, I turned on the faucet and splashed water on my face. Tears trickled down my cheeks.

Why was I crying? What made those tears flow out? Why did I have feelings for a person who did not belong to me?

The mascara and kohl had smudged all over my face. I studied myself in the mirror for a long time and remembered my own family ethics and values. I was prohibited from having feelings for a stranger. I would soon be married to a person whom I'd considered a brother all my life. Sarmad was nothing but a saviour. But with him I had experienced emotions that were still unknown to me. With him I'd rediscovered myself and felt freedom like never before. I had felt independent. I had felt free. I was no longer the girl who would seek help or guidance for doing anything. I had become a much stronger person now. I was ready to go back to my world. Sarmad was right. There was something I could take home— memories, his memories. I could live with his memories all my life. As they say, at some point, you have to realize that some people can stay in your heart but not in your life. This was my reality, and I was ready to accept it happily.

Soon, I would return to my parents and everything would become normal again. I would feel like a normal person again without having to go through any trauma or heartbreak. If only I could make a deal with my heart and make it understand. If only I could stop myself from falling in love with him. If only . . .

I cautiously stepped out of the washroom, keeping my emotions in control. Sarmad was already lying on the couch, his eyes open and a cigarette dangling from his lips. A few papers and a notepad were kept on the coffee table. I wondered what he had been doing all this while. Also, I was a bit shocked to find him smoking. I'd never seen him with a cigarette before. I came up with an idea to lighten the atmosphere and cheer him up.

'Do you know a cigarette a day reduces your life by eleven minutes?' I sat on the edge of the bed, just across his couch.

He instantly came back to reality and looked at me.

I tried to smile at him. Of course it was a fake smile; I couldn't let him know how sad I felt inside.

'How do you know that?' he asked in a whisper, trying to sit up.

He put off his cigarette right away.

'I did some research on it for one of my subjects at the university,' I replied, crossing my arms.

'Oh, okay . . .' He became quiet for a moment. 'I . . . don't really smoke.'

'What happened today?' I tried to probe him.

'Nothing,' he snapped. 'I think we should get some sleep. We have a long journey tomorrow.'

'Yes, you're right.' A lump of disappointment burned in my throat. 'Goodnight, Sarmad,' I said as I looked in his eyes.

'Goodnight, Mehar,' he said.

Before he could hold my eyes, I broke our gaze and went to make my bed. Sarmad fell asleep in no time.

I tossed and turned in bed, restless and scared. I tried to sleep but in vain. Finally, I got up and checked the time on my cell phone. It was 4 a.m., and still sleep eluded me. The room was engulfed in complete darkness; maybe there was a power cut. Suddenly, I felt thirsty. I got out of my warm blanket, wrapped myself in a shawl and filled a glass with water. As I walked back to my bed, my eyes slowly drifted towards the pieces of paper scattered on the coffee table. I picked them up, trying to understand what was scribbled on them. I couldn't see clearly as it was completely dark in the room. I still picked up his notepad. A face of a beautiful girl smiled back at me. Even though the sketch was incomplete, it was stunning. The girl resembled me. A small smile played on my lips as I realized he had been trying to make my portrait. I put the notepad on the table and slowly walked to the washroom.

Suddenly, I heard a strange sound near the door. As I opened it, I found him standing there. I could hear his breathing as he came closer. A small light flickered on his face.

'What are you doing here?' he whispered, his brows pulled together. He looked a little annoyed.

As he came closer, I realized he was half naked; a plain white trouser hung over his waistline. I felt a strong desire to touch and explore his skin. In the dim light that streamed in through the window, I observed his taut torso. I closed the space between our bodies by stepping closer to him.

'Mehar . . .' he whispered, his lips quivering.

'Sarmad . . .' I murmured, holding his hand and squeezing it lightly. I could hear the desperation in my voice and feel his uneven breathing. My heart thumped loudly in my chest as I felt his strong grip on my hand. Perhaps he also wanted to say something.

Sarmad

As she drew closer, my entire body shivered. Slowly, she wrapped her shaky arms around my neck and ran her fingers through my wet, ruffled hair.

'Mehar . . . this is . . . not right . . . you're not in your senses . . .' I whispered.

Her eyes were closed. Our lips almost touched, breaths intermingled and heartbeats intertwined. For one moment, I wanted to let go of everything for her. I wanted to feel the moment. I wanted to get carried away. We stayed in that position for a long time. The smell of her hair and skin sent shivers down my spine. I'd never imagined that I would stand so close to her. Yet, at the same time, a feeling of guilt enveloped me. I was a monster. She would loathe me once she knows my truth. I wanted to step back when the cruel reality dawned on me but her grip was too strong. I couldn't let it go. The touch of her fingers on the nape of my neck was driving me crazy. Her cheeks glistened with tears as she held me tightly.

'Mehar . . .' I said, concern dripping from my voice.

'I . . . I don't want to let you go, Sarmad. Not now, not tomorrow. Never,' she said as fresh tears rolled down her cheeks.

I fought back my own tears and gulped down a lump in my throat when I heard what she had said.

'I don't understand why this is happening to me. I have never done anything bad in my whole life, then why is god making me go through so much pain? Why?' she cried.

I had resisted all this while, but I couldn't hold back any longer. I lightly wrapped my arms around her waist, making her body shiver.

'Mehar . . . nothing is happening to you. Everything is fine.' I tried to console her.

'Really?' She looked me in the eye now. 'Why don't your eyes match your words then? I *know* what you feel for me, Sarmad. I've seen it in your eyes. I've seen it in your heart. You cannot deceive a woman. You may tell the greatest lies or wear a brilliant disguise, but you can't escape the eyes of the one who sees right through you. I have seen right through your heart. Right through your soul. I know you love me, and you know that too.'

I was taken aback by her words. My startled eyes met hers. I drew my arms back. I was speechless. She stepped closer to me once again and held my face in her hands.

'Isn't there any way we can be together? I want to have a life with you, Sarmad. I want to explore myself with you,' she said, looking in my eyes with love and compassion. 'Let's make a life together. Just you and me.' Another tear trickled down her cheek as she pressed her forehead against mine.

With this, I half smiled and closed my eyes. She didn't know what she had just asked for. I had not felt so weak and vulnerable before. This girl was making me feel defeated.

'Would you want to live your life with someone who took away a part of you?' I asked, making her look up.

She stared at me incredulously, slightly taken aback.

'Would you want to stay with a person who is responsible for destroying the peace of your home?' I asked another question.

'Sarmad . . . what are you saying?' she asked, stepping back.

'Come with me, I'll explain it to you.' I took her hand and led her out.

I opened my bag, took out the wallet and showed her the picture. She was stunned to see that photograph. Her world turned upside down. She took the picture from my hand and stared at it for a long time. Tears welled up in her eyes as she caressed the picture.

'I was at the site when the bomb went off. I saw him die.'

'What . . . ?' she asked. 'You're saying that you were there when my brother took his last breath . . . but . . . but what were you doing there, Sarmad? Did you try to . . . to save him?'

'The people responsible for taking millions of innocent lives can never save one innocent life . . .' I whispered, agony visible on my face.

'What do you mean?' she asked, wiping off her tears.

'When I said I took away a part of you and was responsible for destroying the peace of your home . . . I meant . . .'

'You meant what?' she asked, her eyes wide open in fear.

I held her gaze for a long time before saying anything more.

'Did you . . . you mean you were . . . did you do something to him?' she asked abruptly, a horrified look clouding her face.

I didn't say anything nor did I nod.

'Sarmad! I'm asking you something! SPEAK UP!' she yelled, grabbing me and shaking my bare shoulders. 'Did you kill my brother?'

I simply nodded in return. My face remained expressionless. .

'I am a terrorist, Mehar, and you surely don't want to live your life with one,' I said, tearing up.

Mehar

The truth that unfolded was something I had least expected.
Something inside me died. I felt suffocated and my heartbeat
quickened. I didn't want to trust my ears; I didn't want to
believe what I had just heard. But his teary eyes and defeated
expression made me realize that he was telling the truth. All
this while I'd been living inside a bubble of fantasy. The
moment he pricked the bubble, I stepped into reality—a
dreadful reality. Sarmad was a monster, a killer. He was
a terrorist by his own admission. He was the one who had
planned the Lahore Bazaar blast that had killed hundreds of
innocent people, including my brother. How could I make
the mistake of falling in love with a murderer? How could
I expect a future with a monster? He not only killed my
brother that day but also destroyed the peace of my home.
My mother hasn't slept properly since the day she lost
her only son. Every night she cries in her sleep. My father
doesn't go to bed before looking at his son's photograph.
Everything changed for us. All this happened because of the
person standing in front of me. How can I look him in the
eye again? How can I tolerate his presence? How can I ever
think of forgiving him?

'I know I am a criminal and should be punished. I took away your happiness. You can take my life if you want to . . . I leave the decision to you. My punishment is in your hands, Mehar. I would not want to get shot by anyone else but you. I leave my fate to you . . .' he whispered, his face dull, eyes lifeless.

My body turned numb and my arms felt limp; all my energy seemed to have drained out of me. I didn't know how to react. I felt disoriented and heartbroken.

'Before leaving for Lahore, please decide . . . don't leave me here. I'd die from this guilt,' he said, his voice dry. 'I will wait for your answer : . . '

He picked up his shirt from the couch, slipped it on and walked out of the room. The moment he stepped out, I dropped to my knees and let out a loud, doleful wail. I cried in pain until I ran out of tears. I experienced the same excruciating pain that I had felt when my brother died three years ago.

Sarmad

Day 11

I sprinted as fast as my legs could carry me till I reached a hilly region next to the river. Catching my breath, I kneeled down and let out a deep, painful cry. The moment I feared the most had arrived. My real identity had been revealed to her. Somewhere in my mind, I also felt relieved. I could not encourage her feelings knowing how dangerous it could be for her. I'd made up my mind to embrace every situation that came my way. Exposing the truth about me and my clan could jeopardize my mission but I chose to ignore that. I trusted Mehar regardless of the fact that she could turn me in any second.

I don't remember how long I stayed there whimpering in solitude.

Mehar

Day 11

After Sarmad left the room, I got plenty of time to contemplate what had just happened. Three painful truths unfolded that morning:

1. Sarmad was a terrorist.
2. His group was responsible for the Lahore Bazaar blast which had killed my brother along with many other innocent people.
3. I couldn't ever think of living with a terrorist, not even in my wildest dreams.

I stayed in the same position for a long time; knees on the floor, head bowed and the black and white photograph still in my hands. My tears had dried now. I felt frightened.

After a while, I stood up; my feet felt stronger. Breathing heavily, I searched for Sarmad everywhere in the room. When I was sure he was nowhere around, I managed to get hold of his belongings. I grabbed his travelling bag and rummaged through it. I wanted to know his true identity. I knew terrorists lived with fake identities. It was possible that he had fooled me all this while. I found a stack of papers, mostly maps, a toothbrush, toothpaste, business cards, an ID card and a small leather pouch in his bag. The pouch looked somewhat suspicious. It felt really heavy. On opening the pouch, I was horrified to find a loaded pistol. The sound of the doorknob startled me. As soon as he came in, I grabbed the pistol and pointed it at him. Sarmad's face remained unchanged. Instead of trembling with fear, he smiled feebly and closed the door behind him. I was shocked at his demeanour, and my heart pounded loudly in my chest. With a hesitant expression on his face, he took a step towards me.

'Stop or I'll shoot you!' I bellowed, holding the pistol firmly in my hands.

Fresh tears trickled down my cheeks.

'Then shoot me and end this story. Once and for all,' he whispered, taking one more step towards me.

'Sarmad, I'm serious. I know how this thing works. Stop walking towards me or this bullet will go right into your heart.'

'Like I said earlier, I would like it to be you who kills me rather than someone else,' he said as he took another step.

'Please don't make me do this, Sarmad . . . please don't make me a murderer,' I pleaded, tears rolling down my cheeks.

'Perhaps this is how you would avenge your brother . . . just pull the trigger and kill me, Mehar. Kill me.' He now stood in front of me.

I looked at his heroic, brave eyes, and felt weak in the knees. How could I kill the person I loved so much? How could I kill the person who had saved my life so many times?

'Stop reminding me of what you've done! Stop telling me you're nothing but a monster!' I pressed the tip of the pistol against his forehead.

Unfazed, he glanced at the weapon.

'I can do this . . . you know I can . . .' I whispered, my voice determined.

'I know you can. Pull the trigger, Mehar. What are you waiting for?' he asked guilelessly, slowly raising his hands and placing them on mine.

Quiet yet resolved, I tightened my grip on the trigger. But there was something in his morose eyes that left me distraught. His touch made me weak.

'Nothing I say can relieve you of your pain . . . nothing. I am better off dead. I am done. Please shoot me and release me from this guilt.'

Disconcerted by his words, I gulped, sweat beading on my forehead. The pistol, however, remained in the same position—directed at his forehead.

We remained in that position for a long while—our eyes locked. My heart took a thousand somersaults as I looked deep into his fearless, intense eyes. He cocked his head to one side and smiled at me. As much as I cringed at his expression, I hated the fact that he knew I wouldn't shoot him. In the next instant, he slowly cupped my hands and lowered the pistol. To my disbelief, I surrendered to him without retaliating.

God, what was I doing? Why?

He turned away from me as soon as the pistol was in his hands. He then quickly stuffed his things into his bag.

'Pack your things. The bus to Lahore leaves in an hour. I'll drop you at the bus stop, so you reach home safely.'

'Safely? Do you think I'm safe with you? With a monster? How can I feel secure with the person who took my brother's life? How? Tell me . . . what made you do all of this? Huh? What made you kill my brother? What made you kill hundreds of other innocent people? How does your conscience even allow you to take part in such brutal attacks? How do you even breathe? Oh, wait. Do you even have a heart? What an atrocious monster you are! I can't believe I let you come so close to me. I . . . I can't believe I shared this room with you for . . . for so many days. I fucking hate myself for even developing feelings for you!' I yelled.

Despite my thousand accusations, he continued to pack his stuff.

'I hate you, Sarmad . . . or whatever your fucking name is. I hate you to the core. I will not spare you. God will not spare you. You'll die a thousand deaths for what you've done.'

He zipped his bag and then turned to look at me.

'We have to leave now,' he said. My words didn't seem to affect him.

'Huh? You think you'll be spared for your deeds and escape easily? I will put you and your group behind bars! The army won't spare you. My father won't spare you. Just wait and watch!' I lashed out.

'I'll be waiting for you downstairs.' He reached for his bag and walked out of the room, closing the door behind him.

Without retaliating or screaming at him, I agreed. Not because I was scared of him but because I still could not believe what was happening to me. Everything had changed in a matter of seconds. Perhaps this is why life is termed unpredictable. As I scanned the room, I reminisced about the time I had spent with him. Despite fighting the urge to cry, tears rolled down my cheeks as I looked around. I took whatever items I could and then walked out of the room.

Bari Aapa and the other family members were waiting for me downstairs, gloomy smiles spread on their faces. I instantly realized that he had informed them about our departure. However, Sarmad was nowhere in sight. I cried as I bid them goodbye, especially Jamil. Bari Aapa prayed for our well-being and wished that we become parents soon. On hearing this, my blood curdled.

'Come here whenever you want to. Remember, this is also your home,' Bari Aapa assured me.

Sarmad

'The bus leaves in ten minutes,' I said, looking away. We were waiting at the local bus stand.

She took the ticket from my hand grudgingly, making sure her fingers didn't touch mine. I was hurt by the animosity in her gesture.

'Mehar . . .' I said.

'You don't need to come with me,' she said sternly, looking at the other ticket in my hand.

'I just want to make sure that you reach home safely,' I replied.

'You don't need to conceal your true face any more. I know who you are,' she said, her eyes full of hatred.

'Think whatever you want to. I'm doing my duty. I have to protect you as long as you are with me.' This time I didn't look into her eyes while speaking.

'What's the use of protecting me when you couldn't protect my brother? When you couldn't protect the other innocent people who died that day in the Lahore Bazaar blast?' she whispered, shaking her head in disbelief. 'I don't believe a word that comes out of your mouth!'

'I understand you have nothing for me except wrath . . . and I'm ready to accept that. I will visit Lahore two weeks from now. I know this means nothing to you. But if you ever feel like hearing my side of the story, then meet a person named Khan Baba in the Walled City. You'll find him at the Gurdwara Dehra Sahib near Badshahi Mosque.'

'What makes you think that I would want to know your story? I know exactly who you are!' she whispered. 'You and your team members will not breathe in peace for long. All of you will rot in hell. Soon!'

'Yes, perhaps that's my fate.' I smiled, eyes filling with tears. 'This is the end of our story.'

'Yes, Sarmad . . . you're right. Our story ends here,' she hissed, turned away from me, and then headed towards the bus.

Never in my life had I felt so dejected, hurt and alone. I had no idea that I would yearn for her attention so much. This girl had become an essential part of my world. I didn't know now to explain everything to her. But again I didn't have anything to explain. Everything was crystal clear. I knew who I was and now she knew it too. How could I ever expect her to accept the monster living inside me? How could I expect her to forgive a person who was responsible for her brother's death? How could I expect her to love an extremist? I had never expected her to do all of this but now I wanted her to. Despite not being allowed to have feelings for someone, I had lost my heart to her. What should I do about it? How should I get back my heart from her? How would I stop thinking about her? How would I live with the fact that she would hate me for the rest of her life? My life had become a curse. As my mind remained occupied with countless thoughts, the bus took off, leaving me behind.

Mehar

I couldn't believe I was travelling all by myself. Circumstances had made me take this step. Tears filled my eyes and streamed down my cheeks as I thought of Sarmad. I tried to look out of the window but couldn't see him anywhere. My heart lunged in my chest as I realized that I had been separated from him forever. I would never see his beautiful face, never look into his deep eyes and never touch his skin again. I'd lost him forever.

On reaching Lahore, I hailed an autorickshaw. Familiar with the roads of my home town, I easily managed to explain to the driver where I had to go. I found some money in my bag to pay the fare. I stood outside my house, staring at the road that led to the gate. Gathering courage, I pressed the doorbell. The gatekeeper opened the small gate. He was surprised to see me.

'Asalaam u alaikum, baaji. I'm so glad to see you,' he greeted me with a warm smile.

'Thank you, Ghafuur Baba,' I said, trying to smile.

The moment I reached the main TV lounge, I saw Amma, who was helping the maid clean out the dining table. I was so happy to see her after so many days.

'Amma jaan!' I croaked happily.

'Mehar! You're back!' Amma ran towards me and embraced me in a tight hug.

'I'm so glad to see you after so long! Missed you so much, meri jaan!' Amma hugged me tightly. I couldn't help but bury my face in her chest and cry.

Hearing our voices, Abba appeared in the hallway.

'Samina, who is there?' he asked.

'It's our daughter, General sahib. Mehar is here,' Amma informed him, wiping the tears from her eyes.

A delightful smile spread across his lips as he saw me.

'Abba . . .' I ran into his arms.

'How are you, my bachchey? How did you come back? Did someone drop you here?'

'Yes,' I lied. 'Asma dropped me.'

'Are you hungry? Should I bring something to eat?' Amma asked.

'No, Amma. I'm not hungry. I just want to lie down for some time. I'm really tired. You know how long the journey is.'

'*Chalo phir*. Rest now. We will chat once you wake up,' Amma said.

I nodded in response.

I'd been away from my home for eleven days. Though it might seem like a small number, for me it held a lot of significance. Eleven days. With Sarmad. Or whatever his name was. I didn't even know his real name.

The maid, Nasreen, greeted me and tried to inquire about my trip as I walked to my room. However, I didn't say much except for 'yes' and 'hmm'. I was not in the mood to talk about anything. I wanted some alone time. It went without saying that I'd already started missing someone. As Nasreen kept my belongings in the room, I parted the curtain of the window and looked outside. I wondered where he had gone and what he would be doing at that moment.

What if he's planning his next attack?

I cringed at the horrendous thought. I didn't even have his number.

'*However, if you ever feel like hearing my side of the story, then meet a person named Khan Baba in the Walled City. You'll find him at the Gurdwara Dehra Sahib near Badshahi Mosque.*'

His words rang in my ears. I put my hands over my ears. I didn't want to hear that voice ever again. I didn't want to know his side of the story. Never.

'Baaji?' Nasreen asked, surprised by my unusual behaviour.

'Haan?' I responded, looking at her.

'You okay, na?' she asked.

'Yes . . . I'm fine,' I said, bewildered.

'Would you like me to get you something?'

'Just a mug of chocolate malt.'

'Sure. I will bring it right away.' Nasreen left, closing the door behind her.

I allowed my mind to wander a bit more as I plonked myself on the bed. I caressed the bed sheet and the pillow. I had missed my bed and room so much. It wasn't long before my thoughts rushed back to Sarmad. All I could think about was his eyes, his voice and his touch. I was not happy to return. Nothing seemed right. The eleven days spent with him seemed like eleven centuries. Spending another eleven minutes without him seemed like hell.

Sarmad

I had been separated from her for only a couple of minutes, and my world had already started falling apart. I'd never wanted someone so much in my life before. Walking down a road in Mingora aimlessly, I spotted a local phone booth. The chilly breeze blew into my face, making me shiver. However, I did not stop. Tears trickled down my face as I thought of her. I paid the guy at the phone booth to make a call. After a few rings, a female voice answered.

'Hello?' she said.

'I didn't know getting separated from someone could hurt so much, Nafisa,' I whispered, a tear rolling down my cheek. 'It's killing me. Deep inside. Now I understand what I made you go through . . . '

'Sarmad . . . what are you talking about? I can't hear you properly. Are you okay?' Nafisa asked, sounding confused yet worried.

'No . . . I'm not okay, Nafisa.' I paused, holding the phone tightly in my hands. 'I'm in love with someone. And . . . it's not okay. It hurts . . . it hurts a lot . . . I'm sorry . . . ' I hung up the phone.

Mehar

I woke up with a jolt to find myself alone in the room. Everything seemed strange. Though nothing had moved since I'd left, everything seemed odd. It felt strange not to wake up in the same room where I had stayed with *him* for eleven days.

After waking up, the first thing I thought about was Sarmad. I missed him. I missed him badly. There was nothing that could make me deny how badly my heart ached for him. Dressed in a plain, cream-coloured khaddar salwar kameez and maroon woollen shawl, I walked downstairs. I could see Abba sitting in the study room. He sat on his rocking chair, with a newspaper in his hand. I walked towards him and slowly sat on the ground, close to his feet. He immediately saw me and folded his newspaper.

'Morning, mere bachchey. You're up early today. Did you sleep well?' he asked.

'Yes. I missed you so much, Abba jaan,' I said.

'How was your trip?'

On the mention of the trip, Sarmad's face flashed across my mind. Abba sat silently on the chair and looked at me thoughtfully.

'I would have come earlier if I had not met this family . . . a very loving family based in Mingora.' I smiled as I told him the truth, remembering Bari Aapa and the others.

'Which family?' Abba asked, taking off his glasses.

I had no idea why I told him the truth. Words had just spilled out.

'On the trip, I met a family in Mingora. They insisted I stay with them for a family wedding, and I just couldn't say no. I had to stay with them till the wedding ended. All of them were hospitable, caring and affectionate. They never made me feel like I was a stranger in their house. They treated me like a family member . . . I got to learn so much from them. Abba jaan, those eleven days were the best days of my life.' And then, unwittingly, I remembered Sarmad and this time it became difficult for me to hold back. 'I didn't know life could be this beautiful, cheerful and . . . meaningful. I was experiencing a new life, it was different from the one I had been leading here.'

Abba kept looking at me thoughtfully.

'I'm sorry if I crossed my limits . . . I'm sorry if I broke any rules. I just didn't know how it happened . . . I just didn't realize how I fell for . . .'

I stopped midway, realizing what I was about to utter in front of my father.

I was about to admit that I'd fallen in love with Sarmad; how ridiculously foolish of me. A tear threatened to roll down the corner of my eye, but I immediately wiped it with the back of my hand and took a deep breath.

'I'm sorry,' I blurted out abruptly, knowing I'd put myself at a huge risk.

After hearing my words, Abba firmly held my hand and planted a kiss on it. I was taken aback by my father's unexpected reaction and looked at him expectantly.

'You don't have to clarify anything, Mehar. I don't want you to apologize. I'm your father. I would never want you to feel guilty for doing something *right*. You got to see the beautiful side of our country. One should always visit such places. This is your age to enjoy. You ought to experience new things and see the brighter side of life because that's how you will learn. What upsets me is the fact that you had to live there all by yourself and that too with strangers. I had no idea you could manage on your own as you've never been alone before. Any parent would get paranoid in such a situation. However, I'm glad you are back safe and sound. I am grateful to the family who gave you space and comfort in their house. I would like to thank them whenever I meet them.'

Yes, Abba. You should thank them and Sarmad . . .

'Now stop feeling guilty. Cheer up. I want to see my daughter smiling. Haven't seen that smile in a while. And trust me, I kind of missed it.' He giggled softly.

'Abba, are you sure you're not upset with me?' I asked.

'I'm happy to see my daughter back. That's more than enough for me.'

'Love you, Abba jaan. Thank you.' I rested my cheek on his hand.

'I have some good news for you though,' he said.

'What?' I looked up at him, a tear glistening in my eye.

'Your sister is coming to Pakistan next week.'

'What? Sidra is coming?' I exclaimed.

'Yes. We've scheduled your engagement ceremony for next week.' My heart sank. I had almost forgotten that I was soon going to get married to my cousin, Hamza.

Sarmad

Sitting cross-legged inside a cave, the rough ground covered with hay, I tried to capture Mehar's features on a piece of paper. Beads of sweat trickled down my forehead as I worked hard on the sketch. As I gave it final touches, I drew in a deep breath and forced myself to look away. But I failed. Mehar's intense eyes demanded to be looked into. I could not leave them even for a second. I had sketched her portrait because I wanted to hold on to her memory for the rest of my life. I had not only drawn her face but also her soul as I wanted to feel her around me, all the time. This seemed like the only way to live through the growing anguish in my heart, which had only increased after she had left. I did not know for how long I kept staring at her sketch. As I caressed her face with my fingers, I felt an excruciating pain in my chest. I'd fallen in love with her. Unwillingly. Unknowingly. Irrevocably. And what caused me more pain was the fact that I could not fall out of love with her.

Mehar

It was a busy day for me and my mother as we had to prepare a grand lunch at home. Sidra had reached that morning. There was so much that I wanted to share with my elder sister, but I had to wait for the right time; it only seemed possible at night when our parents would be asleep. However, the real dilemma was what would I tell her? Would I be able to speak my heart out? Would I be able to tell her everything about Sarmad? But how would I introduce him to Sidra? As the person partially responsible for our brother's death, or the one whom I had fallen in love with?

Sidra had come alone; her husband was still in Dubai. It wasn't a proper engagement ceremony but only a simple get-together, so that close relatives could meet and greet each other. While Sidra distributed the gifts she'd brought for us, I had my eyes glued to the television.

'It's a beautiful sweater,' Amma said.

'I'm glad you liked it, Amma.' Sidra smiled.

'Even I love the one you got for me,' Abba said, smiling.

'I got this stuff in such a hurry. I didn't even know if I was coming to Pakistan any time soon. Thanks to Mehar's sudden engagement plan,' Sidra said, giving me a grateful look.

'We still hope your husband can make it for the occasion,' Amma said.

'It's okay, Amma. He would have loved to come but you know how his work is.'

'He's very hard-working.' Amma nodded.

Getting distracted, I excused myself and tiptoed to my bedroom. Noticing the uneasiness in my stride, Sidra followed me.

'Hey,' Sidra said, stepping into my room.

'Hey.' I turned to look at her and smiled. 'You want to sleep here or in the guest room?'

'Here, of course. I miss this room a lot.'

'I'm sure you do. This room has equally missed you. Let me get a blanket for you then.' As I walked away, Sidra grabbed my arm.

'Are you okay?' Sidra asked, concern filling her amber eyes.

'Yes, of course,' I replied, my throat becoming dry.

'Hmm,' Sidra mumbled.

'Let me make your bed,' I quickly changed the topic. I was scared to look into her eyes as the dreadful truth could unfold any second.

'It's ready. You can lie down,' I said, switching on the bedside lamp.

'I feel so good to be back at home. I missed you all so much,' Sidra said as she plonked herself down on the bed.

'I missed you too.' I sat on the edge of the bed, staring blankly at the bed sheet.

'Hey, what about your trip? You haven't told me anything yet! Amma and Abba got so worried when they couldn't reach you. I'm glad you returned on time.'

'Yeah, I know. I got them really worried,' I replied, slowly.

'And how was revisiting our childhood?' Sidra asked.

I hesitated to talk about it first, as I knew I would be reminded of him. However, there was *a lot* I needed to discuss with her, let alone the places we had visited as kids. It didn't take time for tears to well up in my eyes.

'Mehar, hey, what . . . what happened?' Sidra asked, wrapping her arms around my shoulders.

I needed someone's shoulder to cry on. Someone who would listen to my heart and make me feel at ease, someone who would console me. And at that moment, only Sidra could handle me.

'Be patient, meri jaan. Tell me, what happened?' Sidra tried to calm me down, rubbing my back with her hand. 'I beg of you. Please tell me why you're crying. Did someone say something to you?'

'No . . .' I blurted out, freeing myself from her embrace. 'Nobody said anything . . . it's just that . . . whenever we're together, I miss his presence even more . . .' I said and started crying again.

'Oh, my baby.' Sidra kissed my hair.

Once again, Sidra held me in a tight embrace, trying hard not to break down in front of me. As I cried, remembering my brother, I could hear my mother silently sobbing outside my bedroom door.

Sarmad

In the midst of a stormy cold night, I walked up to our cottage in Jhelum. As was the norm, the clan had to shift locations time and again. This time they had shifted to Jhelum. I knocked on the door and listened to the hushed voices coming from inside. They had just sat down for tea, and a sudden knock on the door had startled them.

'Who could it be in the middle of the night?' an elderly woman inquired.

'Let me check, Amma,' I heard Nafisa say.

As she unlocked the door, a cold wave of air hit her face, forcing her to shut her eyes. Dressed in a worn-out outfit, I stood in front of her. After recovering from the initial shock, Nafisa grabbed the collar of my jacket and pulled me inside, closing the door behind us.

'O, *khudaya!* Sarmad! You're here!' Nafisa desperately ran her cold hands over my dry, unscathed face.

I, however, chose to remain still.

'Oh, how I have missed you!' She embraced me tightly, rubbing my back with her hands. 'Are you okay?' She pulled herself back to see my face. 'Hey, I'm talking to you!' She held my face in her hands and made me look into her eyes.

'I'm fine,' I replied croakily. 'Need to get warm.' I freed myself from her hold, greeted the other companions and then walked over to the other room.

Nafisa grunted in disappointment.

After leaving Mingora, my plan was to head back to Wazirabad to reunite with my group members and continue working on the mission. My other companions, Haider and the others, were still out there, finding the best possible way to reach our destination. After a brief stop at Jhelum, I had to leave for Wazirabad.

The comforting warmth inside the cottage couldn't take the chill off my hands. Despite sitting near the fireplace for a long time, my hands still shivered with cold.

Nafisa entered the room with small, inaudible steps; she had a cup of steaming kahwa in one hand. Within seconds, I became alert to her presence in the room but didn't move an inch; I remained oblivious.

'I brought kahwa for you. Thought it'd help you warm up,' she said, stepping near the wooden side table.

After putting down the cup on the table near the fireplace, she stared at me for a long time.

I remembered what I'd told her over the phone.

However, she didn't know what I'd actually meant.

Despite my uncanny silence, she felt the urge to talk. Dressed in a sleeveless, navy blue gown beneath, she took off her shawl and slowly wrapped her arms around my neck. I remained stiff, careful not to show any emotion. She traced her finger along the length of my face and then continued down my chest, taking advantage of my unbuttoned shirt.

Tired of fighting the urge, I swiftly turned around, grabbed the side of her neck and pushed her on to the bed. A relieved smile played across her lips as she saw me getting aroused. Within a matter of seconds, I was on top of her, my arms tightly wrapped around her waist. Her one hand stroked my dishevelled hair, and with the other she caressed my back. Everything seemed perfect. The situation. The accelerating sexual tension between us. The relishable warmth around us. Yet something was wrong. I was wrong. As I slowly closed my eyes, *her* beautiful innocent face flashed across my mind. I could see the dismay on Nafisa's face. Within a second, I returned to my senses and got off the bed, releasing myself from her hold. I knew I had disappointed her yet again.

'I'm sorry. This shouldn't have happened.'

Guilt washed over my face; I turned away from her and walked towards the window. Looking crestfallen, she picked up her shawl from the floor and put it around her shoulders. She then walked over to where I stood.

'So . . . what I feared has happened. My prediction has come true; you've fallen for some girl . . . '

I stayed quiet, looking out of the window, a blank expression on my face.

'Now . . . who is she?' she asked blatantly.

Mehar

The next morning, I came down to find my mother and sister in the kitchen. A strong, mouth-watering whiff wafted out, indicating that something special was being prepared for lunch. Holding a stirrer in her hand, Sidra was having an animated conversation with Amma. I also joined them, taking a seat near the kitchen counter.

'Mehar, is everything all right with you?' Sidra asked midway, interrupting her conversation with Amma.

My body froze at Sidra's abrupt question. I was surely not prepared for this.

'What happened, Sidra?' Amma asked, taken aback by Sidra's sudden question.

I lowered my eyes, trying to hide the rising fear in them.

'That's what I want to know, Amma. What has happened? I feel there's something wrong with Mehar.'

'Why do you think so? She is perfectly fine.' Amma cleared the air.

I did not dare raise my head because I was too scared to face them.

'No, I don't think so,' Sidra continued. 'She seems like a different person. She doesn't talk much. She remains in her own fantasy world. And last night, she did something she has never done before—she talked in her sleep.'

I did not like my sister blurting out everything, but at the same time I was impressed by her brilliant observation skills. Out of all the family members, it was Sidra who had noticed the major transformation in me.

'Maybe you're feeling that way because you've met her after a long time,' Amma said as she took the stirrer from Sidra's hand.

'Is Amma right, Mehar? Are all my doubts pointless?' Sidra crossed her arms, looking at me.

Now I had to speak. There was no way I could simply walk away from this awkward situation my sister had put me in.

'Uh, Amma is right. There's nothing like that.' I put on a fake smile, without looking at her. 'Is there anything special about lunch today?' I asked, quickly changing the topic.

Sidra passed me a quizzical look, which I ignored.

'Yes. Your Phupho is coming from Islamabad today,' Amma announced, smiling. 'Rings will be exchanged tomorrow.'

'Oh.' My heart sank. A new shock awaited me.

Sidra noticed my strange reaction.

'Phupho will bring something trendy for you to wear tomorrow.' Sidra hugged me, trying to cheer me up.

'Hmm. I'll just be back.' I managed to escape the situation and hurried upstairs to my room.

Without giving much thought to my upcoming engagement, I grabbed my bag from the cupboard and pulled out my cell phone. I inserted the battery back into the phone and pressed the power button. Within a couple of seconds, the dead cell phone came back to life. I quickly opened the list of dialled numbers to find a way to contact Sarmad. As far as I remembered, I had caught him using my phone once. Even though I knew that he would never leave a hint behind, I still wanted to give it a shot. A number, which I failed to recognize, caught my attention. And it didn't take me long to dial it. After a few rings, an unfamiliar old man's voice answered from the other end of the line.

'Hello? Sarmad?' the man asked.

I was startled to hear his name from the other end of the line. Unable to speak up, I immediately cut the call. But I knew I was closer to finding him.

Sarmad

I was compelled to tell Nafisa about my deep connection
with Mehar. I started off with the day I'd met her at the bus
stop and told her how I had saved her after she fell off the
cliff. I deliberately skipped talking about my feelings but
Nafisa already knew. She could see it in my eyes. The love I
had for her was evident. Our conversation over a steaming
cup of chai got disrupted when Mullah sahib called me and
ordered me to reach the next stop.

I quickly got up and started stuffing my clothes in a bag.
As I walked out of the room, Nafisa, out of habit, followed
me to the door.

'You could stay here for a few more days,' she said.

'I can't,' I said in a rush. 'Mullah sahib wants me back.
Need to finish what we started.'

'All of this should end soon. Sometimes I wish we were
not a part of this.'

'There's no turning back, Nafisa.'

'I know . . . anyway . . . when will I see you again?' she
asked, hope gleaming in her eyes.

'Don't expect anything from me. That's all I have to
say.' I turned my eyes away from her.

'You know how hard that is for me,' she responded, glumly.

'It isn't.' I looked at her. 'It is only hard for me, you know, making you realize every time that we're not meant for each other. I am sorry for all the pain. I am sorry for . . . everything.' I let out a deep sigh, trying not to look into her expectant eyes.

'I hope you find her soon,' she said, trying to hold back her tears.

'I hope that never happens. Every day I pray to god that our paths never cross.'

'You cannot challenge your destiny, Sarmad. Stop saying that.'

'I have every right to challenge it. And I will. Because it's mine.' I looked at her fiercely.

Mehar

As soon as the clock struck 3 p.m., Phupho and her family, including Hamza, arrived. Abba greeted his sister with a warm hug. Hamza, on the other hand, coolly smiled at everyone and took Amma and Abba's blessings. Sidra was quite thrilled to meet her cousin and soon-to-be brother-in-law. They spoke for a few minutes, exchanging greetings and inquiring about each other's health. Amma made all of them sit in the drawing room, and Sidra got busy laying the dining table.

The first thing Sidra noticed after walking into my room was the stuff scattered on the bed and then her eyes landed on me. With a small frown creasing my forehead, I stood near the window and stared incessantly at the phone in my hand. Sidra was disappointed to find me in the same clothes.

'Why haven't you changed till now? What the hell have you been doing?' Sidra started gathering the items lying on the bed, making me come out of my reverie. 'Do you even know that Phupho is waiting for you downstairs?'

'What? Oh. No. I didn't realize.' I tried to help her out with the cleaning.

'You're in such a mess, Mehar. What is wrong with you?' Sidra looked at me with concern.

'I'm fine.' I did not want to meet her eyes. 'I'll quickly get ready.' I passed a quick, fake smile to her and then walked into the washroom, avoiding her question.

As Sidra cleared away the mess, I came out wearing a powder-blue, chiffon salwar kameez.

'Mashallah! My baby looks so beautiful!' Sidra embraced me. 'I can't believe you are all grown up and getting married.'

I smiled in response and nodded. After a couple of minutes, I stepped into the drawing room, trying hard to look happy in front of Phupho and the others. Phupho took me into her arms while Hamza stood up, all ready to greet his fiancée-to-be.

'Mashallah. You are so beautiful. I'd always wanted you to be my daughter-in-law.' She kissed my forehead.

I tucked my hair behind my ears, feeling embarrassed.

'Not daughter-in-law,' Abba interrupted. 'She's your daughter, Khadijah. She has always been yours.' Abba tapped Hamza lightly on his back, to which he smiled.

'Yes, of course,' Phupho agreed gleefully.

I turned around to meet Phupho's husband and her younger son, Hassan, who had always reminded me of Omar. Everyone in the family knew that Hassan and Omar had shared a strong bond.

As I took blessings from Phupha and cheerfully greeted Hassan, my eyes landed on Hamza, who had been staring at me since I came into the room.

'Asalaam u alaikum,' Hamza said.

'Wailaikum asalaam,' I whispered.

He was good-looking and definitely charismatic. Any girl would go weak in the knees after laying eyes on him.

Hamza tried hard to hold my stare for a good one minute but I deliberately broke the gaze and looked away. I felt like I was cheating on *someone*. Above all, I felt like I was cheating on myself.

The day progressed rather slowly. The entire family remained engaged with the guests, while I idled away my time in my room.

A couple of hours later, I joined the rest of the family members in the TV lounge, where they were planning the wedding. I could feel Hamza's eyes on me the whole time, but I chose to ignore him as I did not want to have any awkward conversations with my cousin and soon-to-be husband.

After all the family members had gone to sleep, I sat alone on the hammock in the balcony—my favourite spot in the house. A stack of white paper sheets, kept on the table near the chair, caught my attention. I picked up a sheet and stared at it vacantly. My thoughts still revolved around the old man's voice that I had heard on the phone a few hours ago. And then there was Sarmad. Absent-mindedly, I began making an origami crane. Then I picked another sheet. And another. And so on. I couldn't believe I was finally able to make them. I slowly clapped at my own creations; a smile spread over my lips and my eyes filled with tears. I carried the cranes in the folds of my dupatta and then threw them down the balcony, into the air, one by one. The paper cranes flew across the garden and slowly twirled until they smoothly landed on the ground.

'I need to be with you, Sarmad. I need to know where you are,' I whispered to myself.

Sarmad

On my way to Wazirabad, where Mullah and the rest of the group were waiting for me, I jolted awake from a short nap. I felt as if someone had called out my name—a telepathic connection. With a pounding head and quickened heartbeat, I rubbed my eyes to figure out where the bus had reached. It was dark outside, so it was difficult to recognize the place. I leaned back on the seat, trying to relax my stiffened muscles. Instinctively, I opened the zipper of my bag, reached into it and took out a crumpled paper crane. As I held it in my hands, I thought about Mehar. I continued to hear my name being called out, but I chose to ignore it. In the next moment, I threw the paper crane out of the bus window, slowly releasing myself from the uncanny melancholy.

Mehar

A few close family friends and relatives had been invited for my engagement ceremony. I had also invited my college friends, Asma and Laraib. I needed to have a detailed discussion with them. However, I made it a point not to say anything about Sarmad. They did ask me about what happened while I was in Swat. I lied to them that I stayed with my relatives there and had a really good time.

Sidra helped out Amma and Abba with all the arrangements for the ceremony whereas I, along with my friends and cousins, sat in my room with pursed lips—my eyes cast down the entire time. Dressed in a pastel-peach salwar kameez embellished with gold embroidery, I looked different. I could not recognize myself in the mirror.

'So . . . your cousin! I just saw him downstairs. He's so handsome!' Asma exclaimed excitedly.

'C'mon, Asma. It has always been Hamza for Mehar. We all knew it all along. Both of them were destined to be together,' Laraib commented.

It took me a couple of seconds to process my friends' comments. They were right—absolutely right. It had always been Hamza for me. I knew I was going to end up with him. I knew about it before leaving for the trip. I knew about it before accidentally meeting Sarmad, and I also knew about it before falling head over heels for him. How could I even dare to think about someone else when I knew everything all along? How could I develop feelings for a murderer? I felt like a culprit in my own damn world.

'Mehar . . . come. Let's go downstairs,' Sidra said as she stormed into the room all of a sudden, interrupting my thoughts.

Hamza, dressed in an off-white kurta, was seated in the drawing room with the rest of the family members. As soon as Sidra made me sit alongside him, the guests took out their cameras and started clicking pictures to capture one of the most memorable moments of a couple's lives.

Abba handed me a box and I timidly took it in my hands. Phupho also gave Hamza a ring box. Everybody present in the drawing room cheered for us, and the cameras started flashing all over again. Now, all eyes were on me. All of them expected me to make the next move.

'Chalo, beta,' Amma said. 'Go ahead.'

Without looking up at anyone or hearing any other comment, I hurriedly slipped the ring on his finger. Applause filled the air as the engagement ceremony concluded. Both the families congratulated each other. This was followed by warm hugs and teary smiles. It was Omar whom we missed the most at that moment.

And with this, all the doors to Sarmad shut forever.

Sarmad

Meanwhile, putting aside my desolation, I met my clan members exuberantly. It was a delight to meet Ramez, Karim and Haider who were staying in a cottage along with Mullah sahib, far away from the commercial area of Wazirabad. A secret place had been chosen in order to stay away from the army.

'What information do you have on that girl?' Mullah asked me over lunch.

Hearing this, I stopped eating. A young, feeble Pathan boy served us hot boiled rice and chicken shorwa.

'I . . . I lost track of her.' Lies spilled out of my lips. 'I don't think she is of any use to me. Anyway, she was a brainless person with zero information about her father's whereabouts and missions.' I tried to sound convincing.

'Hmm,' Mullah sighed. 'We shouldn't let go of our mission though. Keep looking out for more information.'

'I already am, Mullah sahib,' I assured.

'What's your next move, son? You all need to move to Lahore as soon as possible. We don't want to miss our main target.'

'We won't miss it, Mullah sahib,' Haider interjected. 'We are already on it.'

'May god be with you,' Mullah prayed.

Mehar

Standing on the terrace, I looked up at the dark sky filled with millions of glistening stars. The chilly February breeze blew across my face. Since the engagement ceremony, I had got plenty of time to think. I was no longer a child, I had become someone's fiancée—someone's responsibility. Even though my each and every heartbeat echoed only Sarmad's name, I was ready to move on in life with Hamza. I knew it was foolish to think about someone who had shattered me into a million pieces, but I couldn't help it. Despite knowing what he had done, I couldn't stop loving him. As my mind whirled with all these thoughts, I heard the sound of soft footsteps coming my way. I spun around to find Hamza standing in front of me.

'Enjoying the cool breeze all by yourself?' he asked, smiling.

I immediately broke our gaze and looked up at the starry sky. I don't know why but his presence made me feel uneasy.

'Hmm.' He took in a long breath. 'The weather of Lahore is nothing compared to that of Islamabad. It's chillier there at the moment. Here, it's more humid.'

I simply did not want to get involved in a 'which city is better' debate with him, so I chose to ignore his comment. I remained quiet, but my mind was ruminating on a plan to escape from the terrace.

'Khair. Leave it. Why are we even discussing the weather right now?' he laughed at his own comment.

I pursed my lips in response and tucked my open hair behind my ears. Hamza took a long look at me and then smiled.

'I . . . I just can't believe what has happened. We're . . . we're engaged.' He chuckled again, running his hand through his perfectly styled hair. 'And . . . we're about to get married. Did you ever think that you would get married to me, like ever?' he asked, crossing his arms. His eyes were fixed on me.

I knew I was in deep trouble as I had an accurate answer for his question. 'NO.' However, I could not bluntly say that to him.

'Well, if you ask me the same question, I'd promptly say "yes"!' he said, without waiting for my reply.

His confession took me by surprise. Clearly, I had never had a private conversation with him before. All of our previous meetings were quite formal, with other family members around us all the time. The last time Hamza had really talked to me was when he had come down to offer condolences on Omar's death. He had tried to console me when all I could do was cry ceaselessly. I shuddered at the thought.

'As cousins, I'd always felt that there was some kind of a distance between the two of us. Every time we met back then, I used to look for chances to speak to you in private. Guess that was never meant to be. We were destined to be engaged first and then start interacting, you know,' he shrugged.

My heart leapt on hearing his words.

'It might sound a bit odd to you but yeah, I've always had a soft corner for you, Mehar.' His voice was suddenly soft, his eyes intense.

I nervously looked down at my hands that I had placed on the railing, not knowing what to say or how to react. My engagement ring sparkled in the moonlight.

'I assume you're as happy with this proposal as I am . . .' He looked back at me. 'Because honestly, this is all I ever wanted. And, it is my promise to you that I'll never ever let a tear escape your eye. I'll keep you happy till my last breath. Always.' He smiled reassuringly.

For some odd reason, his words did not make me feel queasy. I could sense truth in them. Whatever he said felt right. Perhaps it was time to move on—say goodbye to the past and welcome the future with open arms.

Sarmad

In the middle of the night, as the sky turned grey, I poked my head out of the window to look up at the stars. I tried to count them but it seemed like a hopeless idea. With arms crossed over my chest, I stood motionless in the same position for a few more seconds. A shooting star, moving rapidly across the dark sky, caught my attention. Before it disappeared, I squeezed my eyes shut and prayed.

'I wish our paths never cross, Mehar. I wish you never see my face again. All I ever want is to see you happy in your world without me in it. I want you to picture your world without me. That's all I could ever ask for.'

Mehar

I made my way through a street in Lahore Bazaar: it was filled with numerous clothing shops, stalls selling household items and food kiosks. The air was filled with coal smoke, indicating that somewhere far off a barbeque was being prepared.

This market held utmost significance for me, considering *whom* I'd lost here. Clad in a beige-coloured cotton salwar kameez, I walked down the street, observing every minute detail of the market with distraught eyes.

In the next instant, the sound of an explosion caused sudden panic among street vendors, shoppers and pedestrians. In an attempt to save myself from getting crushed under a stampede, I jumped to the other side of the street. As I struggled to catch my breath and wiped the beads of sweat from my forehead, I felt something brush against my shoulder.

A young lad, with his head bowed down and a bloodstained hand placed on his injured arm, breathed heavily and slowly.

'Omar!' I gasped. It suddenly dawned on me that the young lad was my own brother.

'Omar, Omar, Omar! Oh my . . .' I took him in my arms and rubbed his back. 'What's this . . . ?' I moved back to

look at his injured arm. 'How did . . . this . . . this happen?'
My lips trembled with fear as I spoke. 'Has *he* . . . has
Sarmad done this to you? Tell me!' I cried in anger.

Omar shook his head in dismay.

'Tell me, Omar . . . oh god . . . you will bleed to death.
Let me take you to the hospital. I won't let you die . . . This
time, I won't . . . '

'Baaji, there's no use saving a soul that has already
departed from this world . . .' Omar began, his breathing
uneven.

I looked up at him quizzically, my hands trembling with
fear.

'Never let him go . . . never . . .' Omar slowly closed his
eyes, as his voice faded away.

'Sarmad!' I called out as I woke up from the frightful
nightmare.

Sidra, who was lying next to me, also woke up in a
fright, wondering who Sarmad was.

'Mehar, are you okay?' she asked, shaking my shoulder.

I looked at Sidra, trying to catch my breath.

'Mehar! I am talking to you.'

'Yes, I'm fine . . .'. My voice choked. 'It was just a
nightmare. I'm fine . . .'

'I don't think you're fine.'

'I am, Sidra. Why don't you stop worrying about me
and go back to sleep?'

I pretended to go back to sleep, worried about calling
out Sarmad's name loudly in her presence. I knew I owed
her an exclamation the next morning.

There was something I needed to know, something that
was left untold. I could feel that something was missing. I
needed to find that missing piece of the puzzle in order to
make sense of everything.

Still occupied and dazed by last night's dream, I took a lot of time to get out of bed. I kept thinking of ways to reach out to *him*. As I forced myself out of bed, Sidra stepped out of the washroom, tossing the towel on the couch.

'Who's Sarmad?' she asked, as she stood in front of the dressing table.

Abashed by her sudden question, I silently tiptoed towards the washroom. I did not like hearing his name from anyone else's mouth. I hated myself for blurting out his name in front of her.

'I am asking you something, Mehru. You just can't ignore my question.' Sidra turned around to face me.

Her questions made me angry.

In a slightly irritated tone, I said, 'I don't know what you're talking about, Sidra. I might have started sleep talking which is beyond my control, but I don't know who the hell this Sarhad is.'

'Sarmad. That's what you said,' Sidra corrected me.

'Yeah. Whatever.' I looked at her embarrassedly and then bit my lip.

'You've changed a lot. You better get a grip on yourself before the situation starts slipping out of your hands,' she said, drying her wet hair.

'Like I said, everything is fine. Don't worry,' I insisted.

'Get ready. Amma wants to see us downstairs.'

Despite my sister's advice, I was adamant and did not want to change my mind. I'd do anything to get in touch with Sarmad.

Khadijah Phupho and her family were to leave for Islamabad the next day. Therefore, they'd decided to go around for a city tour.

'Would you like to go out with us, Mehru?' Phupho asked, popping a peanut into her mouth. 'You can buy whatever you want.'

Hamza quickly shot a playful look at me, which I completely ignored.

'I'm sorry, what?' I blurted out, feeling more miserable than before.

Sidra glowered at my disrespectful behaviour. Abba and Amma also shared a concerned glance.

'Beta . . .' Phupho seemed a bit offended. 'I was just asking . . . '

Sidra interjected, trying to make Phupho feel better.

'Go with her and shop around!' She patted my back, to which I nodded, confused.

'And we'll also visit the Grand Jamia Mosque located in Bahria Town. I saw some pictures of it on Facebook and loved it,' Hassan joined in.

'Haan haan, why not,' Hamza said, taking a sip of his tea and shooting a quick glance at me.

'Go and quickly get dressed. We're a little short of time,' Phupho said, to which I agreed reluctantly.

As I was walking up the stairs, news about a recent terrorist attack on the television caught my attention. Sarmad instantly crossed my mind.

Was he involved in this attack? Has he always been involved in terrorist attacks in our country?

I came back and sat on the couch. The news not only made Abba extremely distressed, but also disturbed the rest of the family members.

'These attacks are becoming common in our country. We should try to take more effective steps to control this appalling situation,' Anwar uncle grunted.

'Trust me, Abba. We're trying our best to eradicate terrorism from our country,' Hamza assured him.

'I am sure our government is cooperating with the army in the best possible way,' Abba said quietly.

'That's true,' Hamza nodded positively. 'If I'm not wrong, Mullah and his gang are behind this attack.'

The words 'Mullah and his gang' caught my attention. I was quite confident that I had heard this name sometime back. Perhaps, this name was linked to Sarmad and might lead me to him.

Did Sarmad ever say this name in front of me? I tried hard to remember.

'Mullah and gang? Where are they from? Are they linked to ISIS or Taliban?' Abba asked, an inquisitive look on his face.

'They're not linked to anyone, Mamu jaan. I think they have a group of their own. Some foreign source is funding them,' Hamza answered, carefully placing the cup of tea on the table.

I tried to look as impassive as I could.

'Watching such terrible news on TV back in Dubai makes me really scared, Abba,' Sidra said, changing the subject. 'It always reminds me of . . .' Sidra said but then stopped as tears formed in her eyes.

A sudden jab of pain hit my chest as I remembered the night Sarmad confessed his crime in front of me. Grabbing the remote control, I firmly pressed the 'off' button. I could feel everybody's eyes on me.

I ran upstairs to my room. Grabbing the laptop from the couch, I went to the balcony and sat on a chair. As soon as I switched the laptop on, I clicked on Google and swiftly typed 'Mullah and gang' in the search bar. For a moment, I couldn't believe that I was looking up some unknown terrorist group. When nothing relevant showed up, I quickly typed 'Mullah and gang terrorist group Pakistan', to which several results came up. I scrolled through a few web pages to find something concrete that would actually help me find Sarmad. However, all my efforts were in vain.

What if Hamza is right? What if Mullah and his gang are behind all the recent terrorist attacks in the country, including the Old Bazaar blast? What if Sarmad is also a part of this gang?

With too many dreadful options laid out in front of me, I felt my throat constrict. I shut down the laptop and put it on the side table.

I need to find out this 'Mullah and gang'. I need to find Sarmad. Even if it costs me my own life. But how am I going to do it?

There had to be some clue or trail that could lead me to him.

'But if you ever feel like hearing my side of the story, then meet a person named Khan Baba in the Walled City. You'll find him at Gurdwara Dehra Sahib near Badshahi Mosque.'

His words, all of a sudden, echoed in the back of my mind. I thought deeply about what he had said—the words that had come out of his mouth at the time of our separation at the Mingora bus stop.

Who was Khan Baba? How was he linked to him? Why did he want me to meet him?

If there was one person who could help me find the missing pieces of the puzzle, it was Khan Baba. I had to meet this person before Sarmad destroys the peace of this country and sacrifices his own life. I had to hurry before it was too late. I had to stop him.

The question, however, was how would I get to the Walled City all by myself?

Sarmad

I studied the map laid out in front of us carefully, trying to trace our next target location.

'I think this is where we should be heading,' I said, marking a territory with a red marker on the map. 'We should be safe here for the next couple of days.'

'For how long, Sarmad?' Ramez asked, concern filling his eyes.

'What do you mean?' I shot him a baffled look.

'We can't be on the run all our lives. There has to be an end to this,' Ramez declared, as Haider and Karim exchanged glances with each other.

'It's do or die, Ramez. The only end point is death. The sooner you know, the better,' I retorted.

Ramez lowered his head in disappointment.

As I walked away, my phone vibrated in my pocket. I flinched as I saw the caller's name on the screen.

'Hello?' I answered.

'Sarmad . . .' an old, frail voice said from the other end.

'Khan Baba?' I asked, my brows furrowed with concern.

'I think someone is looking for you,' he said, pausing. 'You need to be careful.'

'How can you be so sure of that?' I asked, lowering my voice.

'Someone called on my number a few days back but did not speak. I'm assuming someone knows that we're linked.' *Was Khan Baba really referring to her? It had to be her.*

'Just be careful wherever you are, and visit Lahore soon,' Khan Baba instructed.

'I will be there soon. You don't need to worry,' I said, tears clouding my eyes. 'See you soon.'

'Inshallah. May Allah be with you.' Khan Baba ended the call.

Before tears could well up in my eyes, I shut them once again and wiped them off.

Mehar

The next day, Hamza and his family were to leave for Islamabad. Due to shortage of time, they couldn't go arou d the city. Before they left, Phupho had a private talk with Abba and Amma in the drawing room, where she and her husband fixed the wedding date. Sidra overheard the entire conversation and conveyed to me. I, on the other hand, remained oblivious to the n atter as my mind was somewhere else. I desperately thought of ways to reach the Walled City.

Hamza, however, wanted to have a tête-à-tête with his fiancée, and he had already been granted permission by Sidra and the others. Both of us stood on my balcony, near the railing.

'I guess they are deciding our wedding date downstairs,' Hamza said, smiling shyly.

I remained quiet, my face expressionless.

'The sooner it happens, the better.' He ran his fingers through his hair and looked at me.

I looked down at my hand and closed my fist tightly, not knowing how to respond. I was being thrust back into a situation from where it had taken me quite some time to get away.

'I hope you have my number saved in your phone.'

'Yes, I have it,' I mumbled, looking down.

'Great. I shall . . . take your leave then?' he said, looking into my eyes and wanting me to look back at him.

But I didn't. I looked away, nodding my head.

'Allah hafiz,' he said, disappointment dripping from his voice.

'Allah hafiz,' I replied.

Abba, Amma, Sidra and I bid Phupho's family goodbye. As soon as Hamza's car left, I quickly rushed back to my room, without saying a word to anyone. I waited for the next day.

The next morning, I hurriedly took a shower and changed my clothes. I wore a maroon-coloured churidar and a white kurta, combed my hair into a ponytail and then covered my head with a black embroidered dupatta. I put my phone and wallet in my handbag, took in a deep breath and let it escape in a sigh. I knew I had made the right decision and there was no point holding back. I turned and hurried down the stairs, tucking the handbag under my arm.

'Where are you going in such a rush, Mehar?' Amma asked, perplexed.

Abba and Sidra also looked at me curiously.

'Amma . . . I am going over to Asma's place. We need to work on our final project. It has been so many days since I worked on my dissertation. So I have to go,' I lied.

I had to. I had stayed up all night, working on the plan. Chances of getting caught were low, I believed, as I used to go to my friends' place to study earlier as well.

'You can call your friend over. Why do you have to go?' Abba interjected, peering at me over his glasses.

'Abba, it's not possible for her to come over as she doesn't have a car. That's why I agreed to go to her place,' I replied.

I tried my best to give a valid explanation to my parents before leaving home as I did not want them to get suspicious.

'All right. The driver will drop you at her place then. Make sure you come back soon.'

I didn't feel bad about lying, I felt bad because I was not able to tell them the truth. On my way to my friend's place, tears rolled down my cheeks. I tried hard to suppress them but failed. I had no idea if I would even get there. I had no idea whom I'd meet. I had no idea if I'd find out anything that would make my life better.

As the chauffeur parked the car outside my friend's house, I sniffed and stepped out. Asma's house was situated somewhere in the Gulberg area.

'I'll give you a call as soon as I'm free. Come and pick me up then,' I instructed my driver, to which he obediently nodded.

After my car left, I swiftly adjusted the dupatta over my head and walked down the street to look for local transport. I felt stronger, braver. When I couldn't find an autorickshaw, I hit upon the idea of calling a Careem cab, a newly-started cab service in Lahore about which I'd read on the Internet. Luckily, I had already downloaded the app on my phone. I booked a cab and was asked to wait for a couple of minutes at the bus stop. In the next instant, my cell phone buzzed, indicating the arrival of the cab. I quickly got up from the bench, rushed towards the cab and got in.

'Where to, Ma'am?' the cab driver asked.

'To the Walled City,' I declared. 'Gurdwara Dehra Sahib near Badshahi Mosque.'

'Sure,' he replied.

Despite all the hustle and bustle on the road, the traffic flowed rather smoothly, and we reached the destination in no time. He stopped the cab right in front of the Food Street

Fort Road. I quickly paid the fare and stepped out. Taking in
a deep breath, I forced myself to take a step forward. Since
it was a weekday, there weren't too many people around.
Adjusting my dupatta and holding on to my handbag, I
cautiously made my way to the gurdwara. I did not know if
stepping into a gurdwara was considered forbidden in my
religion, but from what I'd heard, people of all religions and
faiths were welcome there. A square hall came into view,
with a domed sanctum in the centre. A couple of devotees
were sitting on the floor, some ardently praying and the
others involved in light conversations. Imitating them,
I also sat down on the floor, crossed my legs and folded
my hands. Though the ambience of the gurdwara seemed
peaceful, I still felt a tightness in my chest. Not wanting
to sit in that posture, I stood up and rushed outside. As I
crossed the gate, my eyes caught a group of old men sitting
on the pavement outside the gurdwara. Gathering courage,
I walked up to one of them.

'Asalaam u alaikum . . . Sat Sri Akal, guruji. I need your
help,' I said, my voice breaking.

'Sat Sri Akal, *putar*. How can we help you?' one of them
asked.

'Do you, by any chance, know someone named Khan
Baba in this area?'

Two of them exchanged a glance and then looked at me.

'Why, of course! Khan Baba lives nearby. You'll find his
house at the end of the street, just across the gurdwara. The
colour of his wooden door is green.'

'Oh, thank you so much.'

My face lit up. And in that heartfelt moment, be it
temporary, I believed in Sarmad. To my relief, someone
named Khan Baba really did exist.

I followed their direction. I passed many old houses
but none of them had a green-coloured wooden door. At

last, my eyes stopped at the last house in the lane that
had a green entrance door. Surprisingly, the door was
slightly ajar. I gently tapped on it but no one answered.
After knocking on the door thrice, I lost my patience and
without giving it a second thought, hastily barged into
the house. The house had a spooky charm. It was eerily
dark, quiet and uninviting. A musty smell filled my nostrils
and made me nauseous. I flashed light from my cell phone
into the gloom, but the house remained stubbornly dark.
It suddenly dawned on me that Khan Baba was nowhere
in sight.

'Hello?' I called out. 'Is somebody here? Khan Baba?'

The dusty floor creaked beneath my feet as I took a
step ahead. Everything about the house seemed eerie—the
veranda, the dusty windows and the string of cobwebs. A
cluster of photo frames hung on one of the walls. Ignoring
everything around me, I peered at those pictures closely.
The framed photographs were covered in layers of grime
but the faces captured within them were still detectable. I
looked up at them, keenly observing each and every black
and white photograph.

One of them seemed like a family portrait, with the
head of the family seated on a chair, a woman, probably
his wife, and a child with an innocent expression on his
face standing by his side—it looked like a Pashtun family.
The other frame had the same child's photo; a woman held
him in a tight embrace, a smile tugging at the corner of his
mouth. And then my eyes landed on a picture that had the
same boy scribbling something in his notebook, a few paper
cranes scattered all around him. That one picture sent a jolt
of surprise through me. I quickly turned and then tripped
over a wooden shelf kept behind me. I hit the dusty floor
with a dull thud. I hastily rubbed off the dust and tried to
stand up, using the same shelf for support. Right then, a

pile of old books fell off from the shelf and landed on the ground. I hurried towards the door but stopped when a pleasant melody hit my ears. The sound gave me a strong sense of nostalgia and brought forth a buried childhood memory. I sprung around, frantically looking for the source of the sound.

I have heard this melody before. I remember it clearly.

As I rummaged through the dusty books, the melody became louder. At last, my eyes stopped on the object from where the music was coming. An old journal, encrusted with layers of dust, laid lifelessly in my hands. I gasped as I looked at it.

I remembered the journal. I remembered it clearly.

I also remembered the person to whom it belonged. It all came back to me in that one fleeting moment.

Sarmad's Journal

I had never thought I'd write anything in this journal. But I did. Because writing reminds me of the good times—the time I spent with her, and it also makes me appreciate those memories. It gives me pleasure. But do you know what gives me the utmost pleasure and peace? Seeing her calm, composed face. Do you even know who made me start writing in this journal? You guessed it right. Only she could do it.

Year 2000—Eight years old

Mingora, Swat

I still remember the day General and his family arrived at their guest house in Mingora. There was something different about his visit this time as he had not come alone—he had brought, to what it seemed to me, his family along. My Baba, Abdul Aziz Khan, a shopkeeper by profession, owned a small grocery store that was only a few miles away from the General's guest house. Every day, after school, I would drop by Baba's store. Being the only child, I assumed it was my responsibility towards my father. Not that an eight-year-old child could offer any substantial help to anyone but still it mattered to me. For most of the time, I'd just look outside the store's window and stare at the surroundings, observing every minute detail. We lived in a cottage built right across our store on the main highway. The cottage was quite small and could only accommodate three members. Baba, Khan Baba, my uncle, and I were the only occupants.

Baba had been a single parent for the last six years. My mother had eloped with her alleged lover when I was only three years old, abandoning my father and leaving him to handle me all by himself. I still don't understand why he lied to me all those years about her impromptu exit. I knew she had left both of us forever. He still kept her photographs.

On the other hand, Khan Baba was also alone—he did not have a family because he did not believe in getting married. He loved me like his son, and I wouldn't be wrong in saying that he loved me more than my own father.

After school, I would rush to the grocery store, keep my school bag aside and plonk down on the stool near the counter and look outside the window. Baba, being an ardent fan of old Hindi songs, would play some classic numbers on his old tape recorder. As I would sit there, listening to old songs, I would take out a few blank sheets of paper from my notebook and start making origami cranes out of them. I had learnt how to make them in kindergarten from one of the craft books at the library.

One day, the General walked into our grocery store with a little girl. I wouldn't have looked at her if her innocent caramel brown eyes had not held my gaze. There was something unusual about not only her eyes but also her shy, beautiful face. I have to admit that she was the most beautiful little girl I had ever laid eyes on. She did not leave my eyes even for a second, as she stood with her father near the counter.

'Salaam, General sahib,' Baba greeted him animatedly.

'Walaikum asalaam,' General replied. 'How's everything going?'

'Everything is fine, sahib. What can I get for you?'

'Please pack a dozen eggs, a loaf of bread and a carton of milk,' the General said.

'Sure, sahib,' Baba said, beginning to pack the items. 'Is this little girl your daughter?'

'Yes, Abdul. She's my younger daughter, Mehar.'

Her name instantly won my heart. It was not only unusual but beautiful as well. Both of us shared a quick glance, her pink lower lip quivering as she blushed.

'This time I decided to bring my family for a trip to Swat,' the General continued. 'Mehar beta, do you want anything for your siblings or yourself?'

Mehar, who still had her curious eyes on me, shook her head in denial.

Baba laughed at her response.

'Here you go, Mehar beta. I've got some chocolate candies just for you,' Baba said as he offered her some candies, which she accepted reluctantly.

'Say thank you to Abdul uncle,' General said.

'Thank you,' she mumbled.

Her sweet, honey-filled voice melted my heart.

Over the next few days, I caught a glimpse of her on my way back to the grocery store. She usually played in the garden outside her guest house with the other children from the neighbourhood. Whenever I passed by, she squinted her brown eyes and wrinkled her nose in disgust, making me wonder if I was that bad looking. Even then, I found her gesture adorable.

One day, Baba was going to their house to deliver some groceries and asked me if I wanted to accompany him. Unable to hold the excitement in my tiny heart, I jumped at the opportunity and followed Baba as he walked towards their porch. As Baba went ahead to drop off the items at their doorstep, I changed my r... and went to watch her play in the garden. All the kids, holding ...other's hands, walked in a circle, humming a song. I put down ... backpack on the damp grass and stared at her as she walked animatedly in the circle. When she caught me staring, I hurriedly looked away. She stopped moving, hushed her friends and then started walking towards me, her friends in tow. I felt embarrassed when I saw her approaching me with her friends. I looked around for Baba but couldn't find him anywhere. She came and stood next to me; I knew I was in big trouble.

'You're not supposed to be in our territory. Go away!' she yelled.

Unable to defend myself, I picked up my backpack, flung it over my shoulder and walked away.

It annoyed me to a great extent that she had asked me to leave in a harsh tone, and that too in front of her friends. I did not expect her to treat me like that but then again what could she have done? She certainly wouldn't have welcomed me with a warm hug.

I tried my best to avoid her for the next few days but always managed to catch her glimpse on my way back from school. As usual, I got the same disgusted look in return, which, of course, I utterly adored. She would also come to the store often, to buy a few candies with her father and siblings. With the old Hindi songs playing in the background, we would share a few quick glances as she stood over the counter.

One day, as I was on my way back home, I caught her playing with her friends across the Swat River. Out of habit, I crossed the valley and sat down on one of the huge rocks. As far as I could understand, they were playing a game of hopscotch on the concrete ground just near the river bank. Mehar threw a flat stone which landed inside square 4. As she stood on one foot and jumped, a tinkling bracelet slid off her hand and fell into the river. She screamed in horror when she realized what had happened. Her distraught expression was unbearable. I ran towards her as fast as my legs could carry me. She cried loudly as I stood by her side, trying to calm her down.

'What happened?' I asked, my feeble voice coming to life.

'Her favourite bracelet fell into the river,' one of the kids told me regretfully. 'I think she has lost it forever.' Without thinking twice about the consequences, I jumped into the freezing water as the kids gasped in horror. My entire body turned numb as my skin came in contact with the cold water. I don't remember for how long I stayed inside the water but my eyes found the gold bracelet sooner than I had thought. I sprang out of the water and saw that she was sitting remorsefully on the ground with her hands cupped around her small innocent face. All the kids jumped in excitement when they realized I was alive and completely fine. Drenched, I walked up to her and held out my hand with the bracelet in it. She walked towards me gingerly, without looking in my eyes and then brought her hand forward to take the bracelet. I brushed away the wet hair from my forehead to take a good look at her.

'Why did you jump into the river? You could have died,' she said, biting her lower lip.

'I couldn't see you crying,' I boldly declared, without thinking about the consequences.

To my surprise, she smiled at my response.

'Will you come and play with us?' she asked, tilting her head to one side, a small smile playing on her lips.

I smiled at her question and gave her an enthusiastic nod. I was dying to become her friend.

'Great! Let's go then!' she squealed in excitement as she turned around.

'Hey, wait! My name is . . .' I said.

'I don't need to know your name!' she said, cutting me in between. 'You are my superhero. Hence, I'll call you superhero!' she smiled at me.

But just when our friendship was about to blossom, she had to go back with her family. She promised to return soon though, much to my pleasure.

Year 2001—Nine years old

Mingora, Swat

She returned to Mingora the following year in summer. The General visited his guest house every year during summer vacations to give his children a relaxing break. I was happy to see her again. The year might have passed in a blink for the world around, but for me it passed at a snail's pace. That year, rumours about unknown assailants taking refuge in our area were rife. Some of the army troops had flown in, taking control of the situation. They had even started raiding different houses. I tried to ask Baba about the issue but he ignored me and asked me to concentrate on my studies rather than on such useless matters. I gladly disregarded the matter and looked forward to spending more time with Mehar. I was happy to be a part of her friends group now. Whenever she played outside with her friends, she invited me and I happily went. I didn't have many friends in town.

One day, she came to our grocery store and started working on her summer vacation homework. I was busy making paper origamis. As usual, an old Hindi song played in the background.

'Hey, that song is really nice!' she exclaimed.

'Yes. It's one of my favourites from the movie, *Hum Dono*,' I told her. She was referring to the song, '*Abhi na jaao chod ker*'.

It felt good to know that we shared the same taste in music.

'What are you busy doing? Come, let's play outside!' she said, nudging me playfully.

'Wait, Mehar . . .' I said. 'Just wait for a second.'

'But why, Superhero? We should go and play outside before my mum calls me back,' she said, making a sad face.

I held her hand in response, trying to silence her. Her brows lifted in surprise.

'Have you ever seen magic?' I asked her, looking into her twinkling brown eyes.

She shook her head in denial.

I smiled at her reaction.

'Do you want to see it? Now?' I asked.

'Yes,' she whispered.

'Great. Come with me then.' I picked up my school bag, slung it across my shoulder, took her hand in mine and rushed outside.

Within no time, we reached the banks of the Swat River.

'What are we going to do here? Where's the magic?' she asked, looking around curiously.

'Impatient enough?' I asked, teasing her. In response, she stuck out her tongue at me in disgust.

'Okay. No more waiting. Close your eyes first,' I said.

'Really?' she asked.

'Yes. Don't be scared.' I'm here with you. You can trust me. Now, close your eyes.'

She happily obliged and closed her eyes. I didn't know if she really closed her eyes or pretended to do so but I believed her anyway.

I hurriedly took the paper origamis out of my school bag and tried to hold them together in my hands. The cold wind blew into my face, sending chills down my spine.

'Okay.' I exhaled. 'Now, open your eyes slowly.'

'Are you sure, Superhero?' she asked, smiling.

'Yes,' I said.

As she gradually opened her eyes, I threw open my fists and released the paper origamis in the air.

She gasped in awe and cupped her face with her small hands, taking in the view. Both of us stood there in silence as the paper origamis flew up in the air, the wind blowing them all away.

'This is so magical and beautiful . . . I'm amazed. You really are a superhero . . . my superhero,' she whispered, holding my hand in hers and making me fall in love with her.

As we walked down the street, hand in hand, a flash of lightning lit up the sky, the sound of thunder instantly filling the air. Mehar shuddered and I realized that she was scared of thunderstorms. Soon, a heavy downpour filled the gutters and drains around us, drenching our bodies and clothes completely.

'I'm all wet!' Mehar cried.

'Come with me.' I held her hand tightly as soon as a plan hit me.

Holding her hand, I darted towards an isolated wooden cart that was parked across the street. I ducked under the cart and she swiftly slid beneath it. Both of us sat there and observed the heavy rain splash across the road. I could feel her shivering with fear.

'What happened?' I asked her.

'I'm scared.' Tears filled her eyes as she spoke. 'I want to go back home.'

'Are you really scared?' I asked, turning towards her.

She nodded as she looked at me, her body trembling with cold.

'Well, in that case, you should know how to overcome your fears rather than running away from them.'

'How do I do that?' she asked in a feeble voice.

'Let me show you.' I leaned towards her and held both her hands in mine. 'Whenever you're scared, just remember this. Close your eyes, take a deep breath in, hold yourself together and then pray persistently. The fear will slowly go away.'

Her eyes were fixed on me as she listened to me intently.

'Should I try it?' she asked, biting her lower lip in anxiety.

'Do it,' I told her.

In the next instant, she closed her eyes, took a deep breath in and then tightly embraced herself. Her lips moved as she prayed. As I continued gazing at her, I felt a sudden surge of exhilaration in my body. She opened her eyes and looked at me.

'What happened?' I asked, getting anxious.

'I really . . . felt what you said. I am not afraid any more,' she murmured, a smile tugging at the corner of her lips.

'What do you feel then?' I asked.

'I feel brave.'

Realizing that my advice had actually made her feel better, I felt more than pleased.

'Just practise this whenever you're scared,' I told her. 'Okay?'

'I will, Superhero.' She beamed at me with those sparkling brown eyes.

The following day Mehar was to leave with her family. Before getting into the car, she came running through the driveway and reached our grocery store. I tried my best to smile at her despite feeling immensely distraught.

'Hey!' She waved at me animatedly as soon as she came in.

'Hey!' I shot her a smile.

'You didn't come to bid me goodbye?' she asked.

'Uh . . . I . . . had to finish my homework,' I lied. I just couldn't watch her leave.

'No problem. That's why I came here.' She walked into the store and stood over the counter to face me. 'I brought something for you,' she whispered into my ear, leaning towards me.

'Really? What?' I asked, surprised.

She quickly unpacked her backpack and took out a beautifully crafted journal.

'Here you go. A journal.' She handed it to me.

'It's beautiful.' I caressed its surface with my hand. 'But what would I do with it?' I asked, inspecting the journal.

'You will write in it,' she said matter-of-factly.

'I don't write. I can only make paper cranes out of it,' I laughed.

'No, you won't just do that. You will write in it. Keep it as a personal diary so that when we meet next time, I can read what you've written in it.'

'There's one more special thing about this journal,' she told me.

'Really, what is it?' I asked.

'When you open it, a melody plays in the background.'

She took the journal from my hands and opened it slowly. A sweet melody hit my ears as she flipped the pages.

'I love it,' I said, gawking at the journal.

Before I could open my mouth to thank her, her father called out her name.

'I have to go now . . .' she said, pursing her lips together.

'I guess our story ends here.'

'No, Superhero. It has just begun.' She winked at me, leaving me baffled. 'I'll see you soon.'

Year 2002—Ten years old
Mingora, Swat

Since the day she left, I felt miserable. I could no longer concentrate on my classes or my homework. Baba could see that I was distracted. At the store, I paid less attention to the customers and continuously stared out of the window, hoping to see her once again.

Something strange happened one evening. As Baba and I stepped into our cottage, Khan Baba stopped what he was doing and frantically looked at us. He was hiding something in his room, which Baba failed to notice but it didn't escape my eyes. Beads of sweat rolled down his forehead and his entire body shivered.

'Are you okay, Feroz?' Baba asked, shutting the door behind him. I hurried towards my room and stood behind the door, eavesdropping on their conversation.

'I have brought some guns. I'm afraid I will have to hide them in our house for a few days,' Khan Baba said.

'Are you out of your mind, Feroz? You know the army can raid our house any time. We will get into trouble,' Baba said in a worried tone.

'I know, bhai sahib. But don't worry. We will be fine. As soon as I get a message from Mullah, I'll deliver the guns to him.'

Their conversation confused me. I had no idea what they were talking about. I didn't know why the army was raiding every other house, who Mullah was, and why Khan Baba was working for him.

I couldn't sleep that night and kept thinking about the weapons Khan Baba was referring to. When I was sure Baba was asleep, I slowly got up and walked towards Khan Baba's room. To my surprise, he wasn't there. I walked over to the wooden trunk kept by his bedside and stared at it for a long time. For some reason, I knew Khan Baba had hidden something in it. I slowly opened the lid. I couldn't believe my eyes when I saw guns inside the trunk. I shuddered at the sight. Before I could react, Khan Baba shoved me away and shut the trunk.

'What do you think you're doing here, kid?' he yelled. 'You're not supposed to be here.'

I was too shocked to say anything.

'Go back to your room, now!' he shouted.

I hurried back to my bed, slid under my quilt and shut my eyes hard. I hated the fact that I couldn't control my heart. It kept banging loudly in my chest. Thud. Thud. Thud. Thud.

A few more days passed but the raids didn't stop. I heard a few children at my school talk about the raids. One of them had seen his house being raided with his own eyes and valiantly told us about the incident. The guns kept hidden in Khan Baba's trunk flashed across my eyes, making me cringe. Ignoring the thought, I walked back to my class. As I was on my way to the cottage, Mehru's guest house came into view. I wished she would come running towards me. As I continued walking, lost in my own thoughts, I heard a loud bang from my cottage. I went around and tried to peep inside through the back window. Dressed in black clothes and turbans, a few men were yelling at my Baba; one of them held weapons in his hands—the same weapons I had found in Khan Baba's trunk last night. Baba incessantly tried to talk through the matter but it seemed the situation was slipping out of his hands as the men didn't seem convinced. Baba got down on his knees and begged them to forgive him and his family.

'Shut up!' one of the men yelled at him. 'Stop begging. We have been hiding our weapons here for so many days and we've done that before as well. How on earth did the information get out this time? The army knows where our weapons are. We've been caught. Just because of you!' He pointed at Baba. 'As long as the matter was in Khan's hands, nothing ever happened. Since the day he involved you in this, we have been in trouble. You are a threat to our tribe. We just can't spare you now. We will kill you and your bloody son!'

My entire body shuddered when he said that. I lowered myself to hide my face.

'No. No. No! Please. Listen to me once. Everything is safe here. Nobody knows we're involved in this. I'm trying to help you people. I will give you cover here, but please don't say that. I have not betrayed anyone, neither has my brother.'

As Baba continued explaining, a jeep full of armed men stopped outside our cottage and yanked open the door. Before Baba could make them stop, they started firing at the robed men. In defence, they did the same. Both the parties shot at each other relentlessly. I shut my ears tightly as the blaring sound continued. My eyes frantically searched for Baba. My jaw dropped in horror when I saw him lying on the floor, his eyes wide open. Fresh blood oozed out of his head. Before I could react or scream, someone covered my mouth from behind and dragged me towards the backyard.

'Sarmad . . . shh . . . stay quiet. Do not scream. All right?' It was Khan Baba's voice, I realized. His hand was still on my mouth.

'We will avenge those bloody officers. Do you see? We will avenge them. But not now. Just run and hide somewhere far away. Do you hear me? Run and hide somewhere far away. I'll find you. Run before these hounds kill us. Run, Sarmad!'

All I remember was running as fast as my legs could carry me. Clutching my school bag, I ran into the woods. My limbs hurt and my heart was crushed into a million pieces but I did not stop running as I knew that stopping would mean death. I was too young to die. I did not want to die. When I was far away from the cottage, I stopped to catch my breath. I looked around to make sure nobody was coming for me. I heaved a sigh of relief and then sank to the ground. I screamed at the top of my lungs as I realized what had just happened with me. I had lost Baba.

'BABAAAAA!' I screamed. 'Babaaa . . . please come back to me. Please.' Tears rolled down my cheeks. 'I can't live without you, Baba . . . please come back . . . please . . .' I don't remember for how long I cried like that. My world had completely shattered. It didn't matter what turn my life was going to take. I was ready to face anything.

Year 2003—Eleven years old

Mingora, Swat

Khan Baba managed to find me in the woods after a couple of hours and took me with him. When I opened my eyes after what seemed like a long sleep, I found myself on a different bed. I gasped as I got up and frantically looked around. A middle-aged man, dressed in a white salwar kameez, entered the room along with Khan Baba and looked at me for a long time. He took a few steps towards me and stood over me. I, on the other hand, stared at his scarred face with utter distress. He cupped my chin in his hand and looked into my eyes.

'Is this the kid you brought along, Khan?' the man asked, holding my chin.

'Yes,' Khan Baba replied curtly.

'I see.'

He stared into my eyes and I did the same. I shuddered with horror and my heart pounded in my chest.

'I think I will keep him with me. And train him.'

I could not decipher his words as they didn't make any sense to me. I saw Khan Baba nodding his head in response.

'Don't you want to avenge your father's death?' the man asked me.

I could see the wrath in his eyes.

'Don't you want to slay those army officers who brutally killed your father?'

Tears rolled down my eyes as I remembered how my father was killed. Despite his continuous requests, the officers had paid no heed and had killed him in just one shot. I will never forgive what they did to him. I will never forgive them. I will make them suffer every day of their lives and take revenge. I will not spare them.

Year 2013—Twenty-one years old

Lahore, Pakistan

Had I known I'd meet Mehar's younger brother at Lahore Bazaar, I would have done anything to save him from that horrendous disaster. I did not want that plan to be executed and had even tried to persuade Mullah to abort it but he didn't listen. He told me this was the best chance to spread terror in the entire nation and get our demands met on time.

I still clearly remember every detail of that day. His wounded body was lying under the table. I slowly crawled towards him and held his hand in mine. Both of us were badly hurt.

'Are you . . . are you okay?' I asked him, almost choking. 'Hey, you!' I held his injured arm.

'Water . . .' whispered. 'I need water . . .'

I looked around to find a pitcher of water but was not able to see anything except grey smoke.

'I'll get you water,' I told him. 'Are you listening?' I asked him, patting his face.

This time there was no response. I couldn't even see his chest rising. I held his wrist to feel his pulse but there was nothing. Soon, I heard the blaring sound of the ambulance. The metal pieces of his phone were splattered on the ground along with a black torn leather wallet. I reached out for the wallet with my wounded arm and grasped it. I slowly opened it and found a black and white photograph inside. Mehar beamed at me—innocent and beautiful. Her laugh rang loud in my ears. I tried to smile back at her but soon everything started becoming blurry. I realized I was about to faint. Within a few seconds, I lost track of everything. I lost the young boy. And with him, I lost the only possible hope of getting her back.

I wish I could have saved Omar's life. I wish I was not a part of that deadly attack. I cannot face her ever. I'm a culprit. I cannot see hatred in those eyes that once had affection for me. I deserve nothing but death. I have to live with this regret for the rest of my life.

Mehar

Present

Tears rolled down my cheeks and dropped on the pages of the journal as Sarmad's story unfolded before my eyes. I flipped through the journal to see if he had written anything more but there was nothing else. I ran my fingers over his handwriting and imagined him writing his painful story. I closed the journal and pressed it against my chest, in an effort to calm myself down. I could not believe what I'd just read.

Sarmad was someone I knew all along. How did I not recognize him the first time I met him? He had the same eyes, the same brows, the same lips. How could I not recognize the person who had taught me how to fight my own fears? Sarmad must have recognized me when I told him about Omar and Abba. If he did, why didn't he tell me? He tried to save Omar but he couldn't. Why did he keep that from me? Why did he make me hate him? Why? I had to find him. Thousands of memories flashed through my mind. I could feel his presence near me. I put the journal in my bag and wiped the tears that rolled down my face. I looked around the room to see if there was someone who could help me find Sarmad. As I stood up, I heard the door crack open. Someone stepped inside, peering at me.

'Sarmad?' I asked, in the hope of seeing his face.

'He's not here,' an elderly man answered.

'Khan Baba?' I asked, taking a step towards him to see his face properly.

'Yes, you're right. It's me. But I'm sorry, Sarmad is not here.'

I felt a pang of pain in my chest.

'Wh . . . where is he?' I asked, disappointment evident in my voice.

'He is nowhere. Don't look for someone who doesn't exist. You will not find him anywhere. It would be better if you left,' he said, looking away.

'No!' I said, almost immediately. 'He asked me to come here and . . . and meet you. He wanted me to know his side of the story . . .'

'What story?' he interrupted, sounding a bit irritated. 'He's not here. Neither will he come here any time soon. You better leave now. This place is not safe.'

'No. I will not go anywhere until I see him. I will stay here,' I said, my tone resilient.

'Your wish,' he said. 'Do whatever you want to. But he will never come to see you.'

'Tell him, wherever he is, just tell him I will wait for him till the end of time. I'm not going anywhere without meeting him. That's final . . . and if he doesn't come, I might just take my own life,' I said breathlessly, and then walked out of the house, leaving Khan Baba behind.

What I had said was right. I would take my life if he didn't show up because I was sure he was somewhere near. I could feel him around. He could see me. He could hear me. I walked through the bazaar without knowing the way. I didn't know where I was going. I just wanted him to stop me from falling off the edge.

Where are you, Sarmad? Where are you?

Sarmad

'But where did she go?' I asked Khan Baba.

It's true I'd asked him not to give out my whereabouts to Mehar as I knew she would come looking for me any time, any day.

'I have no damn idea, Sarmad. I did what you asked me to. You asked me not to tell her anything about you,' Khan Baba clarified.

'Damn . . .' I ran my fingers through my hair. 'I need to find her before she does something reckless. I can't risk her life. I can't.'

I rummaged through the old books scattered on the floor and looked for my journal. I couldn't find it anywhere. I knew she had it. She had been exposed to the truth. She knew everything. Nothing was hidden from her. In a way, I felt relieved.

'Sarmad, you can't meet her. It can be dangerous. What if she has brought armed forces along? We could get caught!' Khan Baba interrupted my thoughts.

'Don't worry. I know her. There's no danger for us. Trust me,' I said, looking at the door. 'I should get going now. I'll be back soon.'

Mehar

As I walked through the busy streets, a million memories flashed through my mind. I clearly remembered the young Sarmad. My *superhero*. That's what I used to call him. When we first saw each other at his Baba's grocery store, I despised him. Then, one day, he risked his life by jumping into the river to find my gold bracelet. That's when he won my heart. Sixteen years later, I met him again at the bus stop. He saved me from falling off the edge. Had he not been there, I would have been dead by now. I lived with him for several days and yet didn't recognize him. I fell for the same person and still my memories didn't tell me who he was. How on earth was that possible? I already had a strong heart to heart connection with him. This made it easier for me to love him. God, I loved him so much. After knowing his truth, I love him even more. If I am not able to find him, I'll die.

Sarmad . . . *where are you? Please come back . . . please. I need you.*

Sarmad

A thousand ugly thoughts crossed my mind as I desperately looked for her everywhere. What if she was serious about doing something reckless? What if she had gone to take her life?

I ran down the street, looking all around. Where are you, Mehar? Why are you doing this to me? My heart told me she might be inside Badshahi Mosque. I climbed up the stairs that led to the prayer chamber. I scanned the entire place but could not find her. I looked around the entire chamber and all of the seven rooms that were linked to it. However, there was no sign of her. I stopped and heaved a disappointed sigh. Perhaps I'd lost her. Forever. I fell down on my knees and panted, beads of sweat trickling down my forehead. I wish I'd seen her face for the last time. I wish I'd touched her for the last time. I wish I'd felt her presence for the last time. A wave of cool breeze hit my warm face as I cried sitting in the same position. But this time, the air felt different. A few seconds ago, I couldn't feel her but now I could. I could not only feel her around me but also smell her fragrance.

'He once told me how to overcome my fears,' she said.

'But what should I do when losing him becomes my only fear?' she continued.

I closed my eyes, contemplating what she had just said.

'I thought he'd never want to see me again,' she said in a low voice.

I unfolded my hands and turned to look at her. Clad in a salwar kameez, she stood a few steps away from me. There was something in her expression. She seemed devastated. I didn't know for how long she had been here—waiting for me. Her frizzled hair peeped from under her dupatta. A few strands fell on her forehead. I slowly rose to my feet, my eyes not leaving hers even for a moment. Holding my gaze, she slowly strode in my direction. My heart loudly thumped in my chest.

'I thought he wanted to run away from me as far as he could,' she smirked, taking another step towards me. 'I thought . . . his guilt was much bigger and significant than the love he had for me.' She stopped, closing the distance between us.

I heard her gasp as our breaths intermingled and hearts beat in sync. She smelled the same. Whatever she had said was true. I could not deny it.

'You're right,' I said, almost breathless. 'He never wanted to see you.'

Disappointment flickered in her sad eyes as I spoke.

'He wanted to run away from you as far as he could,' I continued as I looked into her eyes. 'But . . . you're not right about one thing.'

She narrowed her eyes in confusion.

'His guilt couldn't be more than the love he has for you,' I said as I held her face in my hands.

She gasped as I touched her, fresh tears rolling down her pink cheeks.

'Why didn't you tell me who you were? Why?' She caught hold of my shirt collar and pulled me towards her.

I remained quiet and motionless, inhaling her fragrance. She was with me. Safe and secure. Nothing else mattered.

'You kept saving my life and did everything for me without demanding anything in return. And I didn't even recognize you.'

'I'll always do whatever I can for you, Mehar. Always. At least as long as I am alive,' I said, looking at her affectionately. 'Because your life is not yours. It's mine. It has always been mine.' I cupped her cheeks once again, making her blush.

She sniffled and then smiled at me.

'I'm sorry, Sarmad. I couldn't recognize you. I'm so sorry,' she said as she squeezed my hand.

'God . . . I've missed you so much, Mehru,' I said, gasping and bringing my forehead in contact with hers. I put my hands on her shoulders.

'I've missed you too, Superhero.'

Forgetting the world around us, we held on to each other as long as we could. Nothing else mattered. Once again, we became the same children who'd met in the valley of Swat and had fallen in love.

Mehar

I wanted to capture that moment forever in my heart and never let it go. He sat opposite me, elbows on his knees, watching me intently. His stare made me giddy. Despite trying, I couldn't stare at him continuously. I don't know for how long we sat next to each other inside one of the prayer chambers of the Badshahi Mosque. He slowly took my hand and interlaced our fingers together, without saying a word. I didn't stop him. Why would I? How could I?

'Why didn't you tell me about yourself when we first met?' I asked him in a whisper.

'I wanted you to recognize me . . . all by yourself,' he said, half-smiling.

'I couldn't . . . my bad,' I said, dejectedly.

He squeezed my hand lightly and then smiled at me. There was something in his angelic eyes and beautiful smile. We stayed silent for a bit before another question popped up in my head.

'How did *you* recognize me?' I asked.

'It wasn't difficult. Your face was imprinted on my mind all this while. I couldn't forget you. At all,' he said, looking at me. 'I recognized you the moment I saw you at the bus stop.' I smiled at him. He gently caressed my palm with his finger.

'Sometimes . . . I wish we were back in those carefree days,' he said, looking away. 'I wish life was easier . . . '

'Nothing has changed, at least for both of us,' I told him, holding his hand in mine now. 'We still feel the same for each other. Don't we?'

He looked at me and nodded.

'I love you, Sarmad, and I'll always feel the same for you.' I drew myself closer to him, wrapping my arm around his and resting my head on his shoulder.

He leaned his head against mine, squeezing my hand tightly. We stayed in that position for some time and then I drew myself back.

'What happened after your father was shot? Where did you go?' I asked.

He took some time to answer. He took in a deep breath and started speaking.

'After I lost my father, Mullah took my custody and Khan Baba moved away to some other city. He did keep a check on me through Mullah sahib and visited often. I had a new family. Mullah sahib took me away from Swat and brought me to a place closer to Waziristan. There I met other members who, like me, also had a disturbed past. After a while, we shifted to Kabul. Mullah sahib took good care of me and soon I became comfortable with his group. And that was the time when I thought of writing down my thoughts. That's when I picked up your journal and began to write . . . '

'But . . . why didn't you go to the army for help? Why didn't you come to us? My father?'

'How could the army help me when they were the ones who killed my father?' he asked.

I shook my head.

'That's not true, Sarmad. Maybe it was all a misunderstanding. Your father was killed in an encounter. The army would never take an innocent person's life.'

'Whatever, Mehru. You shouldn't worry about it. It's not your headache. Just forget it.'

'Sarmad, you're not getting my point. I think you should talk to my father. I'm sure he will find a way to help you get out of this mess.'

'I'm not in a mess. I am here because I want to. I will do whatever I can to avenge my father's death.' He stood up and moved away from me.

'Even if it costs you your own life?' I asked, standing up.

'Yes,' he said.

'I can never let you do that. Your life is linked with mine now.' I walked up to him and wrapped my arms around his torso. 'Whatever happens, I'm in this with you.'

'Mehru . . . '

'Shh . . . please don't say anything.'

He relaxed his shoulders for a while.

'I've lost you twice. I don't want to lose you again,' I said as I leaned my head against his back. 'We'll sort this out. We'll figure out something. Everything will be fine. Trust me.'

He held my hands and squeezed them hard. He then kissed them.

Sarmad

For one moment, I wanted to believe what she had said. Even though I knew what the truth was, I wanted to believe that everything would be okay. Nothing could be fixed. I could not simply walk away and start afresh. Once you are a part of an extremist group, there is no looking back. I had joined them to take revenge for my father's death. Mehar didn't understand this. Had she been in my position, she would have thought differently. I wanted to forget my reality and live inside the fantasy bubble she had created for me. I wanted to make the most of the moments I was spending with her. Because I knew what would happen next. And I was prepared for it. I didn't care if Mehar's return in my life had evoked my feelings. I wouldn't change my mind at any cost but I couldn't let her know about it either. I did not want to make her feel hopeless. I wanted to see her happy. Always.

I hired a local autorickshaw outside Badshahi Mosque and made her sit in it. She held my hand and pulled me in. The driver revved up the engine and drove off. To our surprise, an old Hindi song was playing on the radio, reminding both us of our childhood.

'*Abhi na jaao chor ker, ke dil abhi bhara nahin.*'

'Remember this song?' I asked, raising a brow.

'Yes,' she whispered, beaming. 'How can I forget it?'

As I listened to the song, she held my arm and leaned her head against my shoulder. I can't describe how much I loved being close to her. I took her hand in mine and interlaced our fingers together. I wished I could somehow know what was going on in her head. If only I was a mind reader . . .

I had no idea how much time had elapsed when we stopped outside her house. The driver killed the engine, bringing the vehicle to a sudden stop. I could see that she was finding it hard to let me go. I felt the same. She slowly drew herself back and stared into my eyes. I looked back into them, trying to read her emotions. I could see fear in her eyes; fear of never seeing me again; fear of losing me and never finding me again. As I stared at her, I caught a tear escaping her eye. She swiftly wiped it in an effort to hide it from me but I noticed it.

'I know what you're thinking,' I whispered. 'I am not going away from you.'

She looked at me and tried to smile, her eyes still watery.

'Wherever I'll go, I'll keep in touch,' I said, reassuringly. 'Wait.' I fished out a small black diary from my pocket and scribbled down a number on it. 'You can keep my number and call me whenever you want to. It's a private number. Don't save it on your mobile phone.'

She took the piece of paper and looked down at it.

'I'm keeping the journal,' she said, looking at me expectantly.

'It's yours. I wrote it for you anyway.'

She smiled, looking down at our intermingled fingers.

I watched her as she got out of the autorickshaw and walked towards the gate. As soon as someone opened the gate, I asked the driver to start the engine.

Mehar

Now that I had seen him and touched him, it became more difficult to stay apart. As I stepped on to the porch of my house, I heard the autorickshaw leave. I felt as if he had been taken away from me. I could feel a lump rising in my throat and a hollow feeling building up inside my chest. I wish I could bring him back and embrace him tightly and never let him go. I realized that I had felt exactly the same when I had lost my brother, Omar.

I entered the TV lounge and found Abba, Amma and Sidra seated on the couch. As I trudged up the stairs, Abba instantly caught me.

'Mehar!' he called from the lounge.

I shuddered at the sound of his voice. He walked up to me.

'What made you so late? And where are you coming from?' he asked. 'The driver was waiting for you outside your friend's house.'

I had no idea what to tell him. Despite trying hard, my mind couldn't make up a story at that moment.

'Mehar? I'm asking something,' he said.

'Yes, Abba. I'm listening. Actually, I went out shopping with my friends and from there came directly home,' I lied, casting my eyes down. I don't know why but I could never look my parents in the eye while lying.

'Shopping? Do you have any idea how late it is? It's 9 p.m.'

'I know, Abba. I'm sorry. We just didn't realize how time passed.'

Amma joined him.

'Forget it, General sahib. You know how girls are. Never mind, Mehru. Have you had dinner?' she asked, her voice calm and polite.

'Yes, Amma,' I lied, even though my stomach growled. 'Now, can I go upstairs and change?'

'Yes, sure, beta,' Amma said.

I briefly looked at Abba and then turned around to climb the stairs. As soon as I stepped into my room, I closed the door and leaned against it, letting out a long, deep sigh.

I had to save Sarmad's life. I had to do something to take him out of that mess. I could not let him destroy his life because of a misunderstanding. I made up my mind to talk to Abba about the entire matter. I'd tell him that Sarmad is that shopkeeper's son, whose shop we used to visit in Swat, and he . this situation due to some circumstances that were beyond his control. His father had been killed in an encounter and he was not a part of any militant group. Abba would certainly find a way to help Sarmad. He had tried to save Omar's life; that was enough to prove his innocence to the world. I quickly took off my clothes and showered. After changing into fresh clothes—a navy-blue cotton salwar kameez—I hurried downstairs to talk to my father. I found him leaning against the leather couch, his eyes fixed on the television. I presumed Amma and Sidra were in the bedroom, probably discussing my wedding. I walked up to Abba.

'Abba,' I said hesitantly.

'Is everything okay, beta?' he asked, peering at me.

'Yes, everything's fine. I just . . .' I sat down next to him on the couch and tucked my hair behind my ears. 'I wanted to help someone—someone innocent, and I thought I could ask you for advice.'

'Who do you want to help? What's the matter?' Abba asked, concern filling his weary eyes.

Just then our doorbell rang, distracting Abba and breaking our conversation.

'It's 10.30 p.m. I wonder who it is at this time,' Abba said. I looked at him as he walked towards the door.

Abba unlocked the door and found Uncle Habib, one of his old mates and our neighbour, standing in front of him. Both of them gave each other a brotherly hug, and then Abba made him sit comfortably in the TV lounge. I paid my regards to Uncle Habib and tried to smile when he cordially greeted me.

'Mehar, why don't you get us some nice coffee?' Abba asked, raising his brows.

'And cookies too,' Uncle Habib added, beaming at me.

'Sure.' I smiled and made my way to the kitchen.

I quietly made the coffee, without informing Amma and Sidra about our unannounced guest. We were used to Uncle Habib dropping in at odd hours. He always came unannounced and every time Abba asked me to prepare coffee for them. I filled the mugs with the beverage and then placed them on a tray. As I made my way into the TV lounge, Abba and Uncle Habib's conversation hit my ears.

'General sahib, it's difficult to understand why young boys join these militant groups. There could be numerous reasons you know . . . not all of them come from corrupt families. Some are forced to join such groups, whereas some are simply brainwashed,' Uncle Habib said.

'Whatever be the reason, Habib, these terrorists have no life or future. They just have to die in the end. And no matter how innocent they are, we can't help them. The army has been given strict orders to kill them in encounters. So there is nothing we can do for them. Good or bad, they are terrorists and we cannot ignore that fact. I am already working on a secret mission to eradicate Mullah's gang,' Abba said in response.

As I overheard their conversation, the tray fell out of my hands, spilling the coffee all over the marble floor. I froze on the spot.

I stayed motionless for a bit, my eyes as brittle as glass.

'Oh, damn,' Uncle Habib slowly muttered.

'Beta, you should have been careful,' Abba said.

'It's okay,' Amma interjected. 'I'll get it cleaned.' She asked Sidra to call Nasreen to clean the floor.

'Are you okay?' Sidra was by my side, holding my shoulders.

I simply nodded and then ran up to my room.

Sarmad

I became a bit restless when she didn't call me after getting back home. I kept staring at my cell phone, expecting her call any minute, but nothing happened. I was stupid not to take her number. I finally threw the phone on my mattress and looked out of the window, staring at the deep blue sky. I lit a cigarette. Khan Baba brought cups of tea and placed them on the table.

'Are you okay?' he asked.

'Hmm,' I mumbled, still staring into the night sky.

'Sarmad . . . I'm concerned for you.'

I turned around to face him.

'What happened, Khan Baba?' I asked, looking into his eyes, trying to read them.

'This girl . . . she . . . she isn't good for you. She could lead you to danger as she belongs to an army family. She can get you arrested.'

'Khan Baba . . .' I raised my hands in defence. 'I've known her for a long time. Much longer than you can even imagine. I told her the truth when I was with her in Swat. If she had to tell her father about me or our group, she would have done it by now. But . . . she didn't. And she won't. Because she . . .' my voice trailed off.

It seemed odd to explain to Khan Baba what we felt for each other because he surely wouldn't get it. He would consider me insane as 'love' was something we weren't allowed to think about.

'Ah.' I ran my fingers quickly through my hair. 'Forget it. Just don't worry. Nothing's going to happen. You need to trust me, okay?' I patted him on his shoulder.

'I trust you, Sarmad. It's the girl I don't trust.'

'Khan Baba . . . please . . . believe me. I won't take any risk. All right?' I put my hand on his shoulder to make him understand.

'All right, if you say so. Just be careful.' He picked his cup from the tray and walked away to the other room.

I let out a deep sigh.

Mehar . . . where are you?

Mehar

I felt disheartened. Devastated. Hopeless. There was only one man who could get Sarmad out of that dangerous group—my father. But if he couldn't help him, then who could? I sat on my bed, thinking about my next move. I had no idea how I was going to help Sarmad. I took out the piece of paper on which he had scribbled his number and quickly dialled it. After a few rings, he picked up.

'Hello? Mehar? Is that you?' he asked. The eagerness in his voice told me that he had been waiting for my call.

'Yes,' I whispered, looking at my fingers.

'I was waiting for your call. I wish I'd taken your number. Are you okay?'

'Not . . . well . . .' I said, my voice breaking.

'What happened? Is everything okay?' he asked, worried.

'Sarmad . . . I want to meet you. Please . . . take me away,' I said as I burst into tears.

'Mehar? Can you tell me what's wrong? Why are you crying? Did anyone say something to you?' he asked, his voice full of concern.

'Please, Sarmad. Don't ask anything,' I said, wiping my tears with the back of my hand. 'Take me away. Far away. Please,' I requested.

'Okay, okay, fine. Stop crying, okay? I'm coming to get you tomorrow morning, all right?' His voice was firm.

'Yes, okay,' I said as I nodded my head.

After ending the call, I locked my room and looked around. I didn't know if running away was the right decision. Not all decisions you make have to be right. Sometimes you have to take a decision and then make it right. I was going to do the same. Running away would give both of us time to think and work out our options. I couldn't risk staying away from him and losing him again. I quickly took out a travelling bag from my cupboard and started stuffing my clothes in it. I opened my drawer and collected all the jewellery and cash and whatever came in my hand.

I considered leaving my parents a note, but realized it wouldn't help in proving Sarmad's innocence. But at least it would make them less worried. I picked up a notebook and started writing the letter.

Dear Abba, Amma and Sidra,

When you find this letter, I would be far away. Please don't get worried. Whatever I am doing is to help an innocent person. Abba, do you remember the shopkeeper whom we used to visit in Swat to get our daily grocery? He was brutally killed in an army encounter. The shopkeeper also had a son named Sarmad. He had become a good friend of mine back then. He was not a part of any militant group.

Abba, today, the same Sarmad needs my help. He was forced to become a terrorist as he didn't have a choice. He is innocent. I know him and trust him. He's a good person. He is the same person who helped me in Swat. He was with me all the time. He was also there

when Omar died. He tried to save him but couldn't. I
want to help him, Abba. I want to prove his innocence.
I want the army to spare him. I will do anything to save
him . . . because I owe him a lot. He has done a lot for me.
Now it's time for me to pay him back. For this reason, I
am leaving home today. I am going to help him. Please
give me some time. I will be back soon. Please don't get
worried. Hope you understand.

Love,
Mehar.

I didn't sleep that night. Sidra tried to talk to me but I did
not open the door to her. After a few light knocks on the
door, she walked away. I heaved a sigh of relief when I
realized she had left.

It was around 5 a.m. when Sarmad texted me to come
down. I had just finished my fajr prayer. I prayed to god for
my family's well-being and Sarmad's safety. I'd do anything
to keep him safe.

Anything.

I slowly tiptoed downstairs, making sure no one saw
me. I made my way to the entrance door and unlocked it.
I was relieved to see Sarmad standing across the gate. I
looked around to see if the guard was there; he wasn't on his
chair. I slung the bag across my shoulder and ran towards
the gate. I unlocked it and stepped outside cautiously. As I
turned around, I found Sarmad standing close to me. I held
my breath for a second as I looked into his somnolent eyes.
It seemed he had not slept well. A small smile lit up his face
as his eyes met mine.

'Where are we going? Another Swat trip?' He let out a
small laugh, looking down at my bag.

I tried to smile at his question.

'Somewhere far away,' I said, touching his arm.

He thought for a bit, looking into my eyes. I couldn't resist the urge of taking him in my arms.

'Do you trust me?' he asked in a low whisper.

'Yes,' I answered gravely, looking at his tousled hair and the wrinkles around his eyes.

He took my hand in his and held it firmly.

'Let's go,' he said, taking me along.

Sarmad

I had no idea why she'd asked me to come. I had no idea where I would take her from here. She was risking her own life by leaving her house without informing anyone. I was worried about her but at the same I was exhilarated.

'Come,' I whispered, taking her hand in mine.

I got two bus tickets for Murree, a hill station close to Islamabad. I did not know why I chose that place. Perhaps because it was far away from Lahore and the people in our lives. I gave her the tickets to see her reaction. However, she crumpled them up in her hands without bothering to look at the destination and walked towards the bus. I quietly followed her.

Neither of us spoke a word during the journey. Throughout, she rested her head on my shoulder and held my hand. She wanted to feel my skin against hers. We reached Murree around late noon with a few stops in between. We fetched a cab from outside the bus terminal, and I asked the driver to take us to a decent hotel. After we reached the hotel, I went ahead to talk to the receptionist and booked us two rooms. One of the staff members picked up Mehar's luggage and took us to our respective rooms. I entered my room and closed the door behind me, running my fingers through my ruffled hair. I had no idea what the heck I was doing here. Leaving everything behind, here I was—with Mehar. I wondered if I'd done the right thing. But one thing was clear. We couldn't hide here all our lives.

Soon, Mehar's family would come looking for us. And they'd take her away from me. Forever.

Mehar

We reached Murree at around 1 p.m. I walked into my room and sat on the bed. Abba must have found and read the letter by now, I thought. I had no clue why I'd done this. I just wanted Sarmad to get out of this situation. I checked my cell phone to see if there were any calls or messages from home. There were a dozen missed calls and messages which I didn't bother to check. I put the phone on the side table and ignored it. My stomach growled as I realized that I had not eaten anything since I left home. I stepped out of my room and knocked on Sarmad's door. I did not understand why he had booked two rooms for us when we could have stayed in one. It's not like we weren't accustomed to living together. He opened the door and stood before me, his eyes weary.

'All okay?' he asked, rubbing his eyes.

'Uh . . .' I hesitated a little. 'I am hungry. Can we go and eat something?'

We walked to the Mall Road and stopped at a local restaurant. I ordered a dish of chicken karahi for myself. Sarmad was having a hard time deciding, so I ordered the same dish for him too. We ate in silence, without talking to each other. He kept stealing glances at me and I did the same. It suddenly started drizzling and the weather became pleasant. We hurriedly finished our meal and rushed back to the hotel. Soon the drizzle turned into a heavy downpour. We stopped at a closed local shop for cover. We stood there for a while and waited for the rain to slow down. I wiped the water from my face and quickly ran my fingers through my wet hair. I wasn't even aware that he had been staring at me for quite some time. As I looked back at him, he quickly shifted his gaze. There was a flicker of embarrassment in his eyes.

'You remember the night when we ran down the road in a similar way and hid under the cart?' I smiled, reminiscing about our childhood.

'Yes,' he whispered. 'I remember everything.'

'I can't believe I couldn't recognize you all this while . . .'

'I thought you'd forgotten me,' he said, smiling.

I shot him a glance.

'I can never forget you, Sarmad.'

He looked back at me, flicking a strand of wet hair off his eyes. We stood there for a while, looking at each other and holding hands. When the rain slowed down, we walked towards the hotel hand in hand. He stopped when we reached my room.

'Sleep well, Mehar,' he said, looking into my eyes.

His stare made me weak in my knees. He freed his hand from my hold and took a step towards his room. Before he could walk away, I grabbed his hand once again.

'Can we sleep in the same room, please?' I requested, not able to look at him. 'Being alone scares me.'

He held my hand and took me to his room. I watched him as he swiftly locked the door with his sturdy hands.

'You should change your clothes before you get sick,' he told me.

'Can you get my bag from the other room?' I requested, and he nodded in response.

I walked into the washroom and turned on the shower tap. Thankfully, the water was warm. A slight knock on the bathroom door indicated that Sarmad had brought my bag. I opened the door and found him standing before me. I slowly took the bag from his hands and closed the door. After taking a long, warm shower, I wrapped myself in a clean white towel and looked at my reflection in the mirror. I could see a major change in myself. The old Mehar could never take a huge step like this and leave home. She could never deceive her family. The girl who now stood before me was someone else—someone completely consumed by love. I loved the person I had become with him.

I put on my undergarments and then a white-coloured cotton salwar kameez. I buttoned up my kurta and walked out of the washroom. He was leaning against the window pane staring outside. An unlit cigarette dangled from his lips. I instantly noticed that he too had changed his clothes. He wore a black-coloured vest and khaki trousers. His strong muscles bulged from under the vest. I put down my bag on the side table and walked over to him slowly.

He looked at me briefly and then smiled. The rain had once again picked up momentum. The thunder rumbled, making my lips quiver in fear. I quickly wrapped my arms around myself and closed my eyes.

'Does the sound of thunder still scare you?' he asked, looking at me.

I slowly shifted my gaze to him and nodded. A small smile played across his lips.

'Are you scared now?' he asked, closing the distance between us.

'Yes,' I gasped as his cool fragrance hit my nostrils.

He came and stood behind me. I had no idea what was about to happen. Within seconds, I found myself wrapped in his arms. He buried his face in my wet hair and interlocked his fingers with mine, sending a pleasurable electric spark through my body. I could hear him moan. We had never been so close before. The thrill of his touch made my heart flutter and sent a million melting sensations through me.

'Are you still scared?' he asked, his lips caressing my ear slowly.

'No . . .' I whispered.

'Do you want me to go away?' he asked, his fingers stroking my arms.

'No. Please just stay like this. Please . . .' I answered in a low voice.

I didn't know for how long we stood in that intimate position. As the thunder rumbled once again, I quickly turned around and wrapped my arms around his neck, our chests touching. The smell of his skin made me crazy. He stroked my back and then embraced me tightly. In his arms I felt like I had conquered the world. It was a beautiful feeling. As swollen drops of rain splattered down, our embrace became more passionate. We devoured each other in that one intimate moment. Breathless, he drew himself back and then held my face in his warm hands. I tried to look into his eyes and put my arms around his torso.

'Just remember one thing,' he said, bringing my face closer to his.

Our breaths intermingled, our hearts thumped.

'No matter what happens tomorrow, no matter how our fates turn out to be, I'll always love you. Please always remember that, will you?' He shook my head a little as he spoke.

I nodded hazily as I intently listened to him.

'I have always loved you, Mehar, and I will always love you.'

He held me in a tight embrace once again and I hugged him back, this time with even more passion than before. I had never wanted anyone so badly in my life, nor had I felt like this before. He slowly drew back and gazed into my eyes.

'You have no idea how badly my heart has ached for you,' he murmured, tucking my hair behind my ears.

'Mine too,' I said with one hand gently placed on his cheek and the other entangled in his ruffled hair.

He looked at me as if he could see through my soul. I brought his face closer to mine and then planted a light kiss on his forehead. I put my hand under his chin and raised his face so his eyes could meet mine. I kissed the tip of his nose, slowly inhaling his scent. And then he couldn't hold himself back. Before I could react or protest, he pressed his lips against mine. I sighed as our bodies became one. I did not want him to stop; he kissed me with such intensity and so much love that it became difficult for me to stop. His one hand embraced my back while the other gripped the back of my neck, making escape impossible. I did not want to escape. I gave up and kissed him back with the same intensity and love. His lips were soft, warm and felt right against mine. I completely got carried away as our kiss grew fervent. I moaned as his tongue slid into my mouth, reaching for mine. I knew what was about to happen. And I was ready for it.

All of a sudden, he pushed me away, his eyes burning with desire. He turned to the other side, trying to control his heightened emotions. I embraced him from behind, holding him tight, and then made him look into my eyes.

'I want you to want me, Sarmad; to need me. Please. Don't walk away tonight. Please don't go. Please. I love you.

I love you so much. I want this as much as you want it. So please. Don't stop. Not tonight,' I pleaded, tears streaming down my cheeks.

Before I could look back into his eyes or say another word, he took me in his strong arms and carried me to the bed.

Sarmad

I made her lie on the bed, my eyes not leaving hers, and then switched off the lamp kept on the side table. She was right about one thing. I wanted her as much as she wanted me. I don't know for how long I had waited for this moment—to be close to her, to feel her, to touch her. I closed my eyes, wondering if this was really happening. I wondered if we were doing the right thing. She firmly held my hand and pulled me towards her. I fell on top of her, her caramel brown eyes visible even in the darkness. I held her gaze and interlaced our fingers together.

'I love you,' she whispered, smiling.

'I love you more,' I said, rubbing my nose with hers.

'No, I love you more,' she slowly laughed, her lips against mine.

As I looked into her smiling eyes, she ran her fingers through my hair and then drew me closer. I shut my eyes, closing the remaining distance between us, and then kissed her. The entire night, with our minds, with our hearts and with our bodies, we made love. Pure love.

Mehar

Suddenly, I felt different. And complete. Last night, I'd given him a sacred part of me and he'd given me a sacred part of him. He had not only touched my body but also my soul. I'd given him my soul. And when souls meet, no force can pull them apart. As I opened my eyes around dawn, I found his arm wrapped around my waist. The room was dark except for a small ray of light that came in through the window. I looked at him but he was asleep. It was the first time I'd seen him sleep so peacefully. There was no worry on his face, no weariness around his eyes. I slowly caressed the scar that ran from his face to his bare chest. I couldn't believe what had happened last night. I blushed as memories of the night flashed through my mind. As I smiled remembering the beautiful moments, he took me by surprise by kissing my fingers. I suddenly realized he was awake.

'You're up,' he said, brushing his lips against my fingers.

'Yes,' I murmured as colour filled my cheeks. I couldn't look into his eyes as I felt shy.

'Did you sleep well?' he asked, drawing his naked body closer to mine.

We were wrapped under the same blanket.

I nodded, still not looking at him.

'And won't you ask me how I slept?' he asked, tucking my hair behind my ears.

I looked up at him, expecting him to answer his own question.

'I haven't slept like this in ages, Mehar. Undoubtedly, it was the best night of my life.' He smiled as his eyes twinkled.

'And you know what? I had a dream last night. A very beautiful dream,' he continued.

'Dream?' I looked at him. 'What did you see?'

'I usually never dream but last night was different.'

'Would you tell me about the dream now?' I asked eagerly.

He laughed.

'I'll tell you. But not now.' He wrapped his arm around my neck, pulling me closer to him.

'Then when?' I asked.

'Soon.' He buried his face in my hair and kissed the side of my neck, sending shivers down my spine.

'Sarmad, can I ask for something?' I asked.

'Anything,' he whispered, his lips lingering on the skin of my neck.

'If we are able to make it through this situation, would you be able to leave everything for me and start afresh?'

He stopped kissing my neck and looked into my eyes.

'Would you choose me over everything else?' I asked, trying to gauge his reaction.

'I wish that happens, Mehar. I wish . . .' he whispered after a long pause.

'Everything will be fine.' I held his hand and planted soft kisses on his fingers. 'We'll be fine,' I reassured him.

He smiled, bringing his face closer to mine.

'And to answer your question, let me tell you that I have already chosen you over everything else. And I would always choose you—in a million lifetimes, in a million worlds,' he whispered. 'I promise.'

I put my hands in his hair, pulling him closer and then kissed him.

Sarmad

I woke up to check the time on the wall clock and it said 10.05 a.m. Mehar was sleeping next to me, her eyes closed, her breath even. She was the most beautiful woman I'd ever seen. I kissed her forehead softly and then gently freed myself from her hold, trying not to disturb her. I picked up my undershirt from the floor and quietly got dressed. When I switched on my cell phone, I saw a number of messages and missed calls. I quickly dialled a number.

'Hello, Sarmad? Where are you? I have been trying to reach you since yesterday. Where is she?' the man on the line asked, his voice shaky.

'She is with me. Safe and sound. Don't worry. I'll bring her to you tonight.' I ended the call and then glanced over at Mehar who was still serenely asleep under the duvet.

I'm sorry, Mehar, but I had no other option.

Mehar

A wave of fresh air hit my face as I opened my eyes. I noticed that the windows were open and the curtains flew with the wind. Sarmad, wearing the same black T-shirt, was making tea.

'Morning, beautiful.' He turned around to greet me.

'Good morning,' I whispered, resting my back against the headboard. 'What are you doing?'

'I have made tea for you.' He came and sat near me and handed me the cup.

'Oh, thank you.' I took a sip of the sweet tea.

He slid his hand into mine, his touch sending shivers down my spine. He took the cup from my hands and put it on the side table. He slowly slipped inside the quilt next to me. My heartbeat quickened as he came near me and held my hand. I looked into his eyes and kissed his hand. He brushed his thumb across my face.

'Sarmad . . . I want to show you something.'

'What?' he whispered.

I opened my bag and took out an origami crane that I had made.

'Wow. You learnt how to make it,' he said, smiling.

'Yes.' I smiled. 'Finally.'

He kissed the side of my neck, sending a thousand chills through my body.

'Come. Let's fly it.' He looked at my face.

'Really? Are you serious?'

'Yes. Come with me.' He held my hand and made me get out of bed.

We went to the balcony and looked up at the sky. Sarmad stood behind me and made me hold the origami in my hands. Both of us released it into the air together and watched it float. He put his arms around my shoulders and embraced me tightly.

Sarmad took me back to Lahore after lunch. We reached his place at night. The same place where I had found out about him.

'Stay here. I'll be back soon,' he said and walked out of the house.

I sat on the wooden bench and looked at the photographs hanging on the wall. Sarmad still looked the same, I thought. I wondered how I didn't recognize him all this while. I looked around the house and wondered where Khan Baba was. He was nowhere in sight. Tired due to the long journey, I rested my back against the wall and slowly drifted off to sleep.

The sound of someone knocking on the door woke me up. When I realized Sarmad had still not returned, I felt scared. My heart throbbed with fear as the knocks continued. I stood up and hurriedly took out my cell phone from my bag and dialled his number. It was switched off. The knocks on the door became louder. I mustered up the courage and went to open it. And when I did, I found Sarmad standing before me.

'Sarmad!' I gave a gasp of relief. 'Where were you?' I reached for his arms but he didn't hold me back. There was something different about his cold eyes. As I waited for him to speak, another figure emerged from behind him. My jaw dropped in shock and eyes widened as I saw my father standing next to Sarmad. We were both caught, busted. Our game was over. A look of mortification passed over my face as I realized that my father had caught me red-handed with Sarmad. I felt like the most immoral daughter on the face of the earth.

'Abba . . .' I managed to speak. 'I . . . I was just trying to help . . .

'There is no need to say anything,' Abba said, cutting me in between. 'Thank you, Sarmad.' He looked at Sarmad and patted him lightly on his shoulder. 'Thank you for letting me know where my daughter was.'

I was shocked at Abba's revelation. I looked at him and then at Sarmad, but he didn't look back at me. I had no idea what my father was talking about.

'Mehar, I know what you're trying to do—you're trying to help Sarmad. I'm also trying to do the same,' Abba said, looking calmly at me.

I still had no idea what he was talking about. His words made my head spin. I was so damn confused.

'It's true that Sarmad belongs to an extremist group but in reality he works for the army,' he declared.

I shot a perplexed look at Sarmad, but he looked back at me with determination.

'What?' I gazed at them in shock.

'Yes, Mehar. Sarmad is not a terrorist but a secret agent.'

I retraced my steps back, shaking my head in disbelief. All this while, Sarmad had made a fool of me and kept a huge secret from me.

I covered my mouth with my hands, still shaking my head in disbelief. Abba and Sarmad stepped into the room, closing the door behind them.

Sarmad

The shock on Mehar's face disturbed me. I could see hatred in her eyes. I didn't know the truth was going to affect her in a negative way.

'Whatever your father said is partially true. I am working for the army. Not from the beginning though,' I said.

She had now uncovered her face and was intently listening to me.

'It is true that Khan Baba handed me over to Mullah. I was ready to work for them even though my heart never allowed it. I knew I had to avenge Baba's death and kill the people responsible but wasn't fully convinced by what Mullah taught me.

'They wanted me to kill people. Innocent people. And I never wanted to do that. I was against killing. Mullah tried to brainwash me in every possible way and showed me another side of the world. I did listen to him but my heart wasn't in it. He made me a part of every terrorist activity they planned. It's true I was involved in those activities but I did not hurt a single soul myself. I knew everything about the terrorist attacks Mullah planned. I have each and every proof of their criminal activities. Mullah confided in me because Khan Baba had been working with them for a long time. Mullah knew I'd never betray him. And it's true. I never betrayed him. Not until I met General.'

Mehar looked at her father and then looked back at me.

'As you know, I was there when Omar got killed. I was aware of that attack. Mullah had told me about it. When the blast happened, I fell on the ground and fainted. And when I woke up, I found myself sitting on a chair in a dark room, with my hands tied with a rope. I knew I had been caught and there was no escape. My limbs ached badly and I realized that my body was covered with bruises.

'After some time, I saw General walking towards me. I recognized his face instantly. He held my chin, made me look into his eyes and asked me if I knew anything about the blast or if I was involved in it. Initially, I refused and kept my mouth shut for a couple of hours. The General and other army officers waited for me to speak up. But I didn't. I could not betray Khan Baba and Mullah as they'd done a lot for me. A few days passed and I'd still not said anything. One day, the General came up to me and sat down next to me. He asked me who I was and where I'd come from. I told him that he knew me and my father—he used to own a grocery shop just near his guest house in Mingora. He instantly recognized me. I told him how my father was killed in an encounter. The army shot him without confirming if he was a terrorist or not. The General told me the other side of the story. He knew what had actually happened that day.

'The army had been informed that Khan Baba was hiding weapons in his house. And that was true because I'd seen that myself. The army had come to seize the weapons but had found a group of terrorists invading the house. They had no option but to open fire at them. My father, unfortunately, was also inside at that time and got killed along with the other terrorists. The General told me that he

and the entire army was extremely sorry for what happened
to my father, and that Khan Baba was responsible for his
death. Had he not been involved with the terrorists or
helped them, the army would have never intervened. Khan
Baba worked with the wrong people despite knowing the
truth. He had not only put his life at risk but his brother
and son's too. He didn't deserve to live. He deserved
punishment. And the army would do anything to punish
him and Mullah's group.

'A sense of realization hit me when the General told me
the story. He asked me to work for him and the army by
staying with Mullah's gang and collecting evidence. That's
when I decided to do something good. Work against Mullah
and get them arrested.'

As I finished speaking, I saw Mehar wiping her tears.
The General consoled her by putting an arm over her
shoulder.

'He's right, Mehar,' the General said. 'Sarmad is
working with them so that we can get them behind bars for
spreading violence and terrorism.'

After hearing this, she stared at me for a long time and
then went out of the house.

Mehar

I hurriedly ran outside, wiping the tears streaming down my cheeks. I crossed the gate outside the house and sat on the porch steps, my palpitations rising. I did not know whom to believe and whom to trust.

My mind was dazed with taking in too many revelations at the same time. I had no idea whom I had fallen in love with—the Sarmad who I'd met back in my childhood when he was a small boy; Sarmad the terrorist whom I'd encountered in Swat; or the one who worked for my father as a secret agent.

I sat there for some time, contemplating my life as the day's events unfolded in my mind. The dark grey clouds above me roared aloud and soon the rain splattered across the front garden. A few raindrops fell on my cheeks and hands. Abba stood beside me for a while and then sat down next to me. An eerie silence fell between us.

'Sometimes, it hurts to find out the truth,' he said, after a long pause. 'But trust me, truth is always for the better.' He looked at me, taking my hand in his.

I slowly drew in a breath and wiped my tears with the back of my hand.

'When you were stuck in Swat, I wasn't worried, you know . . .'

I looked at him, confused.

'I knew he was there all the time,. looking after my daughter. He was in touch with me all through the journey.'

I broke into tears, covering my face with my hands.

'I'm sorry, beta, but we had to keep this from you. Sarmad was not allowed to share the details of our secret mission with anyone. Not even you,' Abba said, holding me.

'Abba . . . I . . .' I said, trying to control my tears. 'I care for him.'

'I know, beta, and I care for him too. Don't worry. He's in safe hands. We won't let anything happen to him.'

'I'm sorry I ran off with him. I didn't know how to keep him safe. I was . . . just trying to help him . . .' My voice shook and trailed off.

'I know what you've done is not right, Mehar. It's really not right. What if Hamza and your Phupho find out about this incident? I wonder how they would react. Your mother and Sidra are really upset with you. However, at the same time, I do understand what you feel for Sarmad. You were quite attached to him during your childhood. I understand that. He's your friend and you were only trying to help him.'

I looked at my father and then cast my eyes down. I wish I could tell him that he wasn't just a friend. He was more than a friend. He was my life.

'You don't need to worry,' he said.

'Abba, will he be fine?' I asked, my voice breaking as tears trickled down my eyes.

'Yes, Mehar. Of course, he will be fine. We are protecting him the best we can.'

I nodded, wiping my tears.

Sarmad

As I paced back and forth inside the house, I heard a slight knock on the door. I opened it to find the General standing in front of me, his arms folded across his chest. He seemed somewhat distressed.

'I need to have a word with you,' he said.

'Sure. Please come in, General sahib,' I said as I moved aside to let him in.

He stepped into the house, looked around momentarily and then looked back at me.

'Why did you bring her here?' he asked.

For a moment I was quiet. I did not have an answer to his question. Or perhaps I could not answer him. What I felt for her or what she felt for me could not be described. Being a father he would never understand our relationship. He didn't know I'd taken her to Murree. All he knew was that I had brought her to my place in Lahore. And I had to keep it a secret.

'I'm sorry, General sahib, I shouldn't have listened to Mehar. Bringing her here was a foolish decision,' I said, bowing my head.

'Did she ask you to bring her over here?'

'It was a mutual decision.'

'I'd say it was a wrong decision.'

I looked into his eyes for a brief second before looking down again.

'Sarmad, now listen to me very carefully,' the General said, taking a step towards me. 'Son, I know what you've been through in your life. I'm trying my best to end your misery.'

I nodded slightly as I crossed my arms across my chest, trying to understand his words.

'But son, let me be clear that whatever my daughter and you have been fantasizing about cannot come true.'

I felt a sharp jab in my chest.

'I'm not a fool. I can sense everything. I know what both of you feel for each other. I've seen it in her eyes and I've seen it in yours as well.'

I constantly looked down as he continued talking.

'Whatever you feel for each other must be true but it has no future, Sarmad, and you know that very well. My daughter is engaged to my nephew and soon they will be married. So don't make it difficult for her.'

I closed my fists tightly.

'I know she has been in love with you since you spent time together in Swat. When she returned home, I saw it in her eyes. Even though she didn't tell me, I could read her heart. I'm her father after all.'

I nodded.

'I would only request one thing from you, Sarmad, if you can give it to me.'

I hesitantly looked at him, my brows creasing.

'After we get all the evidence and arrest Mullah's gang, I want you to leave this country and go far away from all of us . . . including Mehar.'

I smiled at his words, tears glistening in my eyes.

'I can't believe what you're asking me to do, General sahib. You're asking me to give away someone who has never been mine and will never ever be.'

He firmly nodded.

'You don't have to worry, sir. I'll be gone before she can notice my absence.'

'Thank you, son. Thank you. I really wish . . . things could be different. There could not be a better person than you for my daughter,' he said, patting me on my shoulder.

'Sir, please.' I clasped his hands.

He embraced me for a brief moment, ending it with another pat on my shoulder.

'As soon as I get back to Waziristan, I'll gather all the evidence and I'll hand it over to you,' I assured him.

'Good luck, kid. I'll wait for your arrival,' the General nodded.

I nodded back, a triumphant smile on my face.

Mehar

One of the workers dragged my luggage towards the car. I had to leave for my house in the next few minutes. I did not realize when Sarmad came and stood next to me, all of my senses suddenly reacting to his presence. I folded my arms tightly across my chest but did not dare to look at him even though my entire body ached for his touch.

'I know you're angry with me, and you have every right to be,' he said, taking a sigh. 'I did whatever I could to keep our country safe. I have risked my own life by working secretly for the army.'

I continued staring out of the window and chose to remain quiet.

'I've been lying to you from the beginning because I had to. I had to keep the truth from you. That's how everything was planned. I just couldn't break the rules.'

I took a deep breath.

'I may have lied to you about my identity but there's one thing that I have always been honest about—my feelings. I have never lied to you about my feelings for you. I have always meant it, still mean it, and will always mean it when I say I love you . . .'

I held my breath for a second before turning to look at him.

'My love for you has never been a lie. It's all that I have with me now,' he smiled as tears welled up in his eyes.

Without thinking of the consequences, I hugged him. He slowly put his arms around me and rested his chin on my head.

'I love you, Sarmad. My love and respect for you has increased a thousand fold. I am proud of you. You are my superhero,' I said while holding him tightly.

'I love you too,' he whispered and then pulled me back. 'Now, you have to go back to your father. We need to part ways.' He held my face in his hands. 'I need to hand over all the evidence to the army so that I can be free.'

'I can't be apart from you for a long time. You have to come back to me,' I said.

'Yes, I'll come back as soon as possible.'

'Promise?'

'Yes,' he nodded, kissing the top of my head and then taking me back in his arms.

Sarmad

I did promise her that I would come back but I knew I wasn't permitted to fulfil it. Yet again, I was going to hurt her feelings. At around 4 a.m., I called the General from a private phone. He had asked me to meet him at the Garrison Officers Mess.

When I reached the place around noon, I saw a couple of official vehicles parked in the parking lot. I flung my bag over my shoulder and then waited for the General outside the gate. He showed up after a couple of minutes, with two men by his side. The General spoke to the guards and they let me in without frisking me.

'Asalaam u alaikum, Sarmad,' said the General, shaking my hand.

'Walaikum asalaam, General,' I responded.

'This is Major General Waqar Ahmad, my former colleague, and this is my nephew, Hamza,' he said, introducing the other two men.

I shot a glance at Hamza, knowing who he was—Mehar's cousin and her betrothed. For some reason, he appeared a perfect fit for her. Broad shoulders, sleek hair, determined eyes. He smiled at me warmly as I shook hands with him.

'I have told Waqar and Hamza about your brave efforts and they're really proud of you. In fact, the entire army is proud of you,' said the General.

I tried to smile in response but failed.

'Let's go inside,' General said.

They made me sit inside the drawing room for a while and offered me tea and snacks. I could see the General speaking with the Major General as they stood in the doorway. I unzipped the bag, fished out all the files and devices from it, placed them on the coffee table and then waited for them.

'I believe you have brought all the evidence,' the General said, looking at the items laid out on the table.

'Yes, I have,' I said.

'I request you to hand them over to us.'

For some reason, I had an odd feeling and hesitated for a moment. I knew that what I was about to do could ruin the rest of my life. But then again, did I really care about my future? I was always ready to embrace death as it never scared me.

'Don't worry, son. I won't let anything happen to you,' the General reassured me.

I nodded back at him and handed over all the evidence I had against Mullah and Khan Baba.

'Thank you,' the General said.

'Here is your passport and flight ticket,' the Major General said, handing over some documents to me. 'You won't face any difficulty while boarding the plane. We have cleared your past record.'

I looked at the documents in my hand.

'You're safe to go, buddy,' said Hamza, patting me on the back.

'I have a request,' I said.

'What is it?' the General asked.

'Before the army goes to raid Khan Baba's place, I need to see him for the last time.'

'Sure . . .' the General nodded.

I nodded back at him and got to my feet. I bid them goodbye and headed towards the only place I knew in Lahore—Khan Baba's residence. It was almost midnight when I reached there.

I wanted to meet him so that I could bid him a final farewell. Soon, the army would arrest him for his wrong deeds.

He had always been involved with the extremists. Despite my father's persistent requests, Khan Baba did not stop working with them. It was because of him that my father lost his life. Now, it was time for him to pay for what he'd done.

The house was dark when I creaked open the door. I stepped inside the room. I put down my bag that was now empty except for a few garments and leaned on the bed. I stared into the darkness as a feeble sound of footsteps caught my attention.

'There you are Sarmad, always without warning. You're full of surprises,' he said as he sat down on the edge of the mattress.

I could not see his face in the darkness.

'Where have you been, bachcha?' he asked.

'Had gone to complete a few things,' I said.

'And, have you succeeded?'

'Yes.'

He stood on his frail feet and walked over to the mantle to light a candle. The room lit up in the glow of the candlelight, letting me see Khan Baba properly.

'You look tired, Sarmad jaan. Why don't you take some rest and sleep for a while?'

'Yes, I should.'

'Would you like anything?' he asked.

'No, I'm fine. Thanks.'

I slid my arm underneath the pillow and shut my eyes.

I did feel sorry for Khan Baba considering all that he'd done for me after Baba left us forever. But there had to be an end to his and Mullah's evil deeds. It was time for them to pay for their wrongdoings.

I woke up to the crowing of a rooster early in the morning. I rubbed my eyes and scanned the room. Everything looked at peace. However, I couldn't feel Khan Baba's presence inside the house.

'Morning, Sarmad jaan,' Khan Baba said, as he stepped into my room.

'Good morning. You're here.'

'Yes. Where else would I be?'

'Nowhere.'

'It's Friday today. Get up and go to the bathroom. I'll arrange clothes for you.'

I nodded, walking towards the bathroom.

As I stepped out after taking a bath, a towel wrapped around my torso, my phone's screen showed a 'missed call'. It was Mehar. I had not contacted her since the day she left my place. ˉ suddenly realized how much I missed seeing her face and hearing her voice.

I put down my phone on the mantel and searched for my clothes. A pair of neatly ironed salwar kameez and a grey waistcoat laid out on the mattress caught my attention. Khan Baba must have bought these for me.

'I got these for you. Thought you will look good in them,' Khan Baba said, appearing out of thin air.

'Thanks, Khan Baba,' I said, without feeling guilty for what I'd done.

I took my time getting dressed and stood in front of the mirror putting on the crisp white salwar kameez.

'Mashallah. There's *noor* on your face, just like your Baba used to have,' Khan Baba said, standing behind me.

I gawked at my reflection in the mirror.

'Put on the waistcoat as well.'

'Do I have to?' I raised my brows.

'Yes. It will look good on you. Let me help you wear it.'

I stretched out my arms behind my back so that he could help me wear the waistcoat. To my surprise, it fit perfectly.

'See? I told you that you'd look handsome,' Khan Baba giggled softly.

The sound of his giggle brought a smile to my lips. I turned around to give him an embrace. Perhaps the last embrace. He held me tightly in his arms.

'Oh Sarmad . . . What did you think, huh? That you would be successful in deceiving me and I wouldn't even suspect you?'

His words startled me. I pulled myself back to look at him.

'I know you are working for the army now.'

I blinked my eyes in disbelief. How did he find out?

I closed my fists, my jaw muscles tightened.

'Mullah had been watching your every move since the day you returned from Swat. He doubted you. At first I didn't believe him and disregarded his false accusations but he proved them right . . . you have disappointed me, Sarmad. You have broken my trust.'

'I did what I should have done years ago, Khan Baba. Mullah and his gang, including you, deserve punishment for your actions. Baba lost his life because of your involvement in Mullah and his gangs' activities. I lost my father forever. And then you compelled me to join a terrorist's group instead of ensuring a normal life for me. You ruined my life. Now it's time for you to surrender quietly,' I told him, my eyes filling with tears.

'Do you think I would ever surrender to the army?' he asked, half a smile twitching at the corner of his lips.

'Yes, you will. I know you will.'

'I'd rather embrace death than fall into the hands of those bloody hounds,' he said, gritting his teeth.

I creased my brows, baffled.

'As soon as I learnt of your betrayal, I swallowed a bottleful of poisonous tablets.'

Khan Baba held out his hand, showing me the empty bottle.

'No!' I shrieked. 'No! You can't do this, Khan Baba. You can't!'

'I'm sorry,' he mumbled, lowering himself to the ground.

I saw him lose consciousness; a foamy froth appearing at his mouth. I got down to the floor, resting his head on my lap.

'You can't do this to yourself! Do you understand? You can't!' I cried as tears fell down my cheeks.

'I'm sorry, Sarmad jaan, for ruining your life . . . for not making you the person you could have been. But you're still a lot better than me,' he said, his eyes closing.

'Wake up, Khan Baba, wake up.'

I lightly tapped on his cheeks in an attempt to keep him awake.

'I'm sorry, Sarmad, but I have done something dreadful once again. God will never forgive me for this.'

'What . . . what do you mean?' I asked, shaking his head to try and keep him conscious.

'The waistcoat that you're wearing . . . it has a bomb.'

'What!' I was appalled at his revelation. I could not even feel anything concealed in the waistcoat.

'The bomb is timed to explode within a few hours. If you try to take it off, that will also set it off,' he told me.

Sweat trickled down my forehead.

'I'm sorry . . . I did what Mullah asked me to. I am
sorry . . . please try to save yourself if you can . . . please . . .'

His voice faded, his breathing stopped and his lips
pursed together.

I lowered my head to hear his heartbeat. There was
nothing.

Mehar

Sarmad had not contacted me for a few days. I was worried. I tried to call him but there was no response. I decided to wait for him to call me back. When I returned home, Amma and Sidra did not seem pleased with me. They did not talk to me and looked at me with contempt in their eyes.

Abba did try to explain the entire situation to them but they loathed the fact that I had escaped with Sarmad. Sidra tried to start a conversation and asked me if I was romantically involved with him. I wished I could tell her the truth. I wished I could tell her that there was much more that I felt for him. I owed him a lot. But telling her would do nothing but aggravate the situation and further disrupt the peace of my home.

Sarmad called me around noon when I was sitting in my balcony on the hammock.

'Sarmad?' I said, my heartbeat accelerating.

'Mehar . . .' he said, his voice breaking.

'Where are you?' I asked him. 'You did not call me. I want to meet you.'

'I want to meet you too. Badly.' His voice sounded weak over the phone as if there was no energy left in him.

'Have you surrendered everything that Abba had asked for?'

'Yes, I have . . . I am desperate to see you, Mehar,' he whispered.

'Where can I meet you?' I could hear the longing in his voice.

'Could you come over to the Wazir Khan Masjid?'

'Yes, I'll be there as soon as I can.' I hung up and rushed to change my clothes.

I was finally going to see him again. There would be no intervention from the army, the terrorist group, or any other party. We would be free of all hurdles. I chose a bright red-coloured salwar kurta from my wardrobe, wondering if he would like to see me in red. I blushed as I imagined him looking at me. I quickly changed my clothes and covered my head with a yellow dupatta.

'Mehar, where are you going?' Amma asked as I hurried towards the doorway.

'Amma, I have to be somewhere right now. It's urgent. I'll be back soon. Promise.' I closed the door behind me and bumped into Hamza on my way. His sudden appearance shocked me.

'Asalaam u alaikum,' I said as I looked down, embarrassed.

'Walaikum asalaam. Are you going somewhere?' he asked.

'Yes,' I said firmly.

It was time to tell him everything about Sarmad. If not now, I could never tell him. He had the right to know the truth.

'Hamza, I have to tell you something that I should have told you way before . . . there's someone else I . . .' My voice trailed off.

'You love Sarmad, right? Is that what you were going to say?' He crossed his arms over his chest and looked at me.

My heart stopped beating. I wondered if I had heard
him right. I looked at him with bewilderment.

'Mehar, I know all about him. Mamu told me
everything.'

A tear escaped from my eye but I wiped it off immediately.

'I have met him. He's a good guy, you know. What he is
doing for the army is incredible. Not everyone has that sort
of valour. That man deserves a bravery award.'

I smiled at him, realizing Hamza had also seen the real
side of Sarmad.

'And more than that, he deserves you, Mehar. He
deserves to be with you. He deserves a life with you.'

Hamza stood closer to me, taking my hands in his. 'He
has been suffering since childhood. He has been through a
lot. It's time for him to live a normal, happy life. It's time
for him to live his dreams. With you.'

I looked at him, tears gleaming in my eyes, and then
nodded.

He took off the engagement ring from my finger and
did the same with his. 'You're free from this relationship,
Mehar. You have been his, you are his and will always
be his. Don't worry about Mamu. I have explained him
everything. He has agreed. You just tell Sarmad about this
now. Go to him.'

'Can you . . .' I hiccupped, tears streaming down my
cheeks. 'Can you take me to him? He's waiting for me.'

Sarmad

I exited the house, leaving Khan Baba's body behind. I called up the General on my way to Wazir Khan Masjid to inform him about Khan Baba's death. He listened to me quietly and expressed his sorrow over the issue. He said the troops would be there to take charge of his body. He also told me that the armed forces were on their way to attack Mullah and his tribe. Soon all of them would be under arrest.

'Don't worry, Sarmad. Everything is under control,' the General had said over the phone. 'Mehar's on her way to meet you. She has some good news for you.'

I couldn't respond to him. I couldn't even tell him about the bomb planted inside my waistcoat that would explode any time. I felt like screaming out loudly. My heart ached with pain. And then I thought about the good news that Mehar was about to deliver to me. I had called her just so I could see her face for the last time . . .

I sat inside the masjid, waiting for her. After a few seconds, I realized I was sitting at the wrong place. What if the bomb exploded and killed the people around me? I stood up and rushed out of the masjid as fast as I could. I stopped only when I had reached a deserted area, far away from the masjid and other local buildings. I couldn't see a single soul near me. I hushed my breath and stilled my thoughts as I looked around me. Soon, I would fall into an abyss and never return.

Mehar

I called Sarmad as soon as we were close to the masjid. He told me to meet him at the rear of the building.

'I think he's outside the masjid. I need to go there,' I told Hamza, as I got out of the car.

'Shall I come with you?' he asked, getting out of the car.

'Don't worry. I'll be safe.'

'I'll wait for you right here in that case.'

'Thank you, Hamza. Thank you for everything,' I said, squeezing his hands firmly.

'You're always welcome.'

I rushed to the other side of the masjid and looked for him everywhere. I couldn't see a single person in that area. Everything was quiet.

'Sarmad!' I called out. 'Sarmad!'

'I'm right behind you, Mehar,' I heard him say.

I spun around to find him standing a few steps away from me.

'Hey,' I said, my cheeks blushing.

'Hey,' he said.

'I've missed you.'

'I've missed you too.'

I could see tears forming in his eyes.

'You don't have to miss me any more,' I said, trying to give him a hint.

'Why?'

'I told Hamza about us . . . and he wants us to be together. Abba wants the same for us, Sarmad.'

'What are you saying?' he asked, his voice softening.

'I'm just saying that our right time has begun.' I took a step towards him, closing the gap between us. 'You don't need to hide anywhere, don't have to run from anyone and you certainly don't need to stay away from me.'

He looked at me warily as he took a step back.

'Our love has won, Sarmad. It has won over hatred, terror and death. It overcame every other power. We're one now.'

I took another step forward and he another step back . . .

'We will stay together. Always and forever.'

He retreated once again. I realized that as I closed the gap between us, he increased it once again.

'Sarmad.' I furrowed my brows. 'Why are you moving away from me?'

'Do not come near me, Mehar. I beg you. Please. Stay away,' he said as tears rolled down his cheeks. There was a look of horror on his face.

'What's wrong, Sarmad? What happened to you? Why are you saying this?' I marched towards him, trying my best not to listen to him.

'I said, stay away.' He took a few steps back, increasing the distance between us once again.

'I can't.' I ran into him, throwing myself at him.

He winced as I hugged him.

'Why are you running away from me now that everything is perfectly fine?' I asked, hugging him.

He did not wrap his arms around me. His body remained stiff.

'What's wrong?' I looked at him, and lowered his chin until his eyes met mine. 'Tell me. What's wrong?'

'There is a . . . bomb . . . a bomb . . .' he stuttered.

'Bomb?' I asked, perplexed.

'There's a bomb planted in my waistcoat. It can blow up any time . . . if I try to take the waistcoat off, it will explode immediately.'

'What?' My jaw dropped in shock.

He nodded as he looked into my eyes.

'Who did this?' I asked.

'Khan Baba . . .'

'Oh god . . . no!' I pulled myself off his chest slowly. 'Let's call someone, okay? Let me call Hamza. We'll help you to take off this waistcoat. It won't blow up. It won't.'

'It will, Mehar. Be realistic.' He interjected me.

'We'll do something. We'll call specialists who know how to diffuse a bomb. Abba will know one of them. Let me call him.'

I quickly dialled a number from my phone but Sarmad took it away from me.

'Sarmad, give me my phone. I need to call Abba!'

'No . . . you don't have to. We're running out of time, Mehar. It won't do us any good.'

'Why not? Let me try. Let me call him.'

'Stop it, Mehar. Just stop it.'

'Then what the hell are we supposed to do? Damn it!' I yelled at him.

He smiled at my reaction and it hurt me. How could there be so much serenity on his face in such an alarming situation?

'Sarmad, please . . . please let me call Abba once . . . he'll find out a way. Please don't do this to yourself. Please . . . just think of us . . . please, Sarmad, please . . .' I begged as I cried.

'It's over . . .' He half-smiled, tears glistening in his eyes.

'Please don't say that . . . please . . .' I sank to my knees, crying.

He sat down next to me on the ground.

'Come here.' He took me in his arms but I shoved him away. He then came near me and hugged me. We stayed like that for what seemed like eternity.

'I love you with all my heart and soul. Will you always remember that?' he said softly into my ears. My wails had become fainter now.

'I have always loved you, Mehar, and will always love you. You gave me a new reason to live. To smile. To love. To be happy. You told me what happiness is like. You changed my life and turned it beautiful. I'll always be thankful to you. Always.'

I wrapped my arms around his neck and breathed against his chest, my tears silently falling on to his waistcoat.

'The moments you've given me in this life are enough . . . trust me. I don't need anything else now. I am complete. I have lived my life to the fullest in the moments I have spent with you.'

I stood still in his arms and listened to him quietly, tears streaming down my cheeks.

'And now, I want you to live your life.' He pulled us apart and held my face in his hands. 'I want you to get married and have kids . . . god . . . you'll be an amazing mother, Mehar. I can already see that.'

A faint smile flickered over my face at the thought of becoming a mother.

'See the world. Go around it. Make your kids discover new places. Will you?' he asked.

I hastily nodded.

'And also help them learn to make paper origamis, okay?'

I nodded.

'Promise me that you'll be happy.'

I nodded again.

'And promise me that you'll live your life to the fullest . . .'

I nodded once again.

'Promise me, Mehar . . . say it.'

'I promise,' I said in a feeble voice. 'I promise.'

He hugged me once again, caressing my hair slowly with his hand.

'Do you remember the dream I had once told you about?' he asked, after a heartbreaking silence.

'Yes,' I nodded.

I remembered that just after we had woken up together in Murree, he had told me that he had dreamt while sleeping.

'I remember.'

'Would you like to know what it was about?'

'Yes . . . please . . .' A tear rolled down my cheek.

And then he narrated his entire dream to me as I leaned my head on his shoulder.

After a couple of minutes of silence, my cell phone started ringing. Sarmad held out my phone to me. It was Hamza who was calling to check on me. I did not know whether I should attend his call or not. Sarmad slowly stood up, taking a few steps away from me.

'You need to leave now, Mehar. I don't have much time left.'

'Sarmad, I can't . . . I can't leave you.' I also stood on my feet and followed him.

'Don't be reckless. Now go away!' he yelled. 'Go!'

I felt scared when he yelled at me.

'Go, Mehar. There is no time for thinking. Go now. Hurry!'

I retreated a few steps before turning my back on him.

How could I leave someone whom I loved so much? How could I give up so easily? He was asking me to go away and let him die there all alone. I knew his stare still lingered on me as I walked away. I was leaving him. Abandoning him forever. I was giving up on him. I was giving up on our love. The most selfish act one could ever commit, while in love. I did not know how far I had walked away from him because I no longer heard his voice. My heartbeat stopped for a while. My throat tightened. My arms and legs became numb. I felt lifeless. I felt as if someone was taking away a huge part of me. I felt scared. Very scared. And then I recalled his voice from childhood . . .

'Whenever you're scared, just remember one tip. Close your eyes, take a deep breath, hold yourself together and then pray persistently. The fear will slowly go away.'

I did what he told me to. I stopped right there and closed my eyes and then silently prayed for a few seconds. After a while, as I opened my eyes, I felt fearless. I did not fear anything. Not even death. I spun around and found Sarmad standing a few feet away from me, his face tormented by the pain of parting from me. I smiled at him as a tear fell down my cheek. He looked at me blankly, his shoulders drooping.

'I don't fear anything now, Sarmad. Not even death. A life without you will be a life of no use,' I declared.

I rushed into his arms and wrapped my arms around his neck.

Everything fell into place.

Our love overcame our fears.

And we fell into the abyss of happiness, forever.

Epilogue

The Dream

Sarmad had already said his marriage vows and assumed Mehar had also done the same. He couldn't begin to describe how exhilarated he felt when he said '*qubool hai*' three times in a row.

He was blown away when he laid his eyes on her. Mehar looked ethereal in the red bridal dress. The General and his wife escorted her to the stage and made her sit next to him. He couldn't see her face as it was hidden behind a fancy red-coloured veil. Her sister brought a huge mirror and placed it on their laps. He looked at her beautiful reflection in the mirror and she did the same. He smiled at her, and she blushed. His Baba, the General, along with his wife, Khan Baba and Hamza stood around them, their faces lit with smiles. Bari Aapa and her entire family was also present to witness their union. Omar was also there, beaming down at them.

After the nikah ceremony, Sarmad took her to their new house. It was near the river bank. Sarmad got out of the car and then opened the door for her to step out. She looked into his eyes, blushed and then held his hand. He unlocked the main door and made her step in. Everything about the house was bright and spacious. Neutral-coloured paint adorned the walls, light-coloured curtains hung over the large-framed windows and camel-coloured couches completed the look of the decor. The polished marble floor squeaked as Mehar walked over it.

And then he took her to their bedroom. It had a balcony with a beautiful, scenic view. Mehar gushed with excitement when she saw the bedroom. And, to her surprise, a few colourful paper cranes hung over the balcony along with a wind chime. She wrapped her arms around his neck and kissed him softly. He deepened the kiss, his lips leaving soft trails of kisses all over her face and down her neck.

'I've not found love in you.' Mehar said to Sarmad.

He looked at her adoringly, his face calm and composed. 'I've found life in you.'

'And I have found my heaven in you.' He told her.

'Sarmad . . . does our story end here?' she asked.

'No, Mehar . . . it has just begun.' He smiled, embracing her in a warm hug.

Acknowledgements

How do I begin writing this section? There are so many people who are responsible for making me who I am today.

First and foremost, I would like to thank god for giving me the power to believe in myself and pursue my dreams.

Thank you, Ammi and Abu, for bringing me into this beautiful life and helping me stand on my own.

Thank you, Faadi, for being an amazing brother. Even though you haven't read a single word I've ever written, I know you will always be there to support me.

I cannot even begin to explain how much you mean to me, Ashu. No matter how much you grow up, for me you will always be my baby sister. Had it not been for you, I wouldn't have dared to think of becoming a writer.

My ever loving, considerate and supportive editor, Tarini Uppal—thank you for reading my manuscript and turning one of my wildest dreams into reality. I can't forget the day when I read your email stating how much you loved reading the book! I'm so so so grateful to you! Thank you, Meena Rajasekaran, for designing a beautiful cover for my book and giving life to Mehar and Sarmad. Saloni Mital, my copy editor, thank you so much for being patient with me throughout the editing process. With you by my side, we were able to finish it off really soon. I would like to thank the entire, wonderful team at Penguin Random House for making my dream come true and for letting me experience the joy of getting published by an established publisher.

Mehar and Sarmad, the characters of my book, thank you for making me write about you and for being extremely close to my heart, my soul and my life.

Last but not the least, a big thank you to my readers—my ultimate source of inspiration.

Spread love wherever you go.

Love,
Sara Naveed